RAVES FOR
JAMES PATTERSON

"A legendary novelist." —*CNN*

"One of America's most influential authors."
—*New York Times*

"The man who can't miss." —*TIME*

"The page-turningest author in the game."
—*San Francisco Chronicle*

"One of the greatest storytellers of all time."
—*New York Times* bestselling author Patricia Cornwell

"Patterson is in a class by himself." —*Vanity Fair*

"Patterson boils a scene down to the single, telling detail, the element that defines a character or moves a plot along. It's what fires off the movie projector in the reader's mind."
—*New York Times* bestselling author Michael Connelly

BOOKS BY JAMES PATTERSON FEATURING THE WOMEN'S MURDER CLUB

The 23rd Midnight (with Maxine Paetro)
22 Seconds (with Maxine Paetro)
21st Birthday (with Maxine Paetro)
The 20th Victim (with Maxine Paetro)
The 19th Christmas (with Maxine Paetro)
The 18th Abduction (with Maxine Paetro)
The 17th Suspect (with Maxine Paetro)
The 16th Seduction (with Maxine Paetro)
The 15th Affair (with Maxine Paetro)
The 14th Deadly Sin (with Maxine Paetro)
Unlucky 13 (with Maxine Paetro)
12th of Never (with Maxine Paetro)
11th Hour (with Maxine Paetro)
10th Anniversary (with Maxine Paetro)
The 9th Judgment (with Maxine Paetro)
The 8th Confession (with Maxine Paetro)
7th Heaven (with Maxine Paetro)
The 6th Target (with Maxine Paetro)
The 5th Horseman (with Maxine Paetro)
4th of July (with Maxine Paetro)
3rd Degree (with Andrew Gross)
2nd Chance (with Andrew Gross)
1st to Die

For a preview of upcoming books and information about the author, visit JamesPatterson.com or find him on Facebook, X, or Instagram.

THE 24TH HOUR

JAMES PATTERSON

& MAXINE PAETRO

Little, Brown and Company
New York Boston London

The characters and events in this book are fictitious. Any similarity to real persons, living or dead, is coincidental and not intended by the author.

Copyright © 2024 by James Patterson
25 Alive excerpt copyright © 2025 by James Patterson

Hachette Book Group supports the right to free expression and the value of copyright. The purpose of copyright is to encourage writers and artists to produce the creative works that enrich our culture.

The scanning, uploading, and distribution of this book without permission is a theft of the author's intellectual property. If you would like permission to use material from the book (other than for review purposes), please contact permissions@hbgusa.com. Thank you for your support of the author's rights.

Little, Brown and Company
Hachette Book Group
1290 Avenue of the Americas, New York, NY 10104
littlebrown.com

Originally published in hardcover by Little, Brown and Company, May 2024
First trade paperback edition, February 2025

Little, Brown and Company is a division of Hachette Book Group, Inc. The Little, Brown name and logo are trademarks of Hachette Book Group, Inc.

WOMEN'S MURDER CLUB is a trademark of JBP Business, LLC.

The publisher is not responsible for websites (or their content) that are not owned by the publisher.

The Hachette Speakers Bureau provides a wide range of authors for speaking events. To find out more, go to hachettespeakersbureau.com or email hachettespeakers@hbgusa.com.

Little, Brown and Company books may be purchased in bulk for business, educational, or promotional use. For information, please contact your local bookseller or the Hachette Book Group Special Markets Department at special.markets@hbgusa.com.

ISBN 9780316403085 (hc) / 9781538710647 (trade paperback) / 9780316403283 (ebook)
Library of Congress Control Number: 2023952642

10 9 8 7 6 5 4 3 2 1

CCR

Printed in the United States of America

In memory of Laurie Catherine Birney

THE 24TH HOUR

PROLOGUE
SIX MONTHS EARLIER

One

I WAS LATE getting back from the men's jail in San Bruno. I braked the squad car in front of the Hall of Justice, where my good friend Assistant District Attorney Yuki Castellano was waiting at the curb.

She got into the car and asked, "How'd it go?"

Yuki is a prosecutor. Interrogation is her thing.

I said, "An inmate called Brandt got word to me that he knew who shot Holly Fricke and wanted to make a deal. It should have been one-stop shopping, but I had to sign six forms, wait for a free room, wait some more for Brandt to be brought down…"

"And then?" Yuki asked.

"He's a pathetic liar. I heard him out, laughed, and left. Anyway, sorry, Yuki. You called ahead?"

"Yep, yep, yep. Claire said don't worry. She and Cindy are having fun. Said something about caviar."

Yuki grinned into my sour expression.

"Did she tell you?" she asked.

I smiled for real. "Cindy? No. But I have confidential informants."

Yuki laughed her high-pitched musical chortle.

"It's going to be great," she said.

"What part?"

"Allllll of it."

I agreed. Cindy and my longtime friend and partner, Rich Conklin, had finally both committed at the same time to getting married. It was a bell ringer. The two of them had been living together, playing house, for several years, both in love, but still stuck on an obstacle. Cindy was building her dangerous, satisfying career and didn't want to have children—yet. Richie was from a big family, and to him children had to happen. The obstacle had somehow been sidelined. But Cindy was keeping the details to herself. Besides, today's celebration was for Claire.

Cindy, Yuki, and I had saved up for Claire's birthday, and today was the day.

Yuki was perfectly dressed in a pencil skirt and a blazer over a silk blouse just right for Xe Sogni, the hottest and most expensive place to eat in the entire Bay Area.

I hadn't had time to change out of my everyday Homicide detective gear: blue pants, button-down shirt, blue blazer, badge on a chain around my neck. I freed my lapel from the shoulder belt and tipped the rearview mirror toward me.

"You look fine," Yuki said.

I said, "Well, hair and makeup didn't show up this morning."

"It's just lunch. Okay?" she said.

"This time with a cake and candles."

We both laughed and I turned my mind to Claire. I wanted her to have a birthday she would remember for years. If we *got* there this year.

As I sweated the noontime rush, traffic slowed even more. Horns blew. I was tempted to hit my lights and sirens, but instead, I pounded the wheel with my palms. "Come onnn."

Yuki looked at me like, *Chill, Lindsay.* And just then the traffic moved.

"And we're off," she said.

I floored it and five minutes later we saw the restaurant just up ahead, a plain brick building disguising a culinary gem. I pulled up to the curb and valets opened doors and whisked the squad car away.

The restaurant's main room was dimly lit, banked on our right with an open kitchen, lined to our left with mahogany dining tables and large contemporary artwork. The air smelled indescribably delicious.

Yuki said, "The Women's Murder Club is in the house."

I followed her finger and saw Cindy and Claire sitting at a table for four near a spiral staircase. They were both grinning. Claire, dressed in navy-blue silk, had never looked happier. Yuki and I pulled out chairs and joined them. Waiters fussed. As Yuki predicted, we were in time for the caviar course presented with a curl of salmon in a scallop-shell dish.

God, this was good.

We were joking and roasting the birthday girl as the next course was served — then a woman screamed, loud enough to lift the roof.

"Nooooooo!"

Our waiter dropped a water glass. I grabbed his sleeve and showed him my badge.

"What's up there?"

"Staff ch-ch-changing room."

I got to my feet, knocking over my chair, and started up the corkscrew staircase. I took two steps at a time, and when I was halfway up, I heard a man shout, "You crazy bitch!"

I pulled my gun and, with my left hand on the railing, I raced to the top of the stairs.

Two

AS OUR WAITER had said, the second floor was a changing room. It was carpeted, about thirty feet square, densely packed with rows of lockers and benches between the rows. The lockers formed barricades and I couldn't see between them from where I stood in the doorway. Even though I was armed, it was dangerous as hell to be here without my partner.

I listened as I scanned the maze of a room. I heard nothing, saw no movement, and then a shadow shifted in a far corner to my left. The shadow was a woman, lying on her side with her back pressed against the wall twenty feet away. I saw that, except for her pink bra that had been pushed up above her breasts, the woman was naked. The dim overhead lighting flickered. The rheostat was to my left and so I dialed up the lights. I reached the woman in seconds and identified myself. She didn't seem to notice.

But I was taking mental notes of her. She was in her twenties; her eyes were puffy and partially closed and she was wheezing out little cries. I spoke to her again, asked her name, but she didn't respond. That's when I saw the fresh bruises encircling her neck and wrists.

She'd been choked and beaten, but she was alive.

I whipped my head around, scanned the area. Where was the damned attacker? Invisible.

I pulled my radio from my blazer pocket, connected to dispatch, and barked out a request for backup and an ambulance. If the attacker was still in the room, he'd heard me and would know that the cops were on the way.

Where was he?

I scoped out the room again from this new angle. There had to be an exit that led down to the kitchen, but I couldn't leave the victim alone to look for it.

Taking a chance, I stood up and shouted, "SFPD! Step out with your hands in the air."

That didn't happen. Restaurant sounds had resumed on the floor below. China clanked, diners laughed. Where was the man who'd cursed loud enough to be heard downstairs over the music and chatter?

And then I saw movement at the far end of a row of lockers. A man was half hidden behind an open locker door. Was this the attacker, or a waiter changing into his work clothes — or one and the same?

With just a sliver view, I made him as a white male, mid-twenties, average height and weight, dirty-blond hair, and he was half naked. The tails of his white dress shirt hung down to mid-thigh, front and back. His underwear and trousers were coiled around his feet.

It was him.

We made eye contact and he panicked, hopping, stumbling, bouncing off lockers as he tried to pull up his pants.

I shouted, "Stay where you are. Show me your hands."

He stopped and, leaning against a locker, held out his palms. He didn't have a gun. I let out a breath and said, "Turn around, close that locker, and put your hands on the door."

"I'm going to get dressed, okay?"

"What'd I just say?"

The subject shut the locker door with a bang, then hesitated. He tried to pull up his pants and I could see him thinking of making a run. I guess I'm psychic. He pushed off from the bank of lockers and, heading away from me, took one step and immediately tripped and fell hard to the floor with a yowl of pain. He was where I wanted him. I holstered my gun and, kneeling alongside him, pulled his arms around to his back and cuffed him.

"Hey," he said with his cheek pressed to the floor. "Listen to me. She set me up. I want to tell you what happened…"

"You have the right to remain silent. You have the right to an attorney…"

"Am I under arrest?"

"Yes, you are. What's your name?"

"Tyler. I work here."

"Tyler what?"

"I'm done talking."

"Fine. Tyler Doe, you're under arrest for aggravated assault, other charges pending."

He spat, "Jesus Christ, what is this? She set me up, goddamnit. I'm telling the truth, okay?"

I finished reading him his rights and he acknowledged none of them. I needed help to get him out of here and the victim needed medical attention.

Where was my backup?

Three

THE VICTIM LOOKED to be in her late twenties. Her body was marked with fresh contusions and lacerations and the bruises around her neck were livid.

I stooped down and again tried to get a response from her.

"I'm Sergeant Boxer. SFPD. Can you tell me your name?"

She groaned and wheezed. If she'd heard me, she was unable to answer or even look up. I pulled my phone from my pocket and speed-dialed Claire, who was still at our lunch table on the main floor.

When Claire picked up, I said, "There's an injured woman up here. Yeah, I called it in. Can you come up and take a look? And tell the manager that the locker room is off-limits to everyone but cops and EMTs. Yes, Yuki can come up."

The victim's backpack was half buried in a pile of her clothes. I unzipped the bag, saw makeup and pens and an assortment of small office supplies. I rooted around for a moment looking for her wallet and phone, then dumped the whole lot of stuff onto the floor. I opened her wallet and, after finding her driver's license, compared her DMV photo to her face. The woman on the floor was named Mary Elena Hayes, age twenty-eight.

"Mary Elena," I said. "Can you tell me what happened?"

Her voice was raspy, but I could make out what she said.

"He raped us."

What?

"There's another victim? Where is she?"

Mary Elena struggled to sit up.

"Lie still," I said. "Help is coming."

She croaked, "I'm Loretta. My name is Loretta." She rolled onto her stomach and sobbed onto the carpet.

Tyler was looking at me from the floor. He said, "Let me talk."

I said, "Hey! We'll take your statement at the station."

Claire and Yuki stepped through the locker room doorway and went directly to the victim. Claire spoke first.

"I'm Dr. Washburn. Can you show me where you hurt?"

Yuki grabbed a towel from a stack on a nearby bench and covered the young woman's body as I asked Ms. Hayes, "How do you know this man?"

Finally, she looked at me. "I just wanted to use the b-b-bathroom."

"Tyler" had said he was done talking, but he was still trying to get his story out. "Listen. Sergeant. I work here. She saw me, and she followed me. She *wanted* this. Understand? This was her idea."

"I hear sirens," Yuki said. "And Cindy's heading up."

I sighed. Cindy is an investigative crime reporter, and although I love her to pieces, she's dogged, and once she saw this scene she'd call it news and would be working. It was the wrong time to talk to the press.

Tyler Doe spoke. "She said her name was Olivia and that I was hot."

"No. Did not," the woman mumbled.

"She did," said our only suspect. "She said she wanted it hard and fast, and right now. I'm just human, Sergeant. She begged me. And another thing—"

Footsteps pounded up the stairs and two uniforms appeared; Nardone and Einhorn, both good cops I'd known for years.

"*Another thing*," Tyler shouted as the two cops pulled him to his feet. "She's *nuts*. First, she tells me her name is Olivia. Then, it's Loretta. Or is it Mary Elena? She lies."

Nardone got a grip on the suspect's shoulders while Einhorn hoisted and zipped up the man's trousers, leaving the belt dangling.

I began opening unlocked locker doors. A jacket hanging from a hook in one of them looked like it could be Tyler's.

I showed it to him. "Is this yours?"

He looked away from me and Nardone slapped the back of his head.

"Answer the sergeant."

"Yes. It's mine," he said.

Tyler's wallet was inside his jacket pocket. His ID told me that his full name was Tyler Richard Cates, showed him at five ten, 160, with green eyes and a Gough Street address. I said to Nardone, "Voucher this and take him to booking. I've charged him with aggravated assault."

"So leave him in lockup."

"You got it."

As the two officers left with Cates through the rear exit, Cindy, panting from the climb, arrived in the changing room and called out to me.

"Lindsay. What happened?"

"Hey, Cindy. You know I can't tell you."

"Off the record?"

"Hah."

"Okay. I know. Anyway, I'm here to tell you that our waiter needs to clear our table. There's a cake. With candles. Oh, and here you are, Claire. We didn't even sing 'Happy Birthday to You.'"

Claire said, "It's okay, Cin. Medical emergency."

The ambulance driver appeared in the locker room with a pair of EMTs who went to Mary Elena Hayes and lifted her onto a stretcher. While Claire filled in the EMTs on her observations, I thought about what Mary Elena Hayes had told me.

He raped us. What had she meant by that?

Cindy sighed as the room cleared out, leaving her without a story. She put her arm around my waist.

"Trouble always finds you, Linds."

I hugged her and said, "Look who's talking."

Cindy smiled at her feet, then said, "We can still kinda make this work. Let's bag the gifts. Box up the cake. Pay up. And then you tell me everything."

"Girl Reporter," I said, giving her a squeeze. "You're incorrigible."

PRESENT DAY

MONDAY

CHAPTER 1

THE *DAYDREAMER* WAS ninety feet of streamlined fiberglass, teak, and chrome. I'd never been on a yacht like this, but today was the day. Bob Barnett, Cindy's agent and lawyer, had treated her to a three-hour excursion on the bay because her just-published book, coauthored with a twisted serial killer, had topped the *New York Times* Best Seller list.

We grouped around Cindy on the main deck as she read Barnett's card out loud.

"Writing Burke's book was an act of admirable courage and determination, Cindy. You're a winner and your book is a new true crime classic. Promise me that you'll relax and have fun today. Try, okay? Love, Bob."

Cindy called out, "Thank you, Bob. Wherever you are."

I seconded that emotion.

A ship's officer showed us through the lounge and passageways to the aft deck, where a cushioned bench rounded the stern and lounge chairs were set up under the shade of the overhanging deck. As the yacht cast off, Cindy took a lounge chair at the center.

Claire and Yuki settled into the chairs flanking hers and I stretched out on one of the long side benches across from them. We were all beaming. It was a picture-worthy moment.

I took a selfie with my friends waving their hands behind me. Phones were passed around for portraits of a memorable day and the breeze blew away the worries of the last week. Yuki lifted her glass, saying, "To a life of happy days."

"Hear, hear."

Claire reached her hand over to Cindy's chair, saying, "So we're soon to become the Women's Married Club."

"Who told you?" Cindy joked.

Claire laughed. "Let's see that blinding green bling on your finger again."

Cindy stuck out her hand theatrically and Claire said, "Wow oh wow."

Yuki said, "Let me see," and Cindy showed her, too.

"It's too gorgeous, Cindy. It's stunning."

"He bought it for me. I don't even want to know what it cost him," Cindy said, first time I'd ever seen her looking shy.

"Really suits you, Cin," I said. I'd first seen the ring years ago. When Rich asked me what I thought of the square cut emerald I'd said, "It's perfect!" The next day, he'd proposed to Cindy at Grace Cathedral. She'd said yes but then later changed her mind.

It had killed Richie, but he'd hung in for love.

Now, Cindy was wearing the ring again. She was getting married.

And she was marrying the perfect man.

CHAPTER 2

CLAIRE PROPPED HERSELF up on the chaise and asked Cindy, "So, tell us again, but this time fill in some details. The juicier the better. What did Richie say?"

"Aw, I don't think I can tell you that."

Yuki said, "You can tell us, Cindy. It's off the record."

We all laughed, Cindy included. So many times we'd discussed a case in front of her and she'd started taking notes. One or all of us would shout, "Off the record."

I said, "Not fair, Cindy. Come on. We've been talking about you and Richie for years."

Cindy said, "Okay, okay."

She let it all out and we didn't interrupt. She said that the other night she'd opened the bedroom closet door and a pile of gun catalogs had slid down from the top shelf, hitting her in the face. Rich was asleep but when she grabbed up the catalogs and dropped them into the trash, the noise woke him up.

"We had a shouting match about whose closet it was—his—and

how sick I was of living in that dark hole with him, and I threatened to move out."

Claire said, "But this was bull, right? You were fighting about something else, am I right?"

Cindy nodded her head. "I was fuming, packing up, and wondering what the hell I was doing when Rich sat me on the bed, grabbed my hands, and said, 'I want to marry you, Cindy.'" She stopped to cough, then went on.

"He said, 'I love you more than anything, more than closet space, more than a clean fridge, more than a dozen kids.' Something like that," Cindy said, looking at each of us. "And he said, 'Marry me? Will you please?'"

We swarmed over her, congratulating her, practically pulling her finger off her hand to see the ring. One of us was crying. I think it was me.

About then, the waiter came out and said that lunch was served. We four grabbed onto one another and staggered against the surprising roll of the deck.

Claire said to Cindy, "By the way, Cin. This is what marriage is like."

We were all still giggling when we reached the dining salon. A large round table was set for eight in the center of the room and four of the places were taken.

It took a few seconds for my eyes to adjust to the darkened interior, and by then, the men at the table had gotten to their feet. They were grinning because they'd totally blindsided us.

"How'd you get here without us seeing you?" I asked Joe, my dearly loved husband.

"I'm a G-man, remember?" he said.

We reached out to our husbands. Cindy hugged Rich, her husband-to-be. Claire gave Edmund a big smack. Joe hugged me and got in a butt grab while he was at it. Yuki's husband, my commanding officer, Homicide Lieutenant Jackson Brady, swept Yuki off her feet—literally—then toasted the newly engaged couple.

TUESDAY

CHAPTER 3

AT SEVEN THE next morning, Yuki sat in the small conference room in the DA's suite of offices at the Hall of Justice. Tyler Cates's trial would begin tomorrow, and she was polishing her already buffed opening statement.

There was a mug of black coffee at her right hand and her laptop was open to the voluminous Cates folder, filled with depositions and videos and her own notes.

The note on the first page of the folder was the key point of her case against Cates: "Show that Tyler Cates knew that Mary Elena Hayes has a severe mental disorder known as dissociative identity disorder (DID), and therefore cannot, could not, give informed consent to sex."

Yuki had put a star next to this point because it was critical to her case. She would maintain that Cates knew Hayes had a mental condition, and she also knew that Cates's attorney would challenge this claim to the bitter end.

Yuki had listed the proofs of rape in bullet points: That although Mary Elena had no firsthand memory of the event, there was abundant medical proof that Tyler Cates had raped her: The bruises, the vaginal tearing, Cates's semen inside her body. The screams of protest witnesses heard down on the ground floor, rising above the ambient sounds in the restaurant. Cates's admission to Lindsay that he'd had sex with Hayes at the scene of the crime. And that the woman he'd had sex with had said her name was Olivia, while the woman who told Lindsay she'd been raped said her name was Loretta. *Anything else?* Cates had ignored his victim's multiple names and identities, and instead had congratulated himself that he was having a lucky day.

Yuki's second chair, Nick Gaines, pulled open the conference room door, and took a seat beside Yuki.

"I read it. I like it," he said of the draft of her opening statement.

"You only like it? Not love it? You're not blown away?"

Gaines had been Yuki's second chair on dozens of trials. Based on his GPA from Harvard Law, he could have been fast-tracked up the ladder at any prestigious firm, but that's not who Gaines was. He was sharp, insightful, had attack-dog instincts and a genuine soft spot for victims of violent crime.

He said, "I'm this close to being blown away, Yuki. I don't doubt you. It's Mary Elena and company. I don't know if there is a defense against Olivia. From the tapes, she's charming and likable. If Olivia comes forward when Mary Elena is on the stand, the jury will love her, and she'll say she was crazy about Cates."

"Schneider will underscore that on cross and we'll have to cancel out our own witness on redirect." Yuki sighed, continuing Gaines's line of thought.

But could she redirect if the house was on fire?

Gaines handed over the thumb drive of interviews psychiatrists had done with Mary Elena, and said he was ready to meet her.

"If you don't mind, Yuki, I want to push her buttons a little."

Yuki thought about it, said, "Risky. But maybe it's worth trying before we go to court."

Gaines said, "Send me the Cates transcripts and video again, okay?"

Yuki tapped some keys on her laptop as Gaines got out of his seat. "Done," she said.

She was gathering up her laptop, handbag, and coffee mug, planning to go back to her office, when her boss, Len Parisi, walked through the conference room door. Yuki sat back down.

San Francisco district attorney Leonard Parisi was known as Red Dog for his grizzled red hair and unflagging "winners win" mentality. As he took a chair across from Yuki, saying, "How's it going?" a cell phone rang. "Wait a second. I have to take this."

Parisi put his phone to his ear, giving Yuki another few moments to order her thoughts. The boss got snappish if she didn't give him a clean-to-the-bone summary of the matter at hand.

Red Dog growled into the phone, "Right. Call me when you have something real," and hung up.

"Sorry, Yuki. This day is shaping up to be a multicar pileup on Route 101."

CHAPTER 4

YUKI CHECKED HER watch. Eight fifteen already.

She said, "It's complicated, Len. Mary Elena has dissociative identity disorder, formerly and still commonly called multiple personality disorder. Much of the time, she's like the rest of us. Has a job, memories—"

Parisi said, "I know, you've told me this before. Several times."

"This time I'm telling you as if you're a juror. See how it plays."

"As I've been saying for months, Yuki. This is a weak, circumstantial case. Your best witness is Tyler Cates and he's not going to convict himself. So, you're at the mercy of Mary Elena's invisible friends."

Parisi had made his point, but she still wanted his support. A loophole. Or a story of a no-win case that he'd turned into a touchdown. But he wasn't going there. He was itemizing all the reasons the Hayes case was doomed. Yuki listened while looking Red Dog in the eye.

When Parisi ran out of gas, Yuki said, "Hear me out, Len. I was with Mary Elena immediately after she was raped. She'd been choked and punched, and fingerprint-shaped bruises were coming up on her inner thighs. The DNA inside her body matched Cates's DNA. We need to convict him—"

Parisi cut her off, saying, "Olivia was behind the wheel when Cates got busy."

"True."

"And she may have seduced him."

"That's what *he* says. But there's more to it than that. How much time do you have?"

"You'll have to discredit Olivia without discrediting Mary Elena. How are you going to do that?"

Yuki pictured it. Cates had told Lindsay that he'd had sex with Olivia and only heard the name Loretta after the fact. Still, it was indisputable that sex had been forced. Though Cates would say Olivia directed him to be rough.

Parisi cut into her thoughts. He said, "Can you bring out the personality who took the attack? Loretta?"

"If only," said Yuki. "It doesn't exactly work that way with Mary Elena. If I stress her out—or Cates's counsel goes after her, accuses her of being a liar, say—in that case, one of Mary Elena's alters might step in to protect her, but we don't know which one. More than one could front her on the stand."

"What's 'front her' mean?"

"Become the dominant personality."

"Okay. So, you're saying that Loretta or Olivia could come out, and Mary Elena wouldn't be there. Consciously. Or another of her alternate personalities could take control, a personality that you don't know?"

"Possibly."

"I don't like this, Yuki."

Yuki thought that was at least the fourteenth time he'd told her that.

Parisi slapped the conference table and stood up.

"You want to ride this case into a box canyon, it's your horse. Go right ahead. I have a meeting."

Yuki nodded and Len Parisi left the room. He was a great prosecutor. He'd never told her she was crazy to take on a case before, no matter how bad the odds of winning. But this one was brand-new territory. She didn't know a single prosecutor who'd ever been dealt a stack of wild cards like this one.

Then again, she'd never had an easy case in her life.

CHAPTER 5

MARY ELENA SAT in a visitor chair across from Yuki's desk, relating a dream she'd had.

"We're in court," Mary Elena said. "TV movie–type courtroom. I'm sitting next to you and someone says, 'Has the jury reached a verdict?' And the jury foreman says, 'We have, Your Honor.' The foreman looked like Sean Penn and I woke myself up like three times."

"How did you feel in the dream?" Yuki asked.

"Scared, I guess," she said. "Who wouldn't be?"

Yuki nodded. Mary Elena said she was "grounded" but, Yuki saw fear in her eyes.

"It'll be all right, Ms. Hayes. I read that Sean Penn is shooting a movie out of the country."

Mary Elena grinned and said, "My grandmother called me Mary Elena."

Yuki said, "My grandmother called me *chiisana neko*. Which means 'little cat,' but you can call me Yuki."

They both laughed and then Yuki said, "I'd like you to meet

Nick Gaines. He's working with me as second chair in our case against Mr. Cates."

"He knows all about…?"

"Absolutely. And he's got a few questions for you."

Yuki grabbed the desk phone and called Gaines. He picked up, and, by the time Yuki had clicked off, was at her open door. He pulled the second visitor chair around so that he triangulated both Yuki and Mary Elena.

He smiled, said, "We have a good case, Mary Elena, but the defense is prepared and they're going to try to win. Here's what we figure is going to be the defense's position. Shall we talk about it?"

"I'm ready. I think."

"Nothing to worry about. This is just you and your legal team doing a practice run. Not a problem, right?"

"Okay."

Gaines said, "Good," and kept going. Yuki thought Mary Elena was not exactly okay, but she let it go. Gaines was smart and even if Mary Elena didn't know him, this was a safe place.

"Here we go," Gaines said.

Yuki saw Mary Elena's face flatten and she heard Parisi's warning in her mind.

This is a weak, circumstantial case… You want to ride this case into a box canyon, it's your horse.

Yuki watched Gaines lean closer to Mary Elena, who, under the force of his stare, pushed her chair back flush against the wall. If Gaines felt her withdrawing from him, he showed no sign.

"Now, Mary Elena. Ed Schneider, Tyler Cates's attorney, is a pit bull."

Mary Elena said, tersely, "I heard."

Gaines nodded and went on.

"The jury is going to want to hear your side. Schneider may call you to the stand and pummel you with questions. So, it's far better if we call you. The defense will still question you, but they won't have as much control.

"Now, according to Cates, you followed him to the second floor. You asked him for rough sex, then when he hurt you, you said that he raped you. Schneider is going to push hard on that. Quoting his client, he'll say that Cates met a woman named Olivia who told him, 'I want you to take me hard and fast and now.' In other words, the defense position will be that the sex was your idea but that you changed your mind after the fact. And that you were in full control of Olivia."

"I didn't know she was out," Mary Elena said. "She doesn't talk that way. I only remember that when I went into the room and was looking for the ladies' room, that guy asked me who I was. I said, 'Elena.' I don't remember anything else until the police came."

"This is important, Mary Elena. Did any of your alters tell Cates that you have DID?"

Mary Elena said, "I can only tell you what I know and what I've said. I went into Xe Sogni to use the ladies' room. A waiter said it was upstairs, so I climbed that spiral staircase. Then I woke up on the floor, naked and hurting everywhere."

Gaines said, "You told Sergeant Boxer that your name was Loretta. You told her, 'He raped us.' You've just said that you were on your way to the bathroom, then woke up on the floor without memory of this rape. That's a contradiction, isn't it?"

"Noooo. I remember going up to the ladies' room. I remember being on the floor. I remember hurting. But I don't remember talking with Sergeant Boxer."

"So, it was a different personality—Loretta—who was attacked by Cates? Where was the personality called Olivia? Did either one of them tell Cates that you have dissociative identity disorder?"

"*I don't know.* Do you understand, if an alter comes out, she is protecting me? I don't know what happened when Olivia or Loretta were fronting. But I knew from the *pain* that I had been raped and beaten. And that had happened. *Do you understand that?*"

CHAPTER 6

THE ATMOSPHERE IN the room was still quivering in the wake of Mary Elena's anguished protest. Yuki tried to signal Nick Gaines to take the intensity down, but he didn't see her. His eyes were fixed on Mary Elena and he kept talking at her.

"Schneider is going to try to trip you up, Mary Elena. You said, 'He raped us.' Forgive me for saying so, but while your body bore the physical evidence of rape, you don't remember a thing about that attack, who said what to whom, if another person was present, if that person was a facet of you, or even if Cates got Olivia's okay. You don't remember what happened in that room, isn't that right?"

Yuki was as transfixed as Mary Elena, who stared at Gaines with her mouth hanging open. She pushed up against the back of her chair, pulled her legs up to her chest, gripped them hard with her forearms — and then blasted Gaines.

"*Who are you?*"

Shockingly, her voice had changed. To Yuki, she sounded like a very young girl.

Yuki said, "Mary Elena?"

Without looking at Yuki, Mary Elena shouted at Gaines. "*You're baddddd. Mama and I don't like you.*"

Gaines put out his hand to stop Yuki from interfering.

"Who are *you?*" he asked Mary Elena.

"I'm Lily. You know I'm Lily. Don't talk to my mama like that."

Yuki said, "Nick, I'll stay with Lily."

Gaines gave Yuki a look like *I've got this,* but Yuki said his name again, louder. He stood up and left the room, closing the door behind him.

Yuki turned back to the formerly composed woman of twenty-eight, now crouched in a desk chair, panting like a frightened child.

"Lily, I want to help. What can I do for you?"

"Go away. Leave me alone."

"Okay. I'll be right outside the door."

Lily didn't answer. Yuki didn't want to leave Lily alone, but witnessing Mary Elena assume a new persona while sitting across from her was unnerving. She needed a plan.

Hesitating, Yuki left Lily in her office and closed the door. She startled when she saw Gaines standing only feet away.

He said, "That wasn't pretty, but we know a lot more about Mary Elena now, don't we?"

"Yep. If she freaks on the stand…"

"Our case flames out of control."

CHAPTER 7

YUKI'S MOTHER HAD once said, "Yuki-eh, you have three trains of thought at same time."

It was true enough. At the moment, those three trains were on parallel tracks, converging on a one-track tunnel. Yuki told Gaines she'd get back to him in a while, then slid into an empty cubicle. Phone in hand, she took her best shot. She called Mary Elena's psychiatrist, Dr. Stuart Aronson.

By the fourth unanswered ring, Yuki prepared herself for a useless, leave-a-message recording, but before that happened, a masculine voice growled in her ear, "Stu Aronson."

Yuki said, "Doctor, this is ADA Yuki Castellano—"

"I've got a patient in the waiting room," Dr. Aronson said. "I'll call you back—"

"I've got an emergency here and need direction," Yuki cut him off.

"Make it fast," said the doctor.

Yuki explained Mary Elena's immediate condition quickly and finished with "What should I do?"

"Put her on the phone. Has to be quick," Dr. Aronson said. "I can only give her five, six minutes."

Mary Elena was still curled up in the side chair, but she looked more relaxed. Her eyes were closed and one foot touched the floor.

Yuki said, "Mary Elena?"

She opened her eyes. "Did I fall asleep?"

"Yes and that's okay. But I was worried about you so I called Dr. Aronson—"

"You called my shrink?"

"Yep. He's here on my phone right now."

Mary Elena unfolded her limbs and sat up in the chair.

"But why? He's very busy."

"He's free now for a few minutes."

Mary Elena said, "I've never spoken with him on the phone before. Why did you call him? I'm okay."

Yuki said, "If I say you were speaking as Lily, do you know who I mean?"

"Oh. Lily. She thinks of me as her mother. Did something happen?"

"I think so. I want to be sure you can go through this trial without harm. I'm on your side entirely, and so is Nick. Do you remember Nick?"

"I don't think so."

"Please take the phone. Speak with your doctor."

"And say what?"

Yuki said into the phone, "Dr. Aronson, Mary Elena is here. Please ask her to hand you off to me before you go. I would appreciate it."

She passed her phone to Mary Elena, and leaving her office, Yuki went back to the empty cubicle. Gaines peered over the top of the partition, and said, "Hey."

Yuki looked up and said, "She's talking to Dr. Aronson. She doesn't remember you, so probably best if you…"

"Got it."

Gaines was back in his office when Mary Elena appeared and said to Yuki, "Dr. Aronson didn't have time to talk with you, but he says he sent you something by email. A video. I told him it was okay."

After Yuki had walked Mary Elena to the elevator, she stopped off at Gaines's office, saying, "I need you, Nicky. We've got work to do."

Yuki woke her computer and clicked on the email from Dr. Aronson.

"It's a therapy session," Yuki said as Gaines pulled up a chair. "Dated a month ago."

"Aronson sent this to you?"

"With Mary Elena's permission."

Yuki opened the attachment and a video began playing. Dr. Stuart Aronson sat in an easy chair. Mary Elena was in a chair across from him, talking.

Yuki and Gaines watched as the session streamed.

CHAPTER 8

CONKLIN'S FOOT WAS heavy on the gas as we sped to the scene of a fatality on Pacific Avenue. The victim had been identified as James Fricke III: well-known billionaire, middleweight philanthropist, sole owner of a Belgian soccer team, and a narcissistic SOB. The man in his early sixties was now a deceased SOB, shot in the street a block away from where his wife, former Olympic gymnast Holly Bergen Fricke, had been killed six months before.

We still had no leads in Holly Fricke's murder investigation, and I was willing to bet that soon we'd be looking at another no-clue homicide—the kind of crime that would go unsolved for years, then become a cold case that haunted good cops and turned them into humorless drunks.

Conklin's mood mirrored mine, but he was expressing his frustration out loud, ranting that Jamie Fricke, the most likely suspect in his wife's death, had gotten himself killed "on purpose." Richie's uncharacteristic outburst shifted into overdrive when traffic suddenly stopped, boxing us in at the intersection of Franklin Street and Geary Boulevard.

My partner swore, got out of the car, and took off at a run toward the bottleneck. I stayed in place with the radio and thought about Holly Fricke. I'd been a fan. I'd cheered her on when I was in high school and she was in the Summer Olympics, picking up the gold medal in gymnastics for Team USA.

I'd followed her when she founded *Spike*, a women's sports magazine, and became a familiar face on late-night talk shows. Then Holly married Jamie Fricke. He was a large man, square-faced, dark-eyed. He exuded power the way Holly radiated goodness. They'd looked happy together. And although they hadn't had any children, babies were named after Holly and deserving high schoolers went to college on her dime.

But now we still didn't know *why* Holly Fricke had been killed or by *whom*, though Medical Examiner Claire Washburn had told us *how*. Holly's cause of death was an onslaught of .40-caliber rounds from an unregistered handgun, every shot fatally precise. Neither her new Bentley nor the jewelry she'd been wearing, estimated to be worth a low seven figures, had been recovered.

Unofficially, we'd chalked up Holly Fricke's murder to armed robbery, but privately none of us really bought that. It was excessive. Holly had been shot in broad daylight. No witnesses. Nothing from her husband or friends. Now that Jamie had been killed the same way, I knew we'd missed all of it: means, motive, opportunity—and suspect.

On day one, Holly's case had been assigned to senior Homicide team sergeants Cappy McNeil and Paul Chi.

Cappy is a wise old hand, a walking chronicle of murders in San Francisco over the last twenty years. His partner, Paul Chi, is as thorough and obsessively detailed an investigator as is humanly possible. It's said he can find a hair in a haystack. Yet a thousand cop-hours spent working her homicide had yielded zip, not even a theory. If Cappy still had hair, by now he'd have torn it all out. Chi had gone dark and quiet, as though in some fathomless funk.

Conklin and I had been brought in to back up this first-class team, but all we'd been able to surmise was that Holly's killer knew her movements, had a strategic mind, titanium nerves, and perhaps, a cloak of invisibility.

When questioned, Jamie Fricke had told us as little as possible. He didn't like cops, which he made clear with his clipped answers and negative attitude. He'd previously been accused of sports crimes, but had skirted the law with handshake deals and payoffs. He brought in his squadron of high-priced lawyers and threatened to hire private investigators.

Somehow, Cappy and Chi had kept the PI threat at bay. But Fricke had offered a quarter of a million dollars as a reward for evidence leading to the arrest and conviction of Holly's killer, which opened our hotline to an unending plague of useless tips.

My thoughts were derailed as horns blew behind the squad car. Conklin came back to the car and got behind the wheel, released the brake, and I called dispatch to say we would be at the crime scene in ten minutes.

I hit the switch that loosed the lights and siren.

CHAPTER 9

CONKLIN PULLED OUR car over on Steiner Street, at the intersection of Steiner Street and Pacific Avenue. The smart, well-kept homes and small businesses in this upscale neighborhood were now penned in by cruisers with flashing lights, the ME's stolid van, and the CSU mobile with its panel doors wide-open.

"Ready?" Conklin asked me.

Ready or not, I opened my door.

Walking toward the barrier tape, I saw CSU investigators in hazmat suits pitching an evidence tent and placing halogen lights around the perimeter for the night shift. Techs put out markers, snapped shots of shell casings, close-ups of the deceased, and of faces in the gathering crowd.

It was only nine thirty in the morning, but from the amount of manpower working in and around the scene, it was clear to me that CSU would be here throughout the night.

Jackson Brady glanced up when Conklin and I ducked under the tape and became part of the too-real crime scene. Conklin and

I stepped gingerly around the inner perimeter until we were a few feet from the bloody corpse of James Fricke III.

Claire stood up from where she'd been crouched beside the victim.

She said, "In my professional opinion, he's dead."

I said, "Duly noted."

She went on, "The shooting was called in by a bystander about an hour ago, so that's our approximate time of death. I count five bullet wounds, one each to head, heart, liver, back, groin. The head shot was probably the kill shot. I'll let you know after I've done the post. Brady has Fricke's wallet, but his watch and wedding ring are missing. His car wasn't here when we arrived. The shooter may have driven it off."

Same as Holly's car, confirming my earlier thoughts that Holly and Jamie Fricke's murders were virtually identical. Both had been shot on Pacific Avenue, both robbed, both murders were overkill. Since Holly and Jamie were married, and both shot to hell, it made me wonder if these had been crimes of passion. But we hadn't heard even a whisper about anyone wanting to kill either of them, let alone both.

Brady's shadow fell across me. He said, "Here ya go," and handed me a man's slim wallet inside a plastic evidence bag.

"Boxer. You're the lead. You and Conklin assemble a task force that includes McNeil and Chi. I know I don't have to say this…"

So, *I* said it. "Don't blow it."

"*Please,* don't blow it," he said.

Crime Scene Unit director Gene Hallows made his way over to me. He is astute, salty, and after decades of science-based crime-busting in our forensics lab, was recently elevated to the top job when former CSU director Charles Clapper was promoted to chief of police.

"Tell me something good," I said to Hallows.

My guess, CSU had found shell casings at this crime scene of the same caliber bullets as those that had killed Holly.

Reading indignation on my face, Hallows said, "I know you'd like me to say I found Fricke's signed confession in his breast pocket along with a suicide note."

"Good one, Gene."

"Have faith, Boxer. We've been here for under an hour."

Car doors slammed to my right along Pacific Avenue. Reporters exited their vehicles and headed toward the crime scene. More vehicles arrived, more press joining the swarm that soon filled Pacific Avenue from side to side. Uniforms formed a cordon outside the yellow ribbon of tape and held back the crowd shouting questions at Brady.

"Is that Jamie Fricke?" "How did this happen?" "Do you have a suspect?" "Lieutenant. Say a few words to our viewers…"

Brady turned and scanned the crowd. I saw what he saw: cameras held high, mics and phones pushed forward, a sound truck that had parked halfway on the sidewalk. Brady shouted back, his voice colored with a southern twang he'd picked up during his earlier years with Miami PD.

"Listen up, y'all. You, Mr. Clancy, Ms. Blume. You know I'm not gonna feed you reporters guesswork while the case is ongoing. Soon as we can clear the area we can open a lane to traffic. You get any verifiable leads, call Homicide, SFPD. You know our number."

A man's voice came at us from the back of the crowd. "I saw it happen. I live right over there."

I snapped my head around until I located the tall, bearded white man pointing to a three-story, white stucco house with bay windows down the street.

He was saying, "I'm Dan Fields. I'm the one who called the police. I was looking at the view when I saw a guy on foot jump out in front of Jamie Fricke's car. Fricke gets out of his Jaguar. Late model. Black. I recognized him from TV. I heard shots and he dropped. The shooter was on foot with his back to me. The whole thing happened so damn fast. Shooter got into Fricke's car and took it east on Pacific."

Brady said, "Thanks for coming forward, Mr. Fields. We'll be needing you to come to the station to make a statement."

I stepped toward the witness, introduced myself and Conklin, and, after escorting Mr. Fields home to lock his doors, we drove him back to the Hall for a long interview — which went nowhere.

CHAPTER 10

I ARRIVED HOME at just after 7:00 p.m. I parked in my usual spot on Eleventh and Lake, took the elevator up, then paused at our front door before letting myself inside.

My mind was still swimming with fresh images of Jamie Fricke's bloody corpse face down on the street, followed by his unveiling on the table in Claire's autopsy suite. I didn't want to carry those images into my home. I've taught myself a little trick that often works: Before I turn the key in the lock, I roll my shoulders forward a couple of times, then back. And last, I shake myself like a wet dog. Then, I go inside.

Tonight it worked.

I walked into a place that was warm and alive with Dean Martin singing "Volare," his voice filling the loft-sized room, accompanied by my husband's glorious baritone. Martha, my elderly border collie and pal since before I met and married Joe Molinari, woofed at the sound of the door opening and welcomed me inside.

I shouted, "Mommy's home!" as I stowed and locked my gun in the case in the foyer. Then I stooped to gather my five-year-old daughter, Julie, and Martha together into a noisy hug before walking to the kitchen area where Joe was making something with pesto sauce. We hugged and kissed, and after I took a peek inside the pot on the stove, he put a glass of Cabernet in my hand and we all headed to the sofa at the far side of the room.

The next few hours went by way too fast.

We talked, laughed, ate. If dinner had been only half as good, it would have gotten five stars. Julie had made cookies with Mrs. Rose, our neighbor and part-time nanny. Once the cookies had turned into a plate of chocolate crumbs, I took our little girl into her bedroom.

I read to her and then she told me a story that she made up as she went along. Allie the Alligator had a toothache, and he had to go to the dentist.

I asked, "So what happens?"

Julie said, "Allie might eat the dentist, maybe."

Joe was listening at the doorway. He said to Julie, "If Allie does eat the dentist, does he have an escape plan?"

"Oooh," said Julie. "Escape plan? I know. He grows wings!"

Joe said, "Really good, Julie Bug." He walked into the room and we both kissed Julie good night and Joe said he'd take Martha for a walk.

Good. Great. I wanted a shower and I was going to have one.

When Joe came back with Martha, he woke me up. I'd fallen asleep on the bed, still wearing my clothes.

"I just lay down for a second," I mumbled to Joe.

"Stand up," Joe said, using his law enforcement voice. I struggled to my feet.

"Arms up," he said.

I held up my arms like a child and let Joe peel off my clothes. He had some trouble with the hooks of my bra, and I laughed at him.

"I'm out of practice," he said.

"Try again. I'm begging you. I can't get my hands around that far."

"Tough day, hmmm?"

"I can be talked into telling you all about it."

"Later. Take your shower or don't. Up to you."

I left the room, promising that I would be quick, but it felt so good to stand under the hot water, I struggled with turning off the taps. When I was finally steeped and steam-cleaned, I stepped out of the shower stall and shuffled into the bedroom semi-draped in a hand towel.

Joe was in bed, lights out, but I could see him by street light. I dropped the towel and slid under the covers and my G-man pulled me close. I put my arms around him and he kissed me between my neck and shoulder.

"You feel so good," he said.

I reached up to kiss him, but he put his hands on my shoulders and held me back. I looked into his eyes.

"I love you, Lindsay," he said. "All the way."

"Prove it," I said.

I can't be sure why our lovemaking only gets better. I wasn't thinking anymore that night. I was lost in Joe, somewhere near heaven.

CHAPTER 11

THE NIGHT BEFORE the trial, Yuki's sleep was split between waking anxiety and frightening dreams. At some time during that fractured night, she had a nightmare that stayed with her. Mary Elena as Olivia was prancing in front of the jury box wearing a pink bra and ripped leggings, flirting with the jurors.

Yuki woke when a siren screamed past the bedroom window, shattering the night irreparably.

Brady stirred, asking, "You okay?"

"Uh-huh. Fine. Go back to sleep, sweetie."

It was 3:17 a.m. In six hours, she would be in court with a clear-cut mission: convict Tyler Cates and get justice for Mary Elena. Disturbingly, sensational reporting on the case had made her the butt of late-night TV jokes and social media wisecracks. Yuki would need to utilize every bit of her law school training and on-the-job experience with the San Francisco DA to send Tyler Cates to jail.

She knew what she had to do, but still one piece eluded her—and it was critical. Did Cates know that Mary Elena had a dissociative disorder, or that she had more than one functional personality? Or did he really believe that he'd had sex with a woman called Olivia?

Yuki stared up at the ceiling and pictured the jurors as she rehearsed her opening statement, reviewing what she knew about them, imagining their faces. She thought about Mary Elena sitting at the counsel table, listening to Yuki tell strangers about the deeply personal traumatic assault that she didn't remember happening.

She thought about Parisi shaking his head, saying, *Yuki, I warned you.*

Yuki closed her eyes and moments later, it seemed, opened them. It was just after 5:00 a.m., and from the hints of pale light filtering through the windows, it would soon be dawn. She rolled onto her side and moved closer to Brady, tucking her knees behind his, exhaling as she laid her cheek against his bare back.

When he felt Yuki's body against his, Brady turned over, reached his massive arms around her, and drew her close. This was what she loved: the scent of him and how she was able to fit so comfortably against him, and how he could slip back into sleep while surrounding her with the best safety zone she'd ever known.

The next time Yuki's eyelids flew open, it was almost six thirty. It took a few seconds to orient herself and remember that she was meeting Mary Elena at eight. She tried to slip out of Brady's grip but he tightened it, cupping the back of her head with one hand, throwing a leg over her hip.

Yuki said, "Lover, I gotta go."

"Court," he acknowledged. Brady opened his eyes and relaxed his hold on Yuki. "Call me at lunch recess," he said. "You're going to do great."

"There are many unknowns," she said.

"You're not one of them."

He tipped her chin up and kissed her. Yuki wanted more but couldn't take the chance. She kissed him lightly and squirmed out of his arms.

WEDNESDAY

CHAPTER 12

ONCE YUKI'S FEET touched the floor, she moved quietly through the apartment. She'd once lived here with her mother. The carpeting was soft and thick, and so were Yuki's memories of Keiko Castellano, bride of an Italian soldier who had died before Yuki was old enough to know him. Keiko had also since passed away, but not before she'd imparted volumes to her daughter over the years on how to be a good wife.

Keiko had been a spiritual woman. Yuki sometimes still heard her mother's voice, even if it was only in her imagination. And sometimes, she answered her.

Now, Yuki stared down at the two suits she'd laid out on the green slipper chairs in the spare room before going to bed last night.

Her mother's voice was in her head. *The striped one, Yuki-eh. Save red for closing.*

"Done," Yuki said out loud.

She dressed in the gray striped suit, projecting herself toward lunch recess, hoping that when she called Brady, she could tell him, "It's all good."

CHAPTER 13

IT WAS JUST after seven forty-five in the morning when Yuki pulled her car into the All Day lot on Bryant Street. She reached out her hand to the shy young man in the booth, who gave her a ticket and without making eye contact said, "Go get 'em."

Yuki said, "Count on it, Lanny, and wish me luck."

"You know I do," he said. "Hurry though. It's fixin' to rain."

"Hmm. Well, I have to wait for someone," she said.

Yuki parked at the rear of the lot in the only spot facing the street. The Hall of Justice, a large, gray, granite block of a building, was directly across Bryant. Yuki undid her seat belt and got out of the car.

Mary Elena would be meeting her in the lot at eight, giving them enough time to go upstairs and meet with Nick Gaines again before heading to the courtroom doors at a few minutes to nine. Yuki hoped that despite Mary Elena's earlier interaction with Gaines, she would recognize that he was a good guy and valuable to them both.

There was still time, but Yuki paced, looking up and down the street for Mary Elena's car. A new potential obstacle appeared to her: it was possible that one of Mary Elena's alternate personalities would tell her to stay in bed, and she'd go for that; ditch the trial due to stress and outright fear.

She pictured Olivia on Dr. Aronson's tape: a vulnerable-looking, very feminized version of Mary Elena. Olivia twisted her hair, crossed and uncrossed her legs, and spoke in a soft voice while looking at the doctor.

Yuki hated the thought, but *had* Mary Elena as Olivia come on to Tyler Cates, as he maintained? Even so, flirting wasn't consent, not for rape, not for aggravated assault, not for sex at all. Legally, if the attacker knew that the would-be sex object had a mental disorder and could not give informed consent, it was a serious crime with a jail sentence penalty.

The sky darkened with rain clouds. Checking the time, Yuki saw that it was ten after eight. *Where are you, Mary Elena?*

She watched the morning rush on Bryant, frozen at the traffic light. A mob of press gathered across the street, reporters from local news stations as well as unfamiliar faces. This much attention to the People versus Tyler Cates was unexpected and a little daunting.

Yuki heard someone call her name over the street uproar. It was Cindy, looking for an opening in the stream of traffic, and about to step off the sidewalk and cross the street toward her.

Yuki waved her off, *no, no, no,* but called Cindy's phone.

"I can't talk now, Cin. Later, okay?"

"Promise?"

"Cross my heart."

As Yuki walked back to her car, a silver Camaro took a turn into the lot and pulled up to the ticket booth.

It was Mary Elena. Shouts came from the gaggle of reporters across Bryant waiting for the light to change.

The young woman looked alarmed as Yuki got into the passenger seat. "Quick," Yuki said, buckling her seat belt. "Make a U-turn and take a right. I'll tell you where to go."

"What's wrong?"

"Hungry press," Yuki said. "I don't want them to interview you. They can't follow us through the back door."

Mary Elena followed Yuki's directions and parked under the overpass on Harriet. Yuki then hurried them down the breezeway to the Hall's back entrance. But her diversionary tactic didn't stop a dozen reporters from racing ahead, blocking their way. Mary Elena spun on her heels yelling, "Go away!"

Her voice was that of a little girl. Her face was flushed and her eyes stretched wide-open. The reporters stopped, a few backing up. Before they could make another move, Yuki had opened the lobby's rear door. Security guards let her and Mary Elena into the building but the press was shut out.

Yuki said, "Lily?"

"Mary Elena," she said. "I'm Mary Elena."

"Oh, good."

Twenty minutes later, Yuki, Mary Elena, and Nick Gaines settled into their seats at the prosecution table in Courtroom 8G. Soon enough, the courtroom would be called to order.

CHAPTER 14

JOE WAS PATCHING a leak under the kitchen sink when his phone rang. He was alone in the apartment—Lindsay was at work and Julie was at school.

He backed out of the cabinet, banging his head on the lip of the counter. Banged it hard. Calling himself an effing dummy, he reached his phone on the third ring and said, "Molinari."

The voice on the line belonged to Craig Steinmetz, section chief of the FBI's San Francisco office.

"Can you come in? I want you to meet someone."

"I can be there in an hour."

"Half hour would be better."

"Okay," Joe said. "If I don't shave."

"Come as you are," Steinmetz said, and hung up.

A half hour and a couple of aspirins later, Joe was signing in at the fifteenth-floor desk when Steinmetz called out to him. The chief stood behind him at the doorway between the offices and reception area. Joe crossed the blue, insignia-embossed carpet to shake hands.

Steinmetz was sixtyish but looked seventy. He'd put on some weight and lost some hair since they'd last worked together, and the older man looked worried.

"I've got an assignment for you, Molinari. I think you'll like it. Even if you don't, you're needed. We've got a situation…"

The chief's voice trailed off as he and Joe entered the corner office. While Steinmetz had changed, his office looked as it always had: a worn blue carpet, plain government-issue oaken desk, two flags—California and USA—and a picture window behind them. Bookshelves were to his left and right, and a half a dozen photos of Steinmetz shaking hands with high-ranking government officials hung on the wall near his desk.

Yet one thing was new.

A well-turned-out thirtysomething Chinese woman sat in one of the chairs facing the chief's desk, hands clasped in her lap. She turned her head to look at Joe as he came toward the desk. He noted her charcoal-gray pantsuit, white men's tailored shirt, minimal makeup, and short wash-n-go hair. He, having dressed for speed, was wearing a khaki shirt, chinos, and work boots. Plus an untrimmed twenty-four-hour-old beard and plumber's putty under his fingernails.

Steinmetz said, "Joe. Have a seat. Meet Bao Wong, director of cyberterrorism, DC office. Bao, this is Joe Molinari."

Joe dusted off his hands on his back pockets, shook hands with Director Wong, and took the chair beside her. Steinmetz gave Bao the thirty-second version of Joe's decades in government service; first, a few years with the FBI, then even longer with the CIA, followed by getting drafted by DHS as deputy director.

"Later, he went back to DC for another tour," Steinmetz said.

Joe said, "I'm a risk assessment consultant specializing in port security, and I have background in cyber threats."

"Actually, I've followed your career, Joe," Bao said. "Great to meet you in person."

Coffee was served in FBI-branded mugs as Steinmetz told the agents about the case that had brought them together.

"Two weeks ago, Oakland Pediatrics' computer network was breached, for Christ's sake. The hospital had a cybersecurity system in place, but some dope in a back office—a doctor, actually—clicked on a phishing site and let the dogs in. The hackers called themselves 123 Boom. Whoever they are, they put Oakland Pediatrics in a twenty-four-hour choke hold. Then, *boom.*"

Steinmetz swiveled his chair so that he faced the street and talked to the glass.

"They input incorrect medical formulas and protocols, resulting in four neonatal deaths. The hospital was underinsured. The ransom was seventeen million in Bitcoin to get their data back. The hospital paid. The encryption keys were returned. The hackers evaporated. The babies stayed dead. Lawsuits pending."

Bao Wong said, "The hackers can take what they got from Oakland, tweak it, and use it on them again. Or they can use it elsewhere."

"'Elsewhere' called an hour ago," said Steinmetz, swiveling back to face the two people who might be a hospital's last resort. "Joe, now they're threatening St. Vartan's. Boom is demanding eighteen million dollars in"—Steinmetz looked at his watch—"forty-seven hours. By 9:00 a.m. Friday, we've either shut these killers down, or St. Vartan's lights go out. They lose all of their patient records, past and present, and whatever archived information they've stored on dead patients. As a sweet farewell, 123 Boom will also have embedded digital land mines in the network."

Steinmetz stood up, seizing his coffee mug. "Please tell Joe the rest, Bao," he said. "I'm meeting with the governor to fill him in. Contact me the moment you have something, and good luck."

CHAPTER 15

JOE AND BAO got into Joe's old Mercedes and headed out to St. Vartan's by way of Van Ness Avenue.

Bao said, "Gotta make a quick call."

She took out her phone and, seconds later, said, "It's me." She listened, then said, "That's so good, Cam. You did it!"

When she clicked off, she said, "My son Cameron's nine. Got the lead in a class play. Lines *and* singing."

She beamed at Joe.

Joe said, "Hey. That's great."

"You'd think so. The lead role is a talking frog. Cam's been practice-belching for weeks now. Driving his mother crazy."

Joe laughed along with Bao. "I've got a little girl. I think Julie would also love to be a frog."

Bao said, "I just don't see the attraction to amphibians."

Joe laughed again, and relayed Julie's alligator-going-to-the-dentist story. Then, with the ticking clock in mind, he asked, "So what do we know about 123 Boom?"

Bao said, "Well, they set off alarms in DC months ago. My team has been working up their methods, embedding moles, tracking this gang's footsteps ever since. Their IP addresses are always in motion, hopping from one country to another. New threats, new names, but we recognize their patterns."

Joe thought how the public perception of ransomware was a hairy guy in Russia making a digitally distorted phone call: *Give me all your money or people will die.*

He said, "Remember when cyber theft was buying and selling credit card numbers on message boards? Some years ago, an airline called me. Their network was frozen. Flights canceled. Even the elevators were dead. And there was a demand for twenty million in crypto, which they paid."

Bao said, "That was huge. I remember it."

"Now," said Joe, "these digital terrorists don't care about stealing data. They're screwing up chemotherapy orders. Killing without leaving fingerprints. And still walking away with the dough."

The two were silent as Joe took a right on Bush Street and headed east.

Bao said, "One of these businesses we're tracking makes kids' toys, goes by the name Skylark. You look at them, it's a functioning, medium-sized company of seven hundred based in Amsterdam. They have a manufacturing floor. Marketing. Sales. And a floating crew of Americans and other foreign nationals, all tech geniuses, one of whom appears to be in or near Northern California with dark web access to the Dutch mother ship. This holdup at St. Vartan's could be part of Skylark's ransomware wing. The pattern fits."

"What's his job? Does he have a name?"

"All we know is that he's the negotiator, likely American, may have lived in this area for years unnoticed. He has an IP address like a chameleon. We want that guy with his phone and computer. If he would just stand still."

The traffic light turned red and Joe turned to Bao.

"More on that," he said.

"After we meet with St. Vartan's response team, their corporate officers, lawyers, and IT head, we'll see how bad the situation is, what can be retrieved. We'll plug in to home base and try to take these killers down before they turn St. Vartan's network into local phone calls only."

Joe was thinking of the hundreds of patients lying helpless and unaware in hospital beds. "Tell me the truth, Bao. What are our chances of stopping them?"

"I just don't know. I really don't, Joe. But we're not alone in this. Our mother ship is bigger and smarter than theirs."

CHAPTER 16

JOE SAID "HELLO" to the unsmiling woman who was waiting for him and Bao when the elevator doors slid open on St. Vartan's top floor.

"I'm Christine, Mr. LaBreche's PA. Please come with me."

Christine's expression was pained, and she walked as if she had broken glass in her shoes. She didn't speak again, just took the lead, put her head down and struck out for the northern end of the corridor.

Joe and Bao followed Christine along the length of the executive floor. When they reached a glass-walled conference room at the far corner, Christine knocked on the door. A blue-suited man wearing a loosened tie around his collar got up from his chair at the head of the table, opened the door, and stepped back as the two-person FBI team entered the room.

"I'm Rob LaBreche, CEO," he said. "The guy that gets hung for this disaster."

He pulled the ends of his tie up under his jaw and, after fake-hanging himself, shook hands with Bao and Joe and offered them seats at the table. LaBreche introduced the seated semicircle of corporate officers by name and function. Joe made a mental note of the heads of the legal and IT departments. Next, LaBreche introduced Sveinn Thordarson, a stocky man in his sixties and the head of Cyber Security Incorporated, a well-known anti-cyberattack firm. He wore a dress shirt and blue tie, no jacket, good quality trousers, and had a short, trimmed beard. Thordarson in turn introduced his partner, Peter Wooten, as an anti-ransomware genius in a young but growing industry, expanding around the world. Wooten was about forty, a wiry six feet tall, red-haired, wearing square, rimless eyeglasses, chinos, and a Hawaiian shirt.

In the all-suited assemblage, Thordarson and Wooten stood out, as did Joe in his khaki shirt and work boots.

LaBreche said to Bao, "You know what I'm praying? That somehow through the arcane tricks of their trade, Sveinn and Pete will quickly restore our system and wall off our permeable network without loss of life. That's what I've been praying for over the last hour. And that you," he said, indicating Bao and Joe, "will find this filth and nail them to the walls of a maximum-security cell for the rest of their lives."

"Amen," said Thomas Walters, the head of IT. "This is madness. Obviously, it's evil to hold hospitals hostage, and more personally, we had an incident response plan in place. Within ten minutes of getting the threat, Thordarson and Wooten were on the phone."

Thordarson said, "Why don't I take it from here, Mr. Walters? First, nice to meet you both," he said to Bao and Joe. "Director Wong, I believe we worked together on that Chem Con breach...?"

"Five years ago. In Santa Rosa," she said. "Right you are. It was a squeaker."

LaBreche tapped his watch. "Sveinn?"

Sveinn Thordarson said, "Let me give you the streamlined summary. The ransom demand was sent to the hospital's top-tier mailboxes this morning. At 8:00 a.m., everyone at St. Vartan's with an executive function or a stethoscope, say two hundred people, received it. Some messages were sent to St. Vartan's email addresses. But at least half of our executives got the warning in their personal mailboxes. That was the panic button.

"Here's a printout of the email," he said, separating it from a pile of papers in front of him.

LaBreche had immediately forwarded the email to Steinmetz upon receipt. Joe and Bao had already seen the one-page printout that read, "Because you hired a low-rent response team, we've got the goods. We can take the entire hospital down below dead pool in five minutes: computers, medical equipment, refrigeration, everything but the flush toilets. Or you can find twenty million in crypto in the next forty-eight hours and deposit it into our wallet in outer space. See link below. Do that and most of your patients will survive. We'll also educate your lame IT director and tell you how to protect yourself in the future. You'll get a call from us at 1:00 p.m. today. Keep your lines open. All we want to hear from you is, 'We sent the crypto.'"

Thordarson exhaled and said, "It's signed 'Apocalypto.' This is an active start-up group and has some of the hallmarks of the older 123 Boom. Possibly it was seeded by Boom. Pete and I have been in touch with Apocalypto, identified ourselves. We let them know that the hospital cannot raise twenty million in any form within the time allowed and if they don't play this straight, we will hand off our investigation to the FBI."

Joe asked, "How much time did you buy?"

"We deposited seven million in exchange for two days' extension," said the head of the premier incident response company west of the Rockies.

"The deposit went to a virtual account on the dark web that is effectively a ghost bank. They can see it but they can't access it until we have proof they're out of our system."

LaBreche wasn't listening. He cut into the conversation, saying, "We've called for any external backup drives that may exist outside the hospital. We're in the process now of transferring as many patients out as we can find beds for, but other hospitals are packed. We have surgery patients on vents — my PA Christine's mother is one of them — and on heart-lung machines. Pete says that Apocalypto has been inside our systems for months. Is that right?"

Bao said, "Very likely."

LaBreche spit curses, paced, and shoved chairs as he circled the conference table.

"So, for sure they've burrowed into everything we have and do. We're not safe until Apocalypto is out of business and the people who ruined this hospital are in prison. Or worse."

Joe said, "That's why your cybersecurity team called us. Sveinn, Pete, tell us where we can help. We're ready."

CHAPTER 17

JOE WATCHED PETER WOOTEN square the papers and pens in front of him. Then he squared them again. Joe thought, *Precise, maybe OCD*. Perfect mental tic for a man in Pete's field. Check it. Check it again. And again.

Pete said, "We've tracked Apocalypto to a server in Bruges…"

"No longer there?" Bao said.

"Correct."

"Lucky guess," she said.

Christine came into the room and whispered to LaBreche, who said to her, "Might as well." Christine wheeled in a coffee cart and several people rose from their places for coffee, but Bao and Joe, the professional hack prevention team, and four top hospital executives who were sweating and making notes on their phones remained seated. They were fighting an enemy they didn't know and couldn't see, while trying to save lives and a very good hospital on an extremely tight deadline.

Pete Wooten said, "So, this morning at 9:03, after extending the deadline and funneling crypto into their blind Bitcoin wallet, we began to drill down on the malware. As I said, Apocalypto was pinging a server in Belgium. Then the signal hopped to another location.

"The program began seeking its point man on the West Coast from somewhere within a hundred miles of the Anglo-Scottish border, then the signal bounced around here in San Francisco."

"Sounds like an airplane was involved," said Joe.

LaBreche, who'd been pacing since accepting an offered cup of coffee, asked, "This hopping is some kind of 'Catch me if you can' kind of thing?"

"Exactly," said Thordarson. "By disguising their location and the program itself, we don't know who and where they are. Makes it hard to erect a defense. But we will locate the source and the target, Mr. LaBreche. That's what we do."

LaBreche looked hopeful, then a blink later, entirely depressed. He stopped his pacing near Joe's chair and said, "I might as well tell you, I had to be talked into working with the FBI. We don't want this to, you know, get out, but Pete convinced me to call in the Feds. Can you actually keep this quiet?"

Joe said, "Honestly? The fact of the attack may leak, Mr. LaBreche, but we won't be advertising our involvement. We understand what's at stake and we'll do everything possible to contain the situation. Maybe we'll come up with something that hasn't been done before. Anything else?"

LaBreche shrugged and Joe took that to be a no.

He said, "We'll check in when we have something to tell you. Pete? Sveinn? Your place or ours?"

CHAPTER 18

RILEY BOONE WAS the bailiff, the law enforcement officer in charge of maintaining court procedure. He was short but stood tall, and Yuki was always surprised by the volume and resonance of his voice as his announcement "Allll rise" caromed off the oak-paneled walls of Courtroom 8G.

A hundred and twenty people noisily stood as one—the counselors and their clients and deputies, the jurors, and the audience in the gallery—as the Honorable Henry William St. John entered through the door from his chambers into the courtroom.

A handsome man in his forties, Yuki thought Hank St. John had classic good looks, like an adman from the sixties—tall, fit, with a pencil mustache, always carrying a book. He stepped up to his enviable desk chair behind the bench, adjusted his robes, and took his seat.

Judge St. John motioned for all but the jurors to be seated. After Boone had sworn in the jury, they filled the jury box and Boone called the court to order. Two court officers took their places with their backs to the double doors of the entrance.

Nick Gaines, Mary Elena Hayes, and Yuki adjusted their chairs, pulling them up to the prosecution table. To Yuki's mind, Mary Elena looked perfectly composed in her nice brown skirt suit, understated makeup, and unruffled expression. She wondered if Mary Elena was recalling the dream she'd told to Yuki days ago about the movie courtroom, unreal but real, although the actual foreperson looked nothing like Sean Penn.

Across the aisle to their left, criminal defense attorney Edward Schneider—six two, 250 pounds—spoke behind his hand to his second chair. The defendant, Tyler Cates, checked out the courtroom. He leaned forward and peered around the bulk of his lawyer, stared across the aisle at Mary Elena. He continued to stare until Schneider's number two whispered, "Stop doing that."

Judge St. John put his hand over his mic and exchanged a few words with his clerk and then his voice broke into Yuki's thoughts.

"Ms. Castellano. Are the People ready to begin?"

Yuki got to her feet. "Yes, Your Honor."

Two seats down from her at the counsel table, Mary Elena moaned softly. "Oh, no."

Yuki turned her head and following Mary Elena's gaze saw two women in the gallery dressed like lunatics. They both wore hats, one with springs coming out of the top, the other with a cross-eyed cat perched on top. They were laughing.

Yuki stood, said, "Your Honor, may I approach?"

St. John waved her in. She spoke with him quietly but urgently, then returned to her table. The bailiff, Riley Boone, went directly to the gallery. Although the women having fun with the idea of a plaintiff with a mental disorder promised to keep their hats under their seats, they were firmly shown out of the courtroom.

Judge St. John addressed the room, saying, "This is a trial.

Serious work is done here and I will not brook funny business. Understood?"

Murmured affirmation buzzed through the room and St. John banged his gavel, returning silence to the courtroom.

"Ms. Castellano?" he said. "Shall we try again?"

Yuki walked to the jury box and put her hands on the rail. She smiled and made eye contact with all twelve jurors and the two alternates, many of whom she'd chosen during voir dire. They made a diverse mix of male, female, blue-collar, and white-collar, from multiple ethnic groups, with ages spanning thirty-six to sixty-eight. Nine were married with children.

Yuki cared about reaching every one of them.

The jurors lifted their eyes to hers and waited for her to speak. She let the silence grow until it was nearly intolerable.

CHAPTER 19

YUKI WAS VERY good at opening statements, laying out the facts of the crime chronologically without actually arguing the case. And now she was sure she was ready. If she rehearsed her opening once more, she'd risk scrambling the entire bowl of eggs.

Keiko's voice was in her head: *Keep it simple, Yuki-eh. You know this.*

Right. After formally introducing herself to the jurors, Yuki brought them back to six months earlier, when victim Mary Elena Hayes had been brutally attacked and raped in the changing room of a tony restaurant in the financial district.

"Here's what happened to Ms. Hayes on that day six months ago," she said. "Ms. Hayes had been to her dentist and was returning to her job at Raymond James, where she works in human resources. It was a long walk and Ms. Hayes needed to use a ladies' room pretty badly.

"She was coming up on a five-star restaurant called Xe Sogni and took a chance. A valet opened the door for her and she quickly found the maître d', Jules Lenoir. She asked him if she could use the facilities. Mr. Lenoir said yes to this well-dressed young lady and pointed her to a spiral staircase."

Yuki continued, "Ms. Hayes took the stairs up to a carpeted room, furnished with lockers and benches — the staff changing room, where at opposite sides of the room are two bathrooms, one for men and one for women.

"Ms. Hayes never reached the ladies' room.

"Within minutes after she'd climbed the stairs, diners on the floor below heard a loud scream and '*Nooooo!*' Mr. Lenoir will testify that he took this scream to be a distressed cry for help."

Yuki let the echo of that virtual scream hang over the jury box, then said, "One of Xe Sogni's clientele that day was a police sergeant having lunch with friends. I was one of those friends, and I, too, heard that scream. The police officer, Sergeant Lindsay Boxer of SFPD Homicide Division, will testify that she ran upstairs. She will tell you in her own words that she saw a nearly naked woman lying on the floor wearing only a pink bra pulled up over her breasts and that this woman had an assortment of fresh bruises on her arms and inner thighs as well as finger marks around her neck. Her eyes were swollen nearly shut and she had a large fist-sized bruise coming up on her left cheek.

"Sergeant Boxer asked this semiconscious young woman what had happened to her and she said, 'He raped us.' Let me repeat that. Ms. Hayes, the victim, said, 'He raped us.'"

Yuki paused to let Mary Elena's words work on the jury and saw surprise on several faces. Images of Claire's birthday lunch and Mary Elena Hayes's bruised body lit up Yuki's own mind, and for a moment she was as good as there at Xe Sogni six months ago.

Back in the present, Yuki walked along the front of the jury box and stopped at the center of the rail, looking into the eyes of the forewoman, Gayle Grabo, and the other jurors. What she saw in their faces confirmed what she'd anticipated. Fully attentive, they waited to hear more.

CHAPTER 20

JUDGE ST. JOHN cleared his throat with meaning and Yuki got the message. *Get on with it.*

The expected time limit for an opening statement is fifteen minutes. Yuki glanced at her watch. She was six minutes shy of fifteen, so she picked up the story where she'd left off, this time with more energy.

She said, "The apparent victim told Sergeant Boxer that her name was Loretta, but when the sergeant located her wallet, the name listed was Mary Elena Hayes. Apart from Ms. Hayes, there was only one other person in the changing room: the defendant, Tyler Cates, who worked in the kitchen. Sergeant Boxer located him half hidden behind a locker door. He was also naked from the waist down.

"At that point, Mr. Cates told Sergeant Boxer that the name of the woman on the floor was Olivia, not Loretta, that she was a liar, and that she had asked him for rough sex. He admitted, and we have his sworn statement, that he'd had sex with Olivia but insisted that she was the one who'd initiated it and directed him as to when and how."

Yuki continued the narrative, stating that Sergeant Boxer had called for help from a doctor. San Francisco's chief medical examiner, Dr. Claire Washburn, then came upstairs. Dr. Washburn gave Ms. Hayes a cursory examination while she waited for an ambulance to arrive. At about that time, backup in the form of two uniformed officers took Mr. Cates into custody to SFPD's Southern Station, right here in this building two floors up.

Yuki said, "Mr. Cates was questioned and he gave a statement to detectives before hiring an attorney. This interview was videotaped and will be entered into evidence by Sergeants McNeil and Chi, who interviewed Mr. Cates, and who will testify and show the videotape.

"But here's the main point. Mr. Cates told the detectives that when Mary Elena came into the room, he called out, 'Hey. Who are you?' And Ms. Hayes told him that her name was Mary Elena.

"That is a seemingly innocuous verbal exchange but let me repeat it again. When asked her name, Ms. Hayes told Mr. Cates that her name was Mary Elena. The answer is pivotal to determining what happened in Xe Sogni that day.

"Let me shift gears for a moment. Ms. Hayes has a mental disorder known as dissociative identity disorder, or DID. It was formerly known as split personality, or multiple personality disorder. In the course of this trial, you will hear from two highly qualified psychiatric experts who will tell you about this disorder and what it means to have alternate personalities. It's possible that while Ms. Hayes is testifying, one or more of those personalities will emerge.

"But for now, the critical point to know and remember is that this syndrome is the psychological result of severe childhood trauma. Some of those afflicted with this disorder may have two or even dozens of alternate personalities who exist to protect 'the body'—in this case, Ms. Hayes—from danger."

Yuki explained to the jurors that it was a crime to have sex with a person whose mental disorder makes it impossible for them to give informed consent.

"Here's how we know that Mr. Cates understood that Ms. Hayes had a psychological disability: Mary Elena Hayes told Mr. Cates her given name, Mary Elena. But she almost immediately felt threatened by Mr. Cates, which caused Olivia, one of her alternate personalities, to emerge. Olivia is a peacemaker and a people pleaser, and she moved Mary Elena out of the picture and dealt with Mr. Cates as best she could.

"But Olivia was no match for Mr. Cates. When she couldn't distract him or otherwise hold him off, another of Ms. Hayes's personalities, a tougher personality called Loretta, stepped in to fight back. Instead, Loretta absorbed the violent abuse. It was Loretta who told Sergeant Boxer, 'He raped us.'

"*Us.* Mary Elena, Olivia, and Loretta."

Yuki turned her head and briefly took in the gallery, the counsel table, and the defense table, where Tyler Cates's expression was as flat as a wall. As Yuki walked back to the prosecution table, she felt all the people in the courtroom watching her.

CHAPTER 21

CINDY THOMAS AND a dozen other avid journalists had stampeded around the Hall of Justice to the back entrance and, once there, had been flatly turned away by security guards. No surprise, really, but Cindy felt personally attached to Mary Elena, who'd been attacked and raped while the Women's Murder Club had been lunching on caviar.

Trying again to get into the courtroom, this time through the front door, Cindy maintained her pole position in the lead while Alison Kiel from the *American Enquirer* questioned her, trying to make friends, hoping to follow her into the Hall. Cindy put on extra speed. By the time she and the rest of the pack reached the Hall's front entrance and cleared security, court was in session.

Cindy adjusted her computer bag, hoisting its weight onto her shoulder as she took the elevator up to the second floor. Clearly, she'd wasted time trying to snare a quote from Yuki or Mary Elena, but hell, she'd had to try. She hoped that Louie Mack, one of the two court officers who manned the doors to Courtroom 8G, would hold "her" seat in the last row and would admit her to the court while it was in session.

Cindy didn't see Louie outside the courtroom as she headed toward it, and then, as if he could see through six inches of oak — he opened the door.

"Anybody else would be left standing in the hall," he said.

"Thanks, Louie. I was chasing a scoop. How'd you know?"

He said, "ADA Castellano texted me. Get in here. Quick."

Cindy edged into her seat, closest to the door. She plugged her devices into the socket in the baseboard and checked the time, again. It was later than she'd thought. Yuki was winding up her opening statement. Damn it. Cindy loved to watch Yuki work and now she'd missed her setup for the trial.

"Shit."

The woman sitting in the seat to her left gave her a hard look. Cindy ignored her and concentrated on Yuki.

CHAPTER 22

YUKI SUBMITTED THREE copies of each of her exhibits to the clerk: the photos of Mary Elena's injuries, the transcript and a thumb drive of the police interview with Tyler Cates before he lawyered up, with a video of the interview. The clerk logged the exhibits and passed them to the judge for his approval. Defense counsel had already seen them so the clerk delivered the exhibits to the jury, who, to Yuki's eye, still looked a little shocked from her opening.

When the exhibits had been viewed and returned to the clerk, Yuki addressed the jurors again.

"As you saw from the photos, Ms. Hayes suffered a vicious attack. Mr. Cates punched her, strangled her, pulled her legs apart, and forcibly penetrated her. As you will see on the videotape, Mr. Cates claimed that Ms. Hayes 'asked for it.'

"It will be up to you to decide if her screams contradict this statement.

"During the course of this trial, we will introduce noted psychologist Dr. Laurie Birney, a specialist in the field of dissociative identity disorder. We will also introduce you to Dr. Stuart

Aronson, Ms. Hayes's treatment psychiatrist, who will testify about her condition and how it affects her emotions and behavior."

Yuki explained, "Alternate personalities, Olivia and Loretta, took over for Ms. Hayes when she was experiencing terrible fear, pain, and stress. This happens when the dominant personality, Mary Elena, is 'bumped' into a dark place that people with this disorder often call 'lost time.' This lost time is a form of amnesia and a hallmark of DID. Accordingly, Ms. Hayes does not remember what happened to her in the changing room at Xe Sogni, but it cannot be disputed. The beating and the rape did occur, and we will prove this to you with medical reports and forensic evidence showing a 100 percent match to Mr. Cates's DNA."

There was a murmur in the gallery that was shut down of its own accord. What would the ADA say next?

Yuki was pacing now, looking down at the floor as she collected her thoughts. Keiko's calming voice was in her head: *Okay now, my daughter, you are doing very well.*

Yuki launched the next and last part of her opening. "The defendant did indeed assault and rape Ms. Hayes. And whether or not he knew what Ms. Hayes's mental disorder was called, he knew that her name and personality changes that took place in his presence were not normal. Still, he violently assaulted her, sexually penetrated her as she screamed for help. Mr. Cates chose to take advantage of the situation, possibly thinking that it was his lucky day."

Ed Schneider objected to Yuki's putting her thoughts into his client's mouth and Judge St. John sustained his objection, ordering Yuki's last comment stricken from the record. Yuki felt it was a price worth paying.

She thanked the court and said, "We've concluded our opening statement."

Yuki returned to the counsel table, nearest to the jury box. She took her seat on the aisle and leaned across Gaines and whispered to Mary Elena, "Okay?"

Mary Elena said softly, "We're fine."

Gaines gave Yuki a hearty thumbs-up and then Judge St. John addressed the defense.

"Mr. Schneider, please proceed with your opening statement."

CHAPTER 23

YUKI HAD NEVER met Ed Schneider, but he was well-known in California as a cutthroat criminal defense attorney with an impressive batting average. Now, Tyler Cates's attorney rose to his feet. He buttoned his jacket and staked out a position behind the podium in the center of the well. Facing the jury box, he began to dismantle Yuki's platform, one board at a time.

"Your Honor, good people of the jury. I don't intend to take an hour to give the defense opening statement. The witnesses will fill you in on the events that took place in Xe Sogni because they were there.

"For now, let me say this.

"The defendant did not know that the plaintiff had a theoretical mental illness that blocks out real words and actions happening in actual present time. Why is knowledge of this theoretical mental illness critical to the prosecution's case?

"It's critical because my client has sworn that he did not know that there was anything wrong with Ms. Hayes. If he had known, it would have meant that Ms. Hayes could not give consent to having sex with him. That is the prosecution's case because sex without consent with a disabled person is a crime.

"There was no witness to the commission of the sex act, let alone that the defendant believed Ms. Hayes was mentally disabled. Ms. Hayes told my client that she wanted to have sex.

"Furthermore, when I say that Ms. Hayes's disorder is 'theoretical,' I mean there is no scientific proof that DID even exists. It's simply theory. Guesswork and make-work for untold numbers of psychiatrists, psychologists, psychiatric researchers, and social workers. However well-meaning, the expertise of these people lies in detecting and analyzing symptoms, then labeling them as mental disorders. They are not scientists, and I repeat, scientific evidence of DID does not exist.

"For example, a theory of another psychological disorder: It's been posited by psychiatrists for decades that depression is caused by a shortage of serotonin, a feel-good neurochemical produced in the brain. Until lately, the theory has been that early trauma causes the human brain to create additional *receptors* for this neurochemical. The effect of many additional receptors, according to this theory, is that the serotonin is sucked up into those receptors so quickly that it does not sufficiently bathe the brain cells with feel-good serotonin, and so the individual becomes depressed.

"Ever hear of a book called *Listening to Prozac*? This book posits that if a patient responds to selective serotonin reuptake inhibitors, like Prozac, they are therefore suffering from a shortage of serotonin, ergo, their depression is a psychiatric disorder and can be treated by serotonin.

"Manufacturers of a huge class of these selective serotonin reuptake inhibitors sold them by the boatload. Not long ago, it was proven that this theory—sold as 'science'—is faulty. SSRIs cured nothing. But Big Pharma pushed the theory disguised as proof and made billions.

"Back to the case at hand. Actually, there is no medication for DID. Psychoanalysis is recommended. Meditation. Learning what trauma triggers the presence of so-called alters. Tranquilizers. In other words, there's no standard of proof that DID exists. I could go down the list of psychological disorders where the proof is in the interpretation of symptoms, not in physical structures or provable disorders.

"Tyler Cates has common sense and a tenth-grade education. He washes vegetables and dishes for a living. He did not know if Mary Elena Hayes had dissociative identity disorder or a vivid imagination or just wanted to get roughed up by an attractive stranger. He didn't know, I don't know, and whatever Ms. Hayes says, I honestly say to her, 'You have a big and active imagination. You put yourself in a situation you couldn't control. You shouldn't do that again.'

"Mr. Cates couldn't take advantage of this so-called mentally disabled person who could not or did not give consent, because only the two of them were present in that changing room. There is no way to establish if Ms. Hayes has such a mental condition or if it just makes for good fiction or a rationale after the fact. At any rate, Tyler Cates didn't know a thing about it. Mary Elena Hayes, by any name, came on to him. He complied with her wishes."

Ed Schneider strode heavily back to the defense table, roughly pulled out his chair, and when it snagged on the table leg, he wrangled it into submission and sat down.

Schneider didn't intimidate Yuki and she'd remained unfazed while he spoke. Now it was time for Yuki to call her first witness.

CHAPTER 24

JOE WRENCHED THE steering wheel, sending his old Mercedes into a hard right turn around the curve on California Street. Bao fell against her seat belt, then was thrown back in her seat as Joe, staying close to Cyber Security Incorporated's Tesla, climbed the forty-five-degree incline of Jones Street. Bao hung on to the armrest, and as Joe took the hilly roads, she told him what she knew about Thordarson and Wooten.

"Sveinn Thordarson graduated MIT with honors in math— Jeez, Joe."

"Sorry, Bao. Keep talking."

"Where do you keep the barf bags?"

"Seriously?"

"Nooooo. As I was saying, Thordarson was then recruited by the Secret Service. Wooten graduated Harvard in the top 1 percent; majored in science and technology. He was snapped up by Intel and was on a management track. By then Thordarson had started his new business and offered Wooten a partnership in his cyber threat defense start-up."

Joe said, "That fits. I see Thordarson as a risk taker. Wooten's precise. I'd guess an intellectual."

"Here," said Bao, reading from her phone. "One of their clients says, 'Wooten can see threats in five dimensions, in or out of the sandbox.'"

"That fits."

"Good guess," Bao teased, bracing against the next curve with her hand on the dashboard.

Joe knew that in tech jargon, a sandbox was an isolated testing environment for trying out code changes and other experimental work. Like tracking cyber threats.

The Tesla pulled up to a ten-story office building on a mixed-use block in the Rincon Hill district. Joe parked behind the CS Inc. company car, and he and Bao joined Sveinn Thordarson and Pete Wooten at the building's entrance.

Inside, the lobby was fronted with a manned security desk, lined with white stone, and punctuated by a half dozen elevators. One of them was marked with a nameplate inscribed CYBER SECURITY INCORPORATED and had a biometric palm print reader below it. Thordarson cleared his guests through security, and Wooten put the flat of his hand on the palm reader. There was a *buzz*, a *thunk*, and the lift doors opened. The four got in and the car sped them directly to the top floor. The doors opened again, this time into a long white room taking up most of the tenth floor.

Joe was temporarily stunned by the pure white light evenly illuminating six long tables, running lengthwise, from back to front of the room, the SOC, or security operations center. Each of the tables held multiscreen computers from end to end. Behind them sat dozens of technology operators wearing headsets, their chairs pulled up to the tables, their eyes fixed on the screens.

There was a soundtrack, the clacking of keyboards and chatter of speech to fellow operators nearby.

Joe and Bao followed Thordarson and Wooten to the office at the rear of the room. Wooten closed the door behind them and Thordarson offered chairs and cold drinks. After all were seated, Joe asked how their process worked.

Thordarson squared the empty space in front of him with his hands. Then he said, "St. Vartan's wants us to work with the Feds and that's what I always recommend. We can track the evildoers but have no authority to arrest them."

Thordarson gave Joe and Bao his full intense attention. He said, "So, our charge is to eject Apocalypto's payload, reset what's been damaged or altered in St. Vartan's network, and set up the next level of protection. In this case, shutter all of the faulty protocols that Apocalypto has put into place in the last weeks or months, malware that is set to drop the instant the two-day extension period expires if the ransom doesn't drop into their bank. Once we've restored their systems, put blocks in place, St. Vartan's is going to be impermeable, and Apocalypto knows it."

"Smart of the hospital to have you at the ready," Bao said.

"Thanks, Director. It's still impossible to stop attacks before they happen, but our warning system did its job and we've been actively working since LaBreche called me three hours ago. Right now we're collecting indicators of compromise. When we're done, God willing, we'll have an impermeable hospital and we'll turn over the attackers' names or pseudonyms, IP addresses, a report on the malware, and other types of indicators to you guys."

"Stupendous," Bao said with a smile. "Now, I think I'll take a diet-something with caffeine. Jet lag."

CHAPTER 25

PETE WOOTEN OPENED the fridge under the table, took out a Diet Coke, held it up.

"Ice?"

"A nice cold can is fine," said Bao.

Wooten handed off Diet Cokes to Bao and Joe, grabbed a Red Bull for himself and one for Thordarson, then clinked cans with all three.

"To Fidelity, Bravery, Integrity," Wooten said, quoting the FBI motto. Bao grinned and Wooten returned a grin, then sat back down in his chair.

Thordarson said to the FBI visitors, "We brought you here to see our process in action. Pete and I developed a real-time attack map for locating cyberattacks."

"Real time how?" Bao asked.

"As you know, the current best practice is to have one person, say FBI or NSA, watching the attackers' end and the internal security folks watching the target—in this case the hospital. Our dream tracker watches both sides at the same time."

"Oh, wow," Bao said. "You're going to give us a demo?"

"Exactly. This is its actual maiden launch. We'd be interested in your read on CS Inc.'s just-minted attack catcher."

"Created right here."

He pointed a remote-control device at the eighty-inch screen on the wall to his right. A diagram appeared on the screen. Joe peered at it. Couldn't quite make out what he was looking at.

Thordarson said, "Can everyone see okay? I'll sharpen the contrast."

Wooten cut the overhead lights, and after Thordarson brightened the picture, Joe walked over to the screen and Bao rolled her chair closer. Now, the 3D diagram was clearer.

"Beautiful," said Joe.

"This program is part sandbox, part dream catcher. It's a perfectly in-scale diagram of the globe. Right now, we're viewing the northern hemisphere. Those pinpoint clusters of light represent individual devices signaling at 1,000 Hz or higher. Here's a sparse concentration of pinpoints in the Arctic," Wooten said. "Those are biologists' devices likely studying and recording lifeforms deep under the ice. And here, this is a military base in Croatia. These blips are coming from search engines powerful enough to hop over continents without being boosted by an outside network. And of course, they use the submarine fiber-optic cable backbone."

Wooten toggled a switch on the remote and the map rotated.

"We're seeking a signal of an IP address launched from a known location in Amsterdam or Bruges or Eastern Europe and coming toward a known location in Northern California, USA."

Sveinn said, "Pete, roll back the tracking record to two weeks ago."

Pete Wooten made some adjustments to the projector, winding back the time stream. The symbols on the diagram rapidly reassembled.

"Here we are," said Wooten. "Two weeks ago."

He jabbed a button on his remote, which brought the rotation and all other movement to a halt.

Wooten said, "Now, retroactively, we've identified devices that have been pinging the IP addresses of companies, individuals, targets of all kinds in Bruges, Amsterdam, Glasgow, and finally setting course for the City by the Bay. We developed an AI program that alerts us to a pair of hits that include Eastern Europe and Northern California. That's when our SOC team"—he pointed to the room outside the office—"runs the IP addresses through our programs to get IDs on the signal. That signal carries the payload and starts the destruction when directed. So far, we don't have those hits."

Wooten pressed a button and the program sped up to present time. Joe found it mesmerizing to watch computer signals break apart and reform. He was impressed by the display, but unless it produced a suspected attacker, it was all lipstick and no pig. As he watched the light array cross the East Coast of the US, the machine beeped.

"There—and none too soon, I should add," Wooten said, pointing to one glowing dot in a cluster. "That dot represents a device bearing a known twelve-digit IP address. It launched from Amsterdam and is searching now from a point in San Francisco."

"It's on the move," said Bao.

Joe added, "Unless my eyes are failing, it's crossing the bay."

Thordarson said, "We're monitoring that signal now. And this tag on the dot identifies the signal as a blacklisted entry. Not necessarily an attack, but an IP address that's pinged a hospital server before. Oakland Pediatrics, I'm guessing. And we watch to see if the next stop is St. Vartan's. Pete and I think that Apocalypto has at least one agent frequenting or living in this area."

Wooten pushed in on the blinking dot. All watched as a dot the size of a pinhead slowly crossed the San Francisco Bay, heading toward the mainland.

CHAPTER 26

I WAS PACING the corridor outside the dozen courtrooms on the second floor of the Hall, waiting to testify in the Tyler Cates trial. Like most detectives, I took all of my cases personally, and I wanted Cates off the street and in a cell for what he'd done to Mary Elena Hayes, and possibly others. I would tell the court what I knew to the best of my ability, while keeping any trace of disgust from my face.

The double doors leading to Courtroom 8G opened. Louie Mack, one of the court officers, said, "Sergeant Boxer? You're up."

He held the door as I walked through. I squeezed Cindy's shoulder and she touched my hand as I passed her sitting in her regular seat on the aisle of the last row. I kept walking, going through the gate in the bar and across the well to the witness box.

Bailiff Riley Boone extended the Bible. I put my left hand on the Good Book, raised my right, and swore to tell the whole truth and nothing but. Then I stepped up to the witness box and took my seat. Below and across from me, my dear friend Yuki Castellano walked toward me. I stole a quick look at Mary Elena, sitting at the prosecution table beside Nick Gaines. Did she remember me? The lights were on, but was she home? I didn't note any flicker of recognition in her eyes.

Yuki stepped over to the witness box in her smart suit and stiletto heels. Suppressing a smile, she said "Good morning, Sergeant Boxer."

I acknowledged her greeting and Yuki asked me if I had responded to a scream for help on the second floor of Xe Sogni on the date in question. I told her that I had, and Yuki questioned me for about fifteen minutes. She asked me about the scream, what I'd found when I arrived upstairs, what I'd seen in the dim light, and if I could identify Mary Elena Hayes. I said I could and did.

"Sergeant, do you remember asking Ms. Hayes to tell you what had happened to her?"

"Yes. She told me, 'He raped us,' and that her name was Loretta."

In response to Yuki's questions, I told the court about finding Tyler Cates half naked at the end of a row of lockers and arresting him for aggravated assault. And that I had asked the ME, Dr. Claire Washburn, to come upstairs, evaluate the victim, and call an ambulance while I kept Cates restrained while awaiting backup.

I said, "Mr. Cates told me that Mary Elena had informed him her name was Olivia, not Loretta, and that she had begged him for sex, 'hard and fast and right now.' I had cuffed him and called dispatch for a team of police officers to come to the restaurant. He was read his rights and arrested, then Mr. Cates was brought back to the station for booking."

"He was questioned at the station?"

"He was," I said. "By two inspector sergeants."

"And apparently, sometime after that, he was arraigned and pleaded not guilty."

"Correct."

"Do you see him in court today?"

"Yes. Mr. Cates is wearing a blue jacket and is sitting at the defense table."

Yuki had no further questions and defense counsel had none, reserving the right to call me at some other time. I was dismissed and left the courtroom.

I found Claire sitting on a bench in the corridor, her ankles crossed, wearing a blazer over her scrubs, reading her phone.

I said, "Hey, girlfriend."

"How'd it go, Linds?"

"Regular," I said. "Just the facts, ma'am."

The guard said to Claire, "Dr. Washburn? You've been called."

Claire has some arthritis in her right knee. She stuck out her arm, asking me, "Mind giving me a hand up?"

I braced and pulled Claire to her feet. Then we hugged, kissed cheeks, and I headed for the fire stairs.

The Fricke task force was waiting for me.

CHAPTER 27

IT ONLY TOOK two minutes for me to take the stairs to the Homicide squad room. I checked in with Bobby Nussbaum, our gatekeeper and squad assistant. He used hand signals to indicate that one of my shirt buttons was open while handing over a short stack of junk mail addressed to me.

I re-buttoned my shirt, then said, "Thanks, Bob," putting a little barb in it. He laughed. Bobby loves his job. I crossed in front of his desk, then walked four paces to the three-desk pod I share with Inspectors Rich Conklin and Sonia Alvarez.

Alvarez is the most recent addition to our Homicide squad. She was previously with Las Vegas Metro's Vice squad, where she'd starred in undercover work. Then she'd been handpicked for the SFPD by our chief, Charles Clapper.

Not long after joining us, she'd proven her tough-cop chops when she and I faced off against a mass murderer in the basement of the Bellagio Resort and Casino. She was all that; good with a gun, as well as being upbeat, fearless, a sharp interviewer, and she can carry a tune. In short, Sonia Alvarez is a pleasure to work with.

I asked her if the task force meeting had started.

"Not yet, but Cappy, Chi, and Conklin are all in Swanson's old office. But that's not all." She pointed to Brady's glass-walled office at the far end of the bullpen. I looked down the center aisle and saw Brady was meeting with two other men, all three standing and filling most of the usable space in that glass bread box. I made out DA Len "Red Dog" Parisi by the color of his tweeds. Chief Clapper filled in the rest of the eight-by-seven room.

Parisi rarely comes upstairs to our bullpen, but no doubt he was here to meet with Clapper and Brady about James Fricke's murder.

I squeezed in behind Alvarez's chair to reach my own so I could check my mail. I couldn't help but notice that Alvarez had her hand inside a bag of potato chips, specialty type, baked in truffle oil. This was her weakness and she'd gotten me hooked, too.

"Please take these," she said shoving the large foil bag over to my desk.

"Hey," I said, "pushing truffle chips is a felony."

She laughed, saying, "I never make you *eat* them."

"Okay. Pushing truffle chips is a misdemeanor in the first degree," I said, pulling open the bag. While feeding my new habit, I peered over Alvarez's shoulder and saw the dazzling image on her computer.

"Fricke Cottage," I commented as the immense mansion in Pacific Heights filled the screen.

"Fricke's man Bevaqua called for you," said Alvarez, referring to Jamie Fricke's house manager, Arthur Bevaqua. "How about taking me along for the ride?"

"Have you heard the expression 'Never volunteer'? Well, too

bad for you, Sonia. I'm putting you on the Fricke task force. Dust the chips off your shirt and come with me to the meeting."

Alvarez beamed. She cleaned up, put the chips in a file drawer, and downed her coffee. I pulled my phone from my pocket, texted Conklin that I was at my desk and would be down the hall in a minute. Then I called Arthur Bevaqua. Bevaqua picked up but his voice cracked so much I could hardly understand him.

After six months of working Holly Fricke's case, I'd logged in so many hours with Bevaqua, I almost felt we were related.

"I'm sorry this happened, Arthur. Stay in the house. I'll be there as soon as possible," I told him.

"Good," he said. "Very good."

Alvarez and I headed down the long corridor to the conference room that had once been Ted Swanson's corner office. Swanson was now deceased but his activities as a sociopathic renegade, responsible for the estimated deaths of more than a dozen cops and crooks and innumerable drug users, had left a stain on Southern Station's reputation. I didn't know if solving the Fricke murders would redeem us, but it would certainly be good for morale.

As we walked, I told Alvarez, "We've inspected every one of the thirty rooms in the Fricke house, spoken with everyone who worked there and is connected to Holly and Jamie. Cappy and Chi went farther afield."

"I'm fresh, Lindsay. Expect the unexpected."

She was right. We could use new eyes on the Fricke family tragedy and Alvarez was something of a lucky charm.

"Task force meeting first," I said. "Then, chez Fricke."

CHAPTER 28

TED SWANSON'S FORMER office was easily the gloomiest office in the Hall of Justice. That's how he'd liked it. Dark. Cold. Out of the way. He hadn't planned on dying in prison but it was what he deserved.

Post-Swanson's-mortem, the walls of his office were used to display crime-scene evidence, and Holly Fricke's morgue photos were still taped where I'd put them. The timeline was sketched in marker pen on the whiteboard. Soon we would fill in James Fricke's movements as we knew them and tape up his morgue shots and pictures of the place where he had died.

Chief Clapper stood by the whiteboard, still speaking with Brady and Red Dog. He nodded a hello toward me and I pulled up a chair at the table. Charlie Clapper's background was Homicide, then head of CSU, and now chief of police. Clapper is the ultimate pro, immaculate in his work and his person. He used to have a sense of humor but left it in the crime lab when he was promoted to the top cop job.

Now, he said to the task force, "I'll make this brief. If we don't find the Frickes' killer or killers, the FBI is taking over the case. Jamie was a white-collar criminal, fixing soccer games overseas. Now that frickin' James Fricke is dead, the CIA is starting an investigation overseas where his soccer team is based and where he surely had enemies. We'll take all the help that's offered," he said. "Northern Station is volunteering two of their three teams from the night shift. They'll report to Lieutenant Brady, who will be keeping me advised."

My old friend and current chief turned to me and said, "I'll be waiting for you to tell me, 'We got him.'"

Next, Parisi spoke to the half dozen of us. "What the chief said. I'll assign an ADA to this case, TBD, PDQ."

Then he spun his 350-pound girth around and left the room, creating a breeze in his wake.

Brady said, "Anyone have anything to add? Any questions? Beefs? Theories? Awright, then. Sergeant Boxer is primary. Cappy is chief firefighter. He and Chi go where needed. Conklin is point man, working from here. Lemke and Samuels as well as Michaels and Wang will pick up new cases that come in and will back us up on Fricke-related incidents. Northern Station cops will become available shortly."

After Brady had scheduled everyone assigned to the Fricke nightmare, he welcomed Alvarez to our task force. Then he dismissed us.

I was determined not to let the Frickes' killer—or killers—evade us, but that was my pride getting brassy. I couldn't afford to either doubt myself or be overconfident. I had to lead.

The sky was overcast, and by the time we signed out an unmarked car, rain was coming down hard. Alvarez took the wheel. The *thwack-thwack* repetition of the windshield wipers and low visibility concentrated my mind, and I turned my thoughts back to Holly Fricke. I pictured her on the parallel bars, on Jimmy Kimmel's late-night show. I had stored an image of her in the audience with schoolkids taking in the Cirque du Soleil. And I saw her lying dead on Pacific Avenue, wearing gray gym wear, her body drilled with bullets, five lethal shots, all of the wounds still oozing red.

Now her husband had suffered precisely the same kind of death. I turned every fold in my brain inside out looking for what I, we, might have overlooked in Holly's case to date. The woman had been admired and loved. She had no record. There had been no unanswered questions except why and whodunit.

I had a sick feeling that working Jamie's murder was going to be just as fruitless as working Holly's had been.

CHAPTER 29

ALVAREZ SPED UP the windshield wipers and was singing a song about rain. I didn't know the song and she only knew some of the words, but it was upbeat and so was she, filling in with "dah dah dah dee dah dah RAIN" when she lost the lyrics.

But I knew why she was so happy. She was getting out of the "house," and I had a feeling that, to her, working on this case was like being assigned to the Zodiac Killer task force.

I turned up the car radio, filling the front compartment with staticky calls from dispatch, and Alvarez didn't seem to notice. A half hour after leaving the Hall, she pulled the unmarked Chevy up to the front gates of a house that looked like a cross between a castle and a wedding cake.

I checked my gear, unbuckled the seat belt, swung my legs out of the car, and bounded up to the intercom at the gates. I pressed the button and said my name. There was an answering buzz and the gates swung open wide.

I got back into the unmarked and Alvarez drove through, then around the circular drive, stopping at the broad steps that rose to the wide expanse of the portico. We walked together to the front door—which sprang open. Arthur Bevaqua stood in the doorway.

Bevaqua was forty and had been with Jamie Fricke for twenty years, working his way up from kitchen aide to right-hand man in charge of the staff at the Fricke house on Pacific Avenue. He was tall, fit, and well-groomed, but his face was swollen from crying, just as it had looked right after Holly was killed.

Our task force had interviewed him for days at a time after Holly's death and he wanted to be questioned more. Anything he could do, he would do. We'd double-teamed him every time we'd gone to the Frickes' home. He had a solid alibi for the time of Holly's death and swore that Jamie hadn't and couldn't have killed her. He hadn't had any clues, leads, hunches about who would have hated Holly or even who could have killed her just to hurt Jamie, who'd been embraced by the 1 percent but widely disliked by regular folk. Theft had been part of Holly's case; neither the very pricey jewelry that she'd been wearing nor her car had turned up. Jamie's watch, wedding ring, and new Jaguar had also been stolen and disappeared.

Had they both been killed for personal property?

People had been killed for much less. But I just didn't believe it.

I looked at the impeccably attired Arthur Bevaqua as water dripped from my hair and soaked my jacket. Alvarez introduced herself and Arthur welcomed us both.

He said, "Step in. Give me a second. I'll get towels."

Alvarez and I took off our shoes and jackets, accepted slippers and towels for our hair, and Arthur told us that he'd set up a light lunch in the solarium.

"Patty insisted," he said of the cook, Patty Delaney.

"Please join us, Arthur."

"I think I will," he said.

He walked us through the high-ceilinged rooms hung with what to my eye looked to be millions of dollars in museum-grade art, including a few old masters featuring rearing horses on gory battlefields. Victorian furniture looked quite at home and Oriental rugs softened and enlivened the stone floors. We followed him through an arched entrance at the western end of the ground floor and entered an enormous solarium with a rounded thirty-foot-high glass-paned ceiling.

Arthur showed us to a wrought-iron table set with linens and silver, surrounded by tall potted palms and hanging succulents. Beyond the glass walls was a stupendous view of the Golden Gate Bridge, Alcatraz, and San Francisco Bay. Arthur pulled out chairs for us, saying, "I'll be right back."

He left and I said to Alvarez, "Train your instincts on him."

CHAPTER 30

ARTHUR RETURNED WITH an ice bucket filled with bottles of sparkling water. He pulled up a chair and joined us as a subdued Patty brought out aromatic bowls of chili—vegetarian for Arthur, with ground, grass-fed beef for us girls—and a basket of warm sourdough rolls. I introduced Patty to Alvarez, offered our condolences, and said we'd catch up with her later.

I was grateful for the lunch, but I was distressed, picturing Jamie Fricke's crime scene washing away in the downpour. That, and knowing I was going to have to question Arthur Bevaqua and the staff again, reopening old wounds.

After the blond, thirtysomething cook had left the solarium, Arthur said, "Sergeant Boxer. Yesterday, I was with Mr. Jamie in his office straightening up, when he got a call on his cell. He told me that he had to leave but he'd be right back."

"Do you know who called him?"

"He didn't say. I got a feeling he'd been expecting the call. And of course, he took his phone with him."

The phone that's now in SFPD's property room, I thought, then asked, "What did you hear him say?"

"He said, 'Seriously? Yes. I'll meet you there in five.' He told me to have Rafe bring his car around. I watched Mr. Jamie get into the Jag and drive off. I never saw him alive again."

I said, "What's Rafe's last name?"

"Talbot."

"Where is he now?"

"He has an apartment over the garage."

Chi and Cappy had interviewed him twice before and found nothing suspicious about him. Their notes mentioned that he had a Kimber handgun and it was registered. Rafe's number was likely in Cappy's notebook, but I took it for mine. To my right, Alvarez asked Bevaqua, "How did Jamie seem to you? Scared? Excited? Pissed off?"

"Excited," Arthur said. "And there's this."

Arthur pulled a sheaf of papers, folded lengthwise, from his inside jacket pocket and handed the sheaf to me. It was a document printout, a work in progress, and it was out of order. A quick look showed me that some lines had been struck out and other lines written in the margins with a ballpoint pen. The new lines had been initialed and dated.

But it was the title on the first page that chilled me.

Alvarez saw the look on my face and tugged the papers out of my hand. I watched her expression and saw that she was as stunned as I. This might be the clue of clues, the piece I'd never seen before that could unravel the mystery of the Fricke murders.

Centered on the top line of the front page were the words "Last Will and Testament of James R. Fricke III."

CHAPTER 31

ALVAREZ, ARTHUR, AND I stood in the doorway of Jamie Fricke's office. I was desperate to read his will but I wanted to do it privately. I clutched the pages and said to Arthur, "How about giving Inspector Alvarez a tour of the place?"

"My pleasure. Downstairs first?"

As they headed for the parlor, I reentered Jamie's office and shut the door. Rich Conklin and I had been in this room with Jamie about a dozen times in the last months. Each time I'd steeled myself for what I knew was coming. Jamie would deflect our questions in the way he had of being rude without crossing the line. No name-calling. No actual bullying. He was just cold, contemptuous, and used as few words as possible.

I'd always let the chill roll off my shoulders into the corners of the room while I watched and listened for tells or accidental self-indicting utterances. Which never happened. Fricke saw himself as some kind of royalty and this room was his seat of power. It felt that way to me, too. More than an office, the room was also a two-story-tall library, a trophy parlor, and a private sanctuary. Fricke's large mahogany desk was at the center of the room resting on a jillion-dollar Oriental carpet. Neat stacks of papers and magazines were piled on a credenza behind the desk, and a multiscreen computer sat in the center of it with the power turned off.

I leaned over and pressed the On button. Light blazed. One screen filled with soccer scores and the other was taken up with a TV show, a pair of sports commentators giving excited play-by-plays to enthusiasts in French.

A fireplace was centered on the wall across from the desk, dominated by a large oil painting of Jamie and Holly, his sons from a previous marriage, and his soccer team, the Bleus, arrayed around them. The trophy case was opposite the door and a pin light beamed down from the ceiling onto the gold cups and photos of winning games behind the glass.

I looked out the window onto the front of the house and called Rich on my cell. I asked him to get Jamie's phone out of the property room and dump the calls, incoming and outgoing.

I said, "He took a call and left the house about five minutes before he was shot."

"Crime lab has the phone now. You okay?" asked my partner, a man I loved like the brother I'd never had.

"Uh-huh. Why do you ask?"

"Your voice."

I cleared my throat. "Is that better?"

"Loads," he lied.

My throat was tight. I hadn't yet gone through the will but I wanted to, badly.

I said, "Rich, ask Red Dog to put a hot rush on a search warrant. The one in my pocket expires at midnight."

"He's done it. Judge Hoffman signed off. I've got it in Brady's desk."

"Thanks. Anything I need to know, text me. I'll check in with you after I've read Jamie's will."

He whistled through his teeth.

"Yeah. His will," I said. "I don't want to get overexcited. But ten minutes after we hang up, I'm going to know a lot more about Jamie Fricke than I do now."

"Do read. Call if you need me. I'm at Brady's desk making paper clip chains."

I laughed. "I'll call you soon."

There was a leather chesterfield sofa and a pair of matching deep brown leather chairs across from Jamie's desk. I switched on a table lamp, sat in one of the chairs, and tried to ready myself for the twenty-six pages of Jamie's last will that were calling out to me from my lap.

CHAPTER 32

I SAT IN the fine leather chair in Jamie Fricke's office, going through his will, cycling old thoughts and new, sure that the motive for Jamie's murder and maybe, God willing, Holly's, too, was just one blink away.

Feelings of imminent solution like this seem real and true and flatter you with your own genius. But I knew not to bet on them. I got a grip on myself, put the pages in order, and flipped to the last one. *Thank you, James* — he'd signed it, and had had it witnessed by Arthur Bevaqua while Holly was still alive.

If only Bevaqua had told us about it sooner.

I kept reading, skipped over long paragraphs of dense legalese, and halfway through found paragraph VI, the bequests. There. "If my wife survives me…"

I skimmed quickly, then forced myself to back up and slow down. In summary: If Holly had lived, she would have inherited the Pacific Heights manse and seventy million dollars in US T-bills and certificates of deposit. There was a two-page list of equities in Jamie's brokerage account that would also have gone to her. A big black X had been drawn with a marker pen through everything Jamie had planned to leave to Holly. He'd dated the changes four months ago and initialed them "JFIII."

But there was so much more to the Fricke holdings, all printed single-spaced, full of "heretofores" and "whereins," and sprinkled with Latin. I kept reading. Well, I skimmed. Assuming Holly's share had been returned to the whole, an enormous sum was now to be divided between Jamie's two adult sons, Leo and Rodney Fricke, the children he'd had with his first wife, Talia.

Two houses in Lucerne, Switzerland, were to be sold, the proceeds bequeathed to Holly's younger sister, Rae Bergen. Why? "For her many kindnesses," he'd written. "God Bless." And there was a margin note, an addendum to Rae's bequest that was too hard for me to read but had been cosigned "J. Borinstein."

Jamie's share in the team would revert to the team's manager. And there was more. Jamie had left three million each to Arthur Bevaqua, Patty Delaney, and two other women: Judy Borinstein, the Frickes' financial manager, and Marilyn Stein, who'd worked as Holly's assistant.

The size of the bequests to the women and to Jamie's right-hand man raised red flags. Why so much to the women? Were they girlfriends? Did the women have something on Jamie that I ought to know? Or did he just love them millions of dollars' worth? No better time than now to look into this munificent transfer of wealth.

CHAPTER 33

THE FIRST NAME on Jamie Fricke's list was Patricia Delaney, the Fricke family cook. Rich Conklin and I had interrogated Patty after Holly's murder and found no reason to suspect her, let alone hold her. She didn't have a police record, she was in the kitchen when Holly had been shot, and the whole household vouched for her — but I absolutely needed to speak with her again.

Judy Borinstein had signed as executor and financial manager. It was likely she wouldn't tell me anything that would betray a confidence, but maybe she had a clue that would break the case. I'd never met her, but I would, as soon as possible.

I'd previously interviewed Marilyn Stein, Holly's former assistant, quite intensely after Holly's death. She'd hired a lawyer, cried throughout the interviews, and said repeatedly, "You don't understand what it's like to work in such close proximity to this family."

I had asked her to please explain, but she would only say, "It's complicated."

I'd wondered if she'd been romantically involved with one of the

Frickes. I'd pressed her. I'd asked if she was more than a friend to Jamie and she refused to answer, just sobbed and kept her arm across her eyes. "Do you have feelings for Jamie?" I'd asked her. *No, no, no.*

Marilyn Stein had quit her job forthwith and moved to New York, where as far as I was aware, she still lived. I had no cause to arrest her, but I got less from Marilyn Stein than from the fortune cookie that comes with my wonton soup.

Her lawyer had said, "That's enough, isn't it, Sergeant? Ms. Stein loves this family. She has a solid alibi for the time of Mrs. Fricke's death. You've checked her alibi, so unless she's under arrest, Ms. Stein has a plane to catch."

I was folding up the will when I noticed a margin note on the reverse of the back page. It read, "To Judy Borinstein, my executor: I've left personal notes to Arthur, Patty, and Marilyn in my desk, center drawer."

The postscript was signed, witnessed, and dated only a few weeks after Holly's murder. Judy Borinstein might know Marilyn's relationship with the Frickes. I had to know.

CHAPTER 34

I HOISTED MYSELF up from the deep brown chair and moved to Jamie Fricke's massive chair behind his massive desk. There was a photo beneath the lamp: a great snapshot of Jamie and Holly looking in love, framed in sterling silver. They had been a handsome couple. Jamie clearly had the charisma of Hollywood leading men like Clooney, Bale, Pitt, Craig. In this picture, he wore sports casual attire and had his arm around Holly, gripping her shoulder in a way that made me feel that he not only loved her, he'd never let her go.

Holly glowed in his embrace. She wore a tennis outfit, her streaked blond curls adding a girlish note to her picture-perfect features. She looked every bit the winner in everything she did.

I was struck again by the sense I'd had at the scene of Jamie's murder, that his death and Holly's were so similar, so closely tied, there had to be a killer—or a reason—in common. Arthur had never given me a hint that would put both Holly and Jamie in a killer's crosshairs. Now, for the first time, I wondered if Arthur could have been looking through those crosshairs himself.

It was a big ugly idea, but as Marilyn Stein had sobbed, "You don't understand what it's like to work in such close proximity to this family." Had Arthur loved Holly? Had they been involved and she'd dropped him? Had he had her killed? Or had Jamie hired a hit man to put her down for cheating on him with Arthur? If so, had Arthur paid Jamie back in kind?

It was another hunch only. But it checked a number of boxes and I couldn't quite shake it. Maybe Jamie had left the answer in a note inside his desk drawer.

CHAPTER 35

THE DRAWER WAS locked.

I had latex gloves in my pocket, so I put them on before I patted the surface of the desk, unplugged the computer, and examined each piece as I put the parts on the floor. I looked under the drawer and opened the paper files in the desk's double pedestal. I did it carefully and thoroughly. I did not find a key even inside the file marked "K." I looked under the lamp, took it apart from base to harp and shade. I still didn't find the key.

I leaned back in the chair, swiveled it, and looked up. I took in the thousands upon thousands of books, pressed together in the stacks twenty feet high. Wheeled ladders on rails reached up to the top shelves. The proper key was probably on Jamie's key chain out at the crime lab. But if Jamie Fricke had hidden another key inside a book, I would need twenty people committed to opening each one, fanning the pages for weeks on end.

Or I could break the drawer from the underside and would be disciplined for doing that, or even sued. But if I found evidence, it would be worth it.

In tossing Jamie's desk, I had cleaned off the surface, thrown the bits and pieces onto one of the leather chairs. I was looking at the fireplace mantel and the painting above it when a small idea bloomed. The framed photo of Jamie and Holly in love that had been on the desk under the lamp was now on the chair face down. I reached that chair in ten seconds, picked up the framed photo, and turned the lovebirds over.

The back of the frame had small catches all the way around, keeping the frame's back in place. After opening half of the catches, I got my fingers under the backing and ripped it off. Then I said "hello" to a small silver key taped behind the photo.

I peeled off the tape, sure that the key would open the drawer and at the same time sure that it wouldn't. Still, I fitted the key into the keyhole in the center drawer and with fifty-fifty odds in mind, I turned the key and the tumblers tumbled. I slid the drawer open.

The contents were disorganized, the drawer filled with business cards and bills and other office litter. I pawed around until I found five cream-colored envelopes each about five by four inches, all bound together with a blue rubber band.

A note to Patricia Delaney was on top of that little stack. I removed it, and using a short, plain letter opener, slipped the blade under the glued flap, pulled out the card, and flipped it over.

CHAPTER 36

THE NOTE CARD to Patricia Delaney read:

"To my darling Pattycakes,

"You know that I love you so very much. I've left you enough money to support you for many years. And I've left you a remembrance of all we've shared. Judy Borinstein has access to my safe deposit box. I hope when you read this, I am in my dotage and yours is the last face I see before closing my eyes forever. Your loving bear-man. J."

What was that?

Jamie and Patty were in love?

As that bombshell exploded in my boggled mind, I opened the next note, addressed to "Dearest Marly." Was Marly a pet name for Holly's assistant, Marilyn Stein?

"Marly, I hope you will always remember that you are the brightest of stars. Some of my best hours on earth were spent with you, our minds and bodies joined, and the earth indeed did move when we were together. My regret that we couldn't formalize our love is profound. That you are reading this note means we will have no more time together. I'm not sure I made it clear how much of my heart and soul belong to you. All my love. James."

I was trying it on. Was that dog, Jamie Fricke, really capable of heartfelt love for Holly, Patty, and Marilyn all at the same time? I wondered if he'd faked it all or if somehow, he was able to split his love many ways. No woman I knew or had ever known would have accepted that. And the next question was, who among them would have had him killed for his infidelities? Or was there a reason that had nothing to do with love?

The third note, inside an envelope the same size as the other two, was addressed to Arthur Bevaqua.

I'd just taken it into my gloved hand when my phone rang. It was Alvarez.

"You have to come out of there, Sergeant. Right now!" she shouted through my iPhone.

I heard scrabbling on the floor above my head, and then the tail end of a scream.

CHAPTER 37

YUKI STOOD BEHIND the prosecution table and watched her friend Claire Washburn raise her hand and swear on the Bible. Once she'd settled into the witness box, Yuki stepped forward and began questioning Claire about her job.

"Dr. Washburn, as San Francisco's chief medical examiner, how often do you examine living patients?"

Claire said, "Going to have to estimate the number."

"Of course. As best you can."

Claire told the court that she did postmortems on roughly a thousand bodies a year, but occasionally when she was called to the scene of an accident or a crime, there were survivors.

"For example?" Yuki asked.

"Say there's been a mass shooting or a fire, with both deceased and living victims at the scene. In that case, I call an ambulance and do first aid immediately; tourniquets, wound compression, chest compressions… The EMTs take it from there."

Yuki said, "Now, taking you back six months to the day in Xe Sogni. How did you come to examine Ms. Hayes?"

Claire explained the birthday lunch, the scream, and the call. "We were having lunch, four of us, including Sergeant Lindsay Boxer. There was a scream for help from the second floor. Sergeant Boxer ran up, and a short time later called my cell, saying, 'Can you come up and take a look?' I went."

Claire was interrupted by a loud yawn from the defense attorney. Yuki turned to glare at Ed Schneider, who didn't give a flip. He actually grinned back at her. Even Tyler Cates cracked a smile.

The judge leaned across his bench and said, "Restrain yourself, Mr. Schneider. Or else. You get me?"

"Yes, Your Honor. My apologies."

The judge told Claire to go on.

Yuki asked Claire, "Can you tell the jury what you saw on the second floor?"

"Well, it took a moment for my eyes to focus. The light was dim."

Claire described the locker room, and how Sergeant Boxer had cuffed the defendant, who was naked from the waist down.

Yuki asked, "Did you see Ms. Hayes?"

"She was lying on the floor in shadow," said Claire, "but I could see from her contorted position that she was in bad shape. An ambulance was already on the way, so I gave Ms. Hayes the best examination I could do without instruments."

"And what did you find?"

"Ms. Hayes showed signs of trauma from a beating. She was bruised all over her body and there were handprints around her neck. Clearly someone had manually strangled her and stopped just short of killing her."

Yuki prompted Claire to go on and Claire commented that "Ms. Hayes seemed disoriented."

Yuki asked for details and Claire explained that along with

giving a different name than the one on her ID, Ms. Hayes was suffering from acute disorientation.

"I asked her to follow my finger with her eyes and she couldn't track it. That lack of eye motility can indicate a concussion or other brain injury. It can also indicate trauma or some form of mental disorder."

"Is the person you found in the locker room inside this courtroom?"

Claire swung her eyes to the prosecution table and said, "Ms. Hayes is sitting right there, wearing a brown suit."

Yuki thanked Claire, and Judge St. John asked the defense if they'd like to cross. Schneider replied in the negative.

The judge asked Claire to step down.

Claire looked up to the judge and said, "Your Honor, okay if the bailiff gives me a hand? I've got arthritis in my knee…"

"Of course, of course."

Bailiff Riley Boone came over to the witness box, offering Claire his arm and a nice smile. Claire leaned on the court officer and got to her feet, thanking him.

"Anytime, doctor."

When Claire had left the courtroom, Yuki called her next witness.

CHAPTER 38

YUKI HAD CHOSEN Dr. Laurie Birney carefully. She was a well-known and highly respected psychologist in her fifties, a top expert in the field of dissociative identity disorders as a practitioner and an educator, and often called as an expert witness in cases like this.

After Dr. Birney was sworn in, Yuki asked questions that elicited her credentials and accomplishments. Then Yuki turned her head to see how Mary Elena was doing. She couldn't read her client's expression—which she thought was a good thing. Yuki also saw Red Dog standing at the back of the gallery. She caught his eye before turning back to her witness.

"Dr. Birney, have you ever treated or even met Ms. Hayes?"

"No, I have not."

"Have you had patients with dissociative identity disorder?"

"Oh, yes. I wrote my first thesis on DID when it was still called 'split personality' or 'multiple personality disorder.'"

"And you're an expert on other dissociative disorders?"

"It seems immodest to say so."

"That would be a yes?"

Dr. Birney smiled and said, "Yes."

Yuki still felt the burn of Schneider's smug opening statement, in which he claimed that psychology was bull. Yuki was damned sure he would use that same argument in his closing statement, too. And it would only take one holdout on the jury to crash her case against Tyler Cates into a wall.

But Schneider hadn't yet gone up against the authority of Laurie Birney. Her soft ways might fool him into taking a chance.

As Yuki turned back to her witness, she noticed peripherally that DA Parisi had moved from the courtroom entrance to the prosecution table and had taken her seat next to Nick Gaines. Parisi was watching. Not signaling. So Yuki walked closer to her witness.

"Dr. Birney, please tell the jury about DID, what was once called multiple personality disorder."

"You don't have to ask twice," said Dr. Birney. "It's my life's work. How long have we got?"

There was appreciative laughter in the courtroom followed by complete silence as Dr. Birney explained DID.

"DID is notable for the patient's missing chunks of memory that cannot be explained by forgetfulness. And the hallmark of DID, the inspiration for movies like *The Three Faces of Eve*, is the presence of at least two distinct and as many as dozens of personalities that are enduring parts of the individual's main personality.

"These fragmented personalities are generally utilitarian in nature in that they come into being to protect 'the body' by serving as a line of defense against further attack or fear of attack."

"This is recognizable, is it not?" said Yuki.

"It can be. Memory loss, disorientation, depression, suicidal thoughts are a number of symptoms that are common in dissociative disorders—and from the point of view of the afflicted person, awakening inside your main personality in a situation you don't recognize, or similarly coming into real time in an alternate personality, can be disabling, especially if the individual has been physically assaulted. With DID, you have no memory of this situation, this assault or circumstance. That's devastating."

There was a loud shriek from the prosecution table behind Yuki. She whipped around to see Mary Elena standing, facing and screaming at DA Parisi, who rose awkwardly to his feet, stepping backward.

Mary Elena yelled, "You go. Go away, Oompah!"

Parisi said, "I'm sorry. I didn't mean..."

"Go away!" Mary Elena yelled again.

Judge St. John banged the gavel and said to the court, "Court is in recess for a half hour. Does that give you and your client enough time, Ms. Castellano?"

Yuki said, "Your Honor, I can't be sure. If that's not enough time, we'll return without the plaintiff."

Bailiff Riley Boone escorted the jurors out the side door to the jury room and at court officer Louie Mack's direction, those in the gallery complied as the room was emptied.

Yuki said, "Mary Elena, come with me."

"My name is Ana. Don't you know me?"

Yuki understood that an alter named Ana was present. Ana seemed larger than Mary Elena. She stood straighter, making her shoulders appear wider. She was angry, furious actually.

Nick Gaines said, "I'll walk Dr. Birney to her car."

Yuki put her hand loosely around Ana's upper arm in order to guide her and said, "Ana. My office is just at the end of the corridor. We'll talk, okay?"

Ana ripped away from Yuki and, glaring at the foot traffic in the corridor, walked alongside, stayed with her to the DA's office suite. Yuki thanked God that they had not run into Parisi.

CHAPTER 39

SONIA ALVAREZ SHOUTED at me, "Quick! Patty's room. Second floor, second room on the right."

I slammed the desk drawer shut, put the key in my front pants pocket, drew my gun, and followed Alvarez up the stairs. Bevaqua lunged past me, stiff-arming Alvarez out of his way and kicking open Patty Delaney's door. Alvarez held her weapon in a two-hand grip. Bevaqua was halfway across Patty's room when Alvarez yelled, "Arthur! Stop! Hands up. Stay where you are."

I didn't get it. "What's happening here?"

"I'd really like to know," said Alvarez.

We were in Patty's bedroom, a peach-colored chamber with a view of the bay through a pair of French doors. It had changed since I'd been here last. Patty had redecorated with a romantic bent.

I looked across the room to Patty, a cherubic blonde in her thirties, about five six, 140, now sitting naked on the edge of her four-poster bed. She pulled a floral quilt around her up to her chin, while heaving deep, wailing sobs. Alvarez had maneuvered Bevaqua so that he was facing the closed bedroom door.

I looked around. The gas fireplace opposite the bed was lit. An oil painting of an entwined nude couple on a chaise longue hung above it. The man's face was hidden in his partner's pale blond hair. There was a full-sized beveled mirror on the ceiling positioned over the bed.

I looked back to Patty, who was sobbing *no, no, no,* hugging pillows and crying into them.

Bevaqua shouted at Alvarez as she patted him down.

"I'm not armed. Don't be crazy, Inspector. I was trying to…Listen, Sergeant, I meant no harm. I'm in charge of the staff. Now more than ever. Okay if I put my hands down?"

"No," I said.

"I'm sorry I shoved you," he said to Alvarez. "Very sorry. I just didn't want for Patty to…"

"To what?"

I was processing slowly, like a first-generation computer, running theories, computing possibilities, weighing scenarios in the absence of facts. According to the note card I'd found in Jamie's desk, he and Patty were in love. The question that seemed to have an obvious answer: Was Bevaqua also involved with Delaney? Of course.

"I want to *console* her," Bevaqua shouted. "To *befriend* her, goddamnit."

"Arthur," I said. "Put your hands on your head."

Alvarez had holstered her gun and frisked Bevaqua up and down, front and back.

"He's unarmed," she said.

I had to be sure. I stooped beside Arthur and checked his ankles, didn't find a gun or any kind of weapon there, either. I said, "Arthur, go downstairs with Alvarez and wait for me at the kitchen table."

"You've got this all wrong."

"Do it or I'm taking you in."

"Okay, I'm going downstairs now. I'm doing what you say."

CHAPTER 40

ARTHUR BEVAQUA SHOT a look over his shoulder at Patty as he left the room with Alvarez. Her gun was in her hand again and she was walking right behind him.

I was confident Alvarez would be sitting across from Bevaqua at the granite kitchen table when I got down there. But at this minute, Patty was still under the covers clutching a blue garment to her face. It was a pajama top. Large man-sized. She was keening now—a terrible sound of bottomless grief that I didn't think could be faked.

I holstered my gun, switched on the overhead light, and looked around the room again. I was seeing things I hadn't noticed while crashing through the doorway with my gun drawn. Baby-blue thong panties on the floor near the Victorian bed; a horse whip over the back of the armchair. I toed a diaphanous curl of a nightgown with my shoe. I said, "Quite a party here, Patty. You and Arthur?"

Patty rolled toward me, propped her upper torso on her elbow, shook her head vigorously, and cried again. "Arthur? Noooo. It was

Jamie!" she bleated. "We made love until sunup. He was right here yesterday morning, his final hours alive. Now I want to die, too."

I'd just seen Patty an hour ago when she served lunch. I had noticed she was downcast but I hadn't imagined this. I had to re-order my thoughts—yet *this* Patty matched with "my darling Pattycakes."

"Do you know who killed him?" I asked this woman who looked vulnerable enough to bleed through her skin.

She shook her head no.

"Patty, you must have some idea. Was Jamie afraid of anyone? Had he been threatened? Did he have anything to do with Holly's murder?"

"*No, no, no.* But he didn't love her anymore. They had no secrets, though. Jamie and I—you're not going to believe me."

"I'm on your side, Patty. Talk to me."

"We were going to get married," she sputtered. "Holly knew, and they were going to get a divorce."

"Who else knew that?"

"It wasn't time to tell. Then Holly got shot…"

Patty searched my face looking to see if I believed her. I hadn't decided. I said, "Please get dressed. We need you to come to the station and give a formal statement."

"Again? You've got to be kidding."

"Arthur's coming, too."

"Why? Arthur didn't do anything."

"Let's go, Patty,"

"Do I need a lawyer?"

"You always have the right to a lawyer."

While Patty pulled on jeans and a cardigan, I opened drawers in her nightstand, then her dresser. Looking for what, I didn't know. A diary. A weapon. Letters from Jamie. Drugs. I had a search warrant for the house and I figured that covered individual rooms. If not, bad on me.

I found nothing but fancy dildos and lubricants along with her workaday outfits and lacy underclothes.

I turned on the closet light, gave her laundry basket a good tossing, moved on to the overhead shelves, feeling up handbags for the weight and shape of a gun. Nothing, nada, zero.

The red-eyed blonde turned to give me a questioning look.

"Do you have a gun, Patty? Tell me now if you do."

"No. I don't have a gun. Arthur doesn't have a gun. He's my friend. He's the only one who knows, knew, about me and Jamie."

She ran from the room and down the stairs. I followed as she turned toward the kitchen. She went into Arthur's arms while Alvarez and I looked on.

CHAPTER 41

THE KITCHEN WAS one of those to-die-for rooms one sees in glossy home decor magazines—marble-tiled walls and floor, with a stone table in the middle of the room—but I focused on Arthur Bevaqua, who had his arms around Patty, cooing, "It's going to be all right."

"Never," she said. "It will never be all right, Arthur."

I pulled out a chair for Patty and one for myself. She sat next to Arthur and I sat beside Alvarez. Arthur looked grief-stricken, as if he'd accidentally backed his car over his dog. The house was big and empty and quiet, except for the sound of Patty's thick breathing and the distant sound of a lawn mower.

I asked the two sitting across the table from us, "Who's caring for the grounds?"

"Joe Casey and Mike Thomas. They're here once a week. They don't come into the house. I hired them. They never met Jamie or Holly."

I asked Alvarez to go outside and get their information and IDs.

"Call for a car and ask them to come to the station for questioning. We know they didn't do it. We just want to know what they've observed."

Alvarez got up from the table and headed out.

I asked Arthur and Patty if they knew or had a good guess about who'd killed the Frickes.

Arthur answered. "Don't you know that I would do anything to know? If only I had a hint or a suspicion as to who killed Mr. Jamie and Mrs. Holly, I would give it up. You wouldn't have to ask. I loved them both."

"Arthur. Think. Who hated them? Who'd been swindled? Who'd been ditched? Who was jealous?"

He said, "Sergeant, no offense. There's a whole world of people the Frickes knew that I never met, or only met to bring a drink to. I opened doors. I hung up coats. I supervised the staff and sometimes I served meals. I kept the press from the door. I was a utility. I knew from things Jamie told me or dictated to me that a lot of people didn't like him. Players and fans from any city with a soccer team that lost to the Bleus. Any man with a woman Jamie had slept with. There were many."

"No," said Patty, fresh tears starting. "You're wrong about that."

"Patty, it's true."

He put his arm around her again and she put her elbows on the table and cried into her sleeves. Then she got up and unloaded the dishwasher.

I said, "Anyone you think we should be looking at?"

"This is just talk," Arthur said, "because I don't know anyone who would have killed either of them. I'm a house manager. Understand? Talk to Marilyn Stein again. She knew everyone who knew Holly."

"Anyone else?"

"Talk to Mr. Jamie's driver. Rafe Talbot. He was totally checked out and cleared before he got this job."

Alvarez poked her head back in the room. She said to me, "Backup is here."

Perfect timing.

CHAPTER 42

I SPOKE WITH Alvarez while standing in the Frickes' semi-circular driveway. "Turn Bevaqua over to Brady, Cappy, and Chi for interrogation, in whatever order." I pictured Cappy or Brady interviewing Arthur, surrounded by morgue shots of the deceased Frickes. He might open up. How many ways could he say, "I have no idea. I have no clue"?

Would Arthur confess? Would he finally spill a name?

I went on, saying to Alvarez, "Turn Delaney over to Conklin."

She and I both knew that Conklin was the best cop with women ever born.

"Brief Brady and sit in on as many interviews as possible," I said. "I'm going to call him and say to take his time getting their statements. Never mind tears and 'swear to God's. If anyone knows who killed the Frickes, it's these two."

I continued, "Keep the gardeners apart. Ask anyone on the team to talk to Casey and Thomas. Lemke and/or Samuels would both be good. If no one else is around, you do the interviews. I'm standing by," I said.

I called for another couple of units. Dispatch said, "On the way, Sergeant."

I walked to the garage, stepped through the open roll-up door. A muscular guy with thick white hair was inside sweeping the floor.

"Rafe Talbot?"

"Yes, ma'am."

I showed him my badge and we went together into his upstairs living quarters.

CHAPTER 43

RAFE TALBOT'S QUARTERS were as plain as a block of wood. Plain double bed covered with a gray sherpa blanket. Sink with a towel bar. A shelf of paperback books.

The kitchen table had a white linoleum top and looked like it had come from a used furniture store. A refrigerator hummed. The few posters on the wall were of rock groups from the 1980s. Beneath the posters sat what looked like a very pricey entertainment unit: a huge TV, abundant sound equipment.

There was no mess anywhere, no laundry, no dirty dishes. I saw no tattoos on Talbot's neck or arms but the shape of his nose suggested that he'd been a fighter or that at least someone had gotten in a punch. I judged him to be fifty-something.

"Sergeant, I have no idea who killed Jamie."

He looked like he wanted to talk, but couldn't find the words. He just couldn't do it. He shook his head.

Finally, he said, "What can I do? How can I freaking help when I don't know and can't even imagine it?"

Jamie Fricke had never warmed any part of me, so clearly there were things about him I just didn't get.

"It was my fault," Rafe Talbot said over and over again. "I should never have let him take the car without me."

And then he started talking in paragraphs.

"Yesterday morning, a little before eight thirty, Arthur told me to bring the car around. But Mr. Jamie said he was just driving over to Steiner Street. He'd be back in five minutes. He didn't say who he was meeting, and I didn't ask. Just drove the Jag to the front door, got out, handed him the keys."

Using my phone as a recorder, I spent an hour with Rafe going over the same well-trodden ground. Holly was loved. Jamie had many women and was apparently loved by some, feared by others. Rafe had only had this job for a couple of years. He knew the staff casually. No one confided secrets to him.

Rafe also had a girlfriend, Greta Schmidt, who worked as a caregiver, day shift. He spent his nights off at her place over in the Sunset district. She spent some nights, like last night, with Rafe. She'd left this morning while it was still dark.

He continued by saying he didn't know of anyone who would have killed the Frickes, but he listed several people who thought that Jamie was a son of a bitch, people Rafe had picked up or dropped off in the car, people who made a comment or two. He started writing names on the back of a grocery store receipt.

"Once I knew who we were picking up, where we were going, I'd close the barrier between the seats and put my earbuds in. I listened to my music when I was driving Mr. Jamie and guests.

"Everyone liked Holly," he continued. "I drove her, too."

I asked, "Did she ever step out on Jamie?"

"She had men friends. And she traveled. This coast, the other one. Overseas. I would drive her to the airport once a month. But if she had a boyfriend, I knew nothing about it."

"You have a record?" I asked him.

"When I was nineteen, I stole a car."

"How much time did you get?"

"Sixteen months at Wasco State, but six months off for good behavior. It was my first and only offense. Nothing since. Not even for speeding. I called Mr. Jamie when I was looking for a job two years ago, and he gave me this one. He knew my father years back."

"What happened to the guy who had the job before you?"

"He moved to Wisconsin to take care of his mother. Robert Corazzo. I have his number."

He wrote it down on the receipt.

"Rafe, our notes on you say that you have a gun?"

"Yes. A Kimber .40. It's registered. Only fired at a range and not in the last two months."

"I need it."

Rafe took the gun out of a high kitchen cabinet and gave it to me. I sniffed the muzzle. Smelled like nothing. Still, I confiscated it and the box it came in. I told him I was going to need an official statement from him at the station later today and to please not get lost.

"I won't go anywhere. Here's a present for you," he said.

He wrapped his hand around an empty ceramic coffee mug, put the mug in a paper bag, and handed it to me.

"My prints. I didn't wash it. My DNA should be all over the lip of it."

"Thanks, Rafe. It's all safe with me."

I let myself out of Rafe's garage apartment, checked out his nondescript gray Nissan just outside, typed the tag number into my phone, and returned to Jamie's office.

CHAPTER 44

JAMIE'S OFFICE LOOKED as I had left it. I gloved up and then opened the desk's center drawer, fished around, and found the other cream-colored envelopes. One was addressed to Marilyn Stein, Holly's former assistant; another to Judy Borinstein, financial manager; and another was addressed to Arthur Bevaqua.

I held the envelope for a moment. The letter opener again did the job. The note card inside had Jamie's handwriting on both sides.

I read every word fast. On the second read, after "Dear Arthur," I fell down the rabbit hole with the rabbit. As we tumbled like weightless astronauts, the rabbit said, "Wrong, wrong, wrong. You got it all wrong. You don't know anything."

CHAPTER 45

I WAS GOING through Arthur Bevaqua's bedroom, which was on the second floor, down the hall from Patty's. Like Patty, he had a bay view. Unlike Patty, his room was painted white. Photos on the wall were of pastel sunrises and blooming sunsets, and a very nice shot of Arthur sitting on a seawall between Jamie and Holly.

Arthur's closet was lined with pressed trousers and white shirts, dress coats and sports jackets. Ties hung from a rack inside the door, and a basket of laundry sat on the floor.

His dresser drawers were filled with neat stacks of underwear and rolled balls of socks organized by color. No evidence of frisky fooling around. His desk faced the windows and had two deep file drawers. I'd started to go through the one on the right when my phone rang. I recognized the name on my caller ID.

I took the call.

A woman said, "Sergeant Boxer? This is Judy Borinstein, James Fricke's financial manager. Your office told me that you're at the house. I'm only five blocks away. Okay if I come over to speak with you?"

I said, "Absolutely. I'll be in Mr. Fricke's office. I'll leave the door open."

When Ms. Borinstein arrived fifteen minutes later, I was sitting in Jamie's chair, going through his files. She was a fifty-something brunette, wearing a mauve-colored silk dress and a silver cross on a heavy chain. The diamond on her ring finger looked large enough to serve as a weapon in a fistfight. She looked formidable and at the same time stressed out, exhausted, and pretty sad.

I came around the desk, and after we'd shaken hands I offered her one of the chairs opposite Jamie's desk and took the other. She didn't look around the museum of Jamie's life, which told me that she'd been here before.

She got right to the point of her visit.

"Sergeant, can you authorize the release of Mr. Fricke's body? He was a congregant at St. Thomas Presbyterian and owns a family plot in their cemetery. As his emergency contact, I'm getting calls about his funeral."

I said, "I'll check with the ME. Hang on."

I speed-dialed Claire and we had five seconds of personal greeting, followed by one question and an answer. I signed off with my BFF and told Ms. Borinstein that the funeral home could pick up Jamie's body tomorrow morning, unexpected circumstances permitting.

"Thank you. My office phones are making us insane."

I said, "Do you have five minutes to talk, Ms. Borinstein?"

"Call me Judy. Of course, I've got time for you. And no, I don't know who killed James Fricke. I don't know who would have had the nerve."

Nerve wasn't the point. Motive was. But now that I had Judy Borinstein's attention, I thought she might tell me a few things I hadn't known before she'd walked through the door.

CHAPTER 46

JUDY BORINSTEIN LOOKED at her sports watch, then turned her blue-gray eyes on me.

I said, "I've been speaking with women who were in love with Jamie. What can you tell me? No judgment, Judy. I'm trying to understand him and the people he knew."

"If you're looking at me, Sergeant," Judy Borinstein said, "I don't go that way. Meaning, married men. Or clients."

I said, "Patty Delaney told me that Jamie wanted to marry her. I suspect he might also have been involved with Marilyn Stein. Both women were torn up by his death. Arthur Bevaqua told me that there were others who were emotionally, sexually involved with Jamie and believed that Holly was old news. Then, someone shot her dead. Judy, do you think Mr. Fricke was planning to divorce Holly?"

Judy said, "In my opinion, absolutely not. And I don't have any idea what bastard might have killed her. It was a sin. Okay. But, between us girls…"

Yes?

"I had a one-week 'thing' with James years ago. One week. In Bermuda. I was single and he was persuasive. The week was memorable, but it wasn't life-changing. I didn't think he was going to ditch Holly then or ever. While we were there, he proposed, which was ridiculous, and we parted as friends. Five years ago, Jamie called me and asked me if I would be his financial manager, handling his estate. Why, yes, I would. Then, after Holly was murdered, I'd say three weeks after, he wanted to update his will. Reallocate his bequests.

"Holly wasn't my client, but always came with Jamie when we met to discuss his business. She was a terrific person. Why was she killed? Why? Why? Anyway, James and I were still cutting and pasting his will when he was shot down. He did sign the hand-edited will that was in progress. I witnessed it."

I said, "Arthur gave me that last draft. I read the lines and between them and didn't see anything about a future new Mrs. Fricke."

Judy Borinstein looked at her watch again and sighed. She said, "When it came to spinning a fairy tale, no one could spin like James Fricke. It was his ego, Sergeant. He loved to sweep women off their footsies, make their sexual fantasies come true."

"Great sex, you're saying."

"Wish fulfillment. Stories were if the girl dreamed of a knight charging through the gates to the village, he'd have a steed and full-dress armor. If she wanted to be treated like a whore or a virgin on successive nights, James was never too bored or too tired to experiment. In my experience, most men treat sex as a form of masturbation. But James liked having a knockout effect on women."

What I was hearing was that Jamie was not just a womanizer; he specialized in creating the feeling of real-life love, but it was entirely contrived.

I said, "He was a narcissist."

Judy laughed. "World champ."

"And how did Holly handle her husband taking his love to town?"

"You know about Holly's parents, Bill and Sassy Bergen?"

"Some."

I'd read Cappy's interview notes and some magazine articles. Bill and Sassy Bergen were party people who'd held major charity events, were world travelers. I'd seen a hundred wedding pictures of Holly and Jamie and read dozens of interviews. But I hadn't met Holly in person and didn't know the Bergens.

"What should I know?" I asked Judy Borinstein.

"Okay, here's what I know or have heard. It was rumored that Bill and Sassy Bergen were hedonists. So, Holly had enough exposure to their lifestyle to be drawn to Jamie and not be affronted by his dalliances. And Jamie told me that Holly didn't get crazy, and neither did he, if either spent a night out. Or a week. That may have been a pitch but I wasn't catching."

I thought about my marriage to Joe. A safe haven. Husband, lover, father of our little girl, all of us eating take-out dinners, watching TV. Joe and I brainstormed our cases, occasionally had a week away together. We were happy.

Judy was digging in her bag for her car keys.

"Just one more question," I said. "Tell me about Arthur Bevaqua."

CHAPTER 47

JUDY BORINSTEIN SAID, "Walk me out to my car?"

I got to my feet. "Sure."

As we left the office, Judy said, "Arthur is a sweetie. You probably know he's been working for Jamie ever since he graduated from Cal State. Jamie bought him a house not far away in Cow Hollow."

"Wait. I thought Arthur lived here. He has a room on the second floor."

"I don't know about that, but Arthur is married. His husband, Simon Bevaqua, is a writer. If I remember correctly, he's been working on a book about the relationship between animals and humans since the Garden of Eden."

My jaw didn't drop, because I'd read the card Jamie left for Arthur.

"I couldn't have left home without you. Wishing you and Simon continued love, health, and a very happy life."

Judy laughed. "I made up the biblical reference," she said. "But as I understand it, Simon's been writing the book for years and years. Arthur signs off on the household expenses, does administrative duties, writes employee checks for Jamie. That's all I know about Arthur except that he was considered invaluable to the Fricke family. Ran things while the Frickes were away, managed the staff and the household budget. I know what he was paid — a lot — and I'd guess he needed the money."

We stopped at her car, a BMW, in the driveway.

Borinstein said, "I just got it. You're thinking of Arthur as a suspect? That's your wheelhouse, Sergeant, but I don't see it. What I see is that pretty soon Arthur's going to have to find another job."

I stood by as Judy Borinstein got into her sharp little Beemer. We mutually agreed to check in with each other as the curtain fell on her visit to the house of Fricke.

I turned back to the house, climbed the steps to the portico, and called Conklin, who was running point for Team Fricke.

He said, "Time check, Lindsay. Nothing new to report."

CHAPTER 48

THERE WAS THE usual scuffle as the folks in the gallery jostled for seats, put away their phones, slid handbags and computer cases under the benches, coughed, whispered, and settled in. His Honor Henry William St. John entered the courtroom through his private door from his chambers to the bench. All rose, then sat back down. The judge exchanged greetings with the clerk and bailiff, who escorted the jury in. Twelve jurors plus two alternates stood while Riley Boone swore them in, announced the trial part and docket number and that court was now in session.

As the room quieted down, crime writer Cindy Thomas of the *San Francisco Chronicle* turned on her recorder. It was a repeat of earlier. Only one thing had changed: Mary Elena Hayes was not in her seat between second chair, Nick Gaines, and ADA Yuki Castellano.

Judge St. John made his customary warnings to the gallery about keeping quiet and penalties for disturbances. Ready to begin, he said, "Over to you, Ms. Castellano."

Yuki stood, saying, "Thank you, Your Honor. The People call Dr. Stuart Aronson."

Dr. Aronson was the reason Yuki had decided to exclude Mary Elena from the proceedings today. The witness was Mary Elena's treating psychiatrist, and although she had given permission for him to explain her condition to a room full of strangers, Yuki felt it safer for her client's mental health that she not be present for the sharing of these intimate details. The reaction from the defense would surely flip her out.

Bailiff Riley Boone stepped out into the corridor for Dr. Aronson, who entered the courtroom, came up the center aisle, and took the witness stand. Dr. Aronson was of slightly less than average height and weight and had less hair than most men in their forties, but his severe expression and firm step communicated that he was to be taken seriously.

After Dr. Aronson had been sworn in and seated, Yuki asked softball questions about his Ivy League education, his teaching hospital background, and how long he'd been treating Mary Elena Hayes. While they were so engaged, Nick Gaines set up a computer on a stand in front of the counsel table.

Yuki said, "Dr. Aronson, it's true, isn't it, that you have permission from the plaintiff to share details of her disorder?"

"That's correct."

"And how is this disorder classified?"

Aronson said, "Mary Elena suffers from dissociative identity disorder, abbreviated as DID. Under extreme stress or danger, her full personality is fragmented, dissociated from her core personality, and one or more alternate personalities come forward and take over, in a sense, to protect her. These alternate personalities are often referred to as alters."

Yuki asked, "Is Ms. Hayes aware of these alters?"

"Sometimes," said Dr. Aronson. "Not all people with DID have the same awareness of their alters. Mary Elena is not generally aware of their behaviors because when they become present, they 'bump her away,' and take over for her main personality. She does know a few and sometimes interacts with them. And some of these alters know one another."

"Was Mary Elena born this way?"

"Not at all. DID is a protective mechanism developed by some victims of abuse and severe trauma. As with many patients I've seen who present with DID, the cause was gross sexual assault, which Mary Elena experienced as a child. I videotaped one of our recent sessions and I've given it to the prosecution. I think seeing this video will explain to the jury how Mary Elena's psychological disorder came about."

Defense Counsel Ed Schneider was on his feet. "Objection, Your Honor. Irrelevant. Dr. Aronson was not under oath and neither was his patient while this demonstration was made. It has nothing to do with my client or the charges against him."

Yuki objected.

"Your Honor, Ms. Hayes's disorder has everything to do with the case against Mr. Cates. We maintain that several of the plaintiff's alters appeared during his assault on her and that he was aware that she was psychologically impaired. As such, she could not stand up to him and he took advantage of her mental disability."

The judge said, "Objection overruled. Carry on, Ms. Castellano."

CHAPTER 49

YUKI SAID, "DR. ARONSON, please continue."

Aronson said, "By way of background, Mary Elena Hayes was under ten years old when she first suffered repeated sexual abuse by her grandfather, whom she called Oompah. Oompah lived in a house behind the Hayes house and would take care of the child in the afternoons while her parents were at work."

Aronson continued, "I've brought a tape of a session I had with Mary Elena taken not long after she was beaten and raped in Xe Sogni."

Yuki nodded at Gaines, and one of the court officers dimmed the overhead lights. Her number two positioned the projector toward a whiteboard that was visible to the jury, the judge, and a portion of the gallery.

A light was projected. The fan whirred and then a moving picture appeared on the whiteboard. In the video, Dr. Aronson sat in a lounge chair in a room painted pale blue. Mary Elena looked as she had looked in the courtroom but was dressed more casually, wearing a large pullover, leggings, and moccasins. She sat in a chair across from Dr. Aronson.

On the tape, Aronson asked his patient, "What do you remember about Oompah?"

Mary Elena shook her head no.

"I'm recording this session, Mary Elena. Please talk to me so I can compare your early memories with your current ones and evaluate your progress."

Mary Elena looked down at her clasped hands in her lap and very softly said, "Okay."

Her psychiatrist said, "Try going back in time. Place your younger self in the kitchen of the house where you grew up. Tell me what you see and hear and feel."

"I've told you."

"I know. Please tell me again."

"'K. The school bus has just brought me home," said present-day Mary Elena in a childlike voice Yuki recognized as belonging to Lily. "The house is empty except for Oompah."

"How old are you?"

"I think, second grade."

"Seven or eight?"

Mary Elena nodded, and her doctor asked, "What does he say to you?"

"Oompah says, 'Hello, darling, how did school go today?' I say, 'It was good. A dad came in for show-and-tell and showed us how to make a whistle with two fingers and a blade of grass.'"

Dr. Aronson said, "And then?"

"I start to go to my room, but Oompah gets between me and the kitchen doorway. He says he's gotten me my favorite snack. Chocolate pudding and Oreos."

The camera in Dr. Aronson's office was steady. A phone rang in an outer room and was answered. Traffic sounds came into the room from the street, but the camera stayed on Dr. Aronson leaning forward in his chair to better hear Mary Elena, speaking in Lily's high-pitched and wispy little-girl voice.

She told her doctor that Oompah gave her the snack in the kitchen and said that he'd spent all morning sorting out inventory in his hardware store and he was awfully tired. He then asked Mary Elena if she was ready for her nap. From the expression of stark fear on Mary Elena's face visible on the recording, she knew what was coming from her previous experience with Oompah. And she was remembering that resisting him would fail.

In the courtroom now, Dr. Aronson spoke up. "See this. On the tape, Mary Elena is her current age of twenty-eight. But her fear has thrown a switch in her mind. She's mentally in the second grade. She backs into her chair and hugs her knees."

On the tape, Mary Elena was saying, "Let's go outside, Oompah. Let's go for a ride in the car. I want to go to the park."

Then her voice changed, though it still sounded young. She said, "He came toward me and I pushed back and the chair fell over and Oompah picked me up. 'What hurts?' he asked me. I told him, 'I just want to go outside. Please, Oompah.' We went to the park."

On the tape, Aronson asked, "Who are you now?"

"My name is Olivia."

In the courtroom, Dr. Aronson said, "Mr. Gaines, please freeze the frame."

Gaines pressed a button and the scene froze.

CHAPTER 50

YUKI STOOD TEN feet away from Dr. Aronson and continued her direct examination.

She asked, "Did you ever call the police about Mary Elena's grandfather, or tell her parents?"

The doctor said, "Oompah had died by the time I started seeing Mary Elena in therapy. Both her parents are now dead, but at that time, she didn't want to tell them, particularly her mother, who was Oompah's only child. But she told me how she tried to protect herself. One of the signal traits of DID is the use of alters."

Yuki asked, "Can you explain more about these alters?"

Aronson described four alternate personalities he'd either met or been told about by Mary Elena. He began with Lily, the childlike alter who had been seen on the video. She was about the same age Mary Elena had been when she was first assaulted. Lily had some power to shame Oompah with her baby talk and manner, but as a grown man, he often as not overrode her.

Aronson explained that a couple of years after Lily's appearance in Mary Elena's mind, Olivia came into being. Olivia's personality was that of an ingenue who used her so-called feminine wiles to distract potential attackers. But Olivia had limited power as a guardian, and soon after Olivia became part of the group of alters, Loretta appeared.

Dr. Aronson noted, "I've only met Loretta one time, and when I asked her if she knew the other alters, she wouldn't answer. I later deduced that she'd been instructed to keep to herself by a fourth alter, Ana."

Yuki asked, "What is the nature of Ana?"

Dr. Aronson smoothed his hair back with his hand and seemed to search for the right words.

Finally, he said, "Mary Elena told me that Ana first appeared when she went to high school. Ana was older than the other alters and assumed a parental role in this grouping. She is authoritative, angry at what Mary Elena has suffered, and appeared when boys tried to get physical with Mary Elena.

"It was Ana who told me that she stood up to Mr. Cates, explaining to him that Mary Elena had a personality disorder. Ana told me that she'd specifically told Mr. Cates, 'Don't bother her. She is off-limits because she has a mental disorder that makes her much younger than she appears.' But he didn't listen to her."

The defendant, Tyler Cates, interrupted loudly, "Oh come on. This is crap," as Schneider added, "Hearsay, Your Honor."

The judge slammed down the gavel and cautioned both Cates and his lawyer. Yuki looked at the jury box. As she expected, she saw shock on the jurors' faces. If they bought that Mary Elena, in the person of Ana, told Tyler Cates that she was psychologically impaired, Cates was cooked.

Yuki asked, "Dr. Aronson, how long have you been treating Ms. Hayes?"

"Currently, for about the last six months. But I was at Handel-Reeves, a noted psychiatric hospital in San Francisco, and treated Mary Elena when as a teenager she was admitted to Handel-Reeves on five separate occasions and diagnosed with dissociative identity disorder, post-traumatic stress disorder, mixed personality disorder, and amnesia."

"Did she know Mr. Cates before the attack?"

"She told me that she did not. She does not know him now."

"Thank you, Dr. Aronson. I have nothing further."

Judge St. John turned to the defense and asked, "Mr. Schneider, do you wish to cross-examine the witness?"

CHAPTER 51

YUKI WATCHED ED SCHNEIDER stump across the well to the witness stand. He greeted the witness, getting his name wrong.

"Dr. Aronstein, how do you know that Ms. Hayes has this DID as opposed to faking it for her own benefit?"

Dr. Aronson didn't correct Schneider's mistake. "I first became her therapist when she was a teenager. Her core personality has aged to match her chronological age, but she still manifests the traits of DID and a few other disorders as well."

"So, you diagnosed her based on traits you observed in a therapeutic environment," said Schneider.

"Yes, that's right."

Schneider took a half turn toward the jury, then pivoted back to the witness. He said, "So you're telling us that the diagnosis of DID is based on hypothesis and/or a theory of intermittent behavior, as opposed to a physical illness like, say, cardiomyopathy."

Aronson asked, "Is there a physical marker for DID? Is that what you're asking me?"

He'd twisted the question just enough to make Schneider sharpen his point to Mary Elena's psychological condition.

"Yes, doctor. That's my question."

Aronson said, "In some cases, there can be a brain anomaly or physical damage that dictates abnormal thoughts and behaviors. But DID is a complicated disorder that is pieced out through interviews over a period of time."

Yuki hoped that Aronson was explaining the disorder in such a way that the jurors, even those who had not had therapy, could understand. He talked about the principal marker of the disorder, the two or more distinct personalities as well as depression and gaps in memory that Dr. Birney had also outlined.

Said Aronson, "These memory gaps cannot be attributed to substance abuse or any other physiological diagnosis."

Schneider said, "So this diagnosis is formed by the attending psychiatrist's analysis, but two such professionals could arrive at different diagnoses, isn't that right, doctor?"

Aronson smiled. "Absolutely. But, in my years with Mary Elena, I've not only observed her. I have been with her when she dissociates, and I have conferred with other psychiatrists at the hospital where we worked. This is how DID is diagnosed."

Yuki shut down her urge to shout, "Yeah!"

Aronson looked calm and competent, but Schneider's expression showed that he hadn't given up trying to discredit the doctor, and by extension, Mary Elena Hayes.

Schneider said, "Question, Doctor. Did Ms. Hayes have control of her body and her conduct on the day in question at Xe Sogni?"

"Yes. But the guile and the physical strength of the attacker would strongly determine the result."

Schneider smiled with his mouth but the rest of his face was stony.

"Dr. Aronstein. It's perfectly clear from what you've told us already that diagnosis of DID is somewhat arbitrary, made of observation, gut instinct, or guesswork—not lab tests or radiology or chemistry. In other words, not provable."

Yuki was on her feet. "Objection, Your Honor. Argumentative."

The judge sustained the objection.

But Schneider talked over the bang of the gavel and the judge's voice.

"—and because psychiatry is not considered a true science, the claim that any single person could know what another person suffers from, if anything…"

Yuki, in her best and loudest courtroom voice, said again, "Objection, Your Honor. Not only is counsel's commentary argumentative, it is irrelevant, immaterial, and clearly prejudicial."

Schneider shot back, "Your Honor, this evidence is central to showing that the case against my client is faulty and based on unprovable theory…"

The judge, in an equally elevated tone, pounded his gavel harder, saying, "That's enough, Mr. Schneider. The jury will disregard."

Despite the judge's gaveling, Dr. Aronson now joined the free-for-all.

"I don't agree that the diagnosis of DID and psychiatry itself is arbitrary. Studies are made over decades, consensus is formed, and diagnoses made that are evidenced by statistics and improvement and relief for the patient, sometimes with medication, sometimes partially, sometimes entirely, for the rest of their lives."

Schneider said dismissively, "I have nothing else."

Yuki's voice rang out in the courtroom. "Your Honor, I move to strike…"

At Yuki's loudly voiced objection, the judge told the clerk to strike Schneider's cross-examination and the doctor's response. He added, "There is a time for closing arguments and this wasn't it. The jury is instructed to disregard Mr. Schneider's commentary. I will see both counselors in my chambers, now.

"Court is adjourned until tomorrow morning at nine o'clock."

CHAPTER 52

JOE AND BAO had been sitting in Joe's car, watching the ferry terminal for over an hour. Ferries had docked, boarded, and launched. In all, ferries had arrived from five points across the bay and hundreds of passengers had disembarked.

Bao had her laptop open. She had uploaded Thordarson and Wooten's threat-catcher program, which indicated computer signals that hopped over oceans and continents. Presently, it showed an enlarged image of Northern California and was alive with pinpoints of light forming clusters and breaking apart. Not a single light came toward or departed from the ferry terminal. There were no hits on St. Vartan's Hospital that were also tagged as having hit on an office building in Amsterdam.

Joe said to Bao, "I'm calling Thordarson and Wooten."

Peter Wooten answered the video call.

Bao said, "We can see you. How's our reception?"

"First-class," said the red-haired cyber tracker from his office on Fremont Street.

Joe said, "Pete, if I'm St. Vartan's, I'm asking, can't you just unplug the hospital network to stop the bleeding?"

"We've taken a few computers off the servers. But if we disconnect the system, there are two possibilities that are as real as death. One, if Apocalypto has booby-trapped the system, it will trigger a complete shutdown and the damage will be biblical. Also, if we disconnect the server, we can't track the signal back to the attackers."

"Okay. My background in cyber threats is out of its league," said Joe.

"Not mine," said Bao.

"Nor mine," said Wooten. "I know you feel like nothing is happening, Joe. We need more time and this is our best chance to pull the line and hook them."

"Got it," Joe said. "All's clear at the ferry terminal."

"Keep the faith," said Wooten. "We're tagging incoming searches, so if they come up again…"

Joe left the conversation to Bao. She lived and breathed cyberterrorism. He wondered why Steinmetz had pulled a risk assessment specialist into a cyberwar with lethal consequences. He listened with one ear as tech talk flowed between the woman sitting beside him and a man who'd spent the last six years of his life becoming a cyber threat catcher.

He heard Wooten say, "We're making progress by process of elimination," then goodbyes, and Bao cut their connection.

"Had enough?" she said to Joe.

"Mmmm. I say we grab a slice then go back to Mission Street."

Bao said, "How do you like your pie?"

"Extra pepperoni with jalapeños."

"I wish I'd bet on that."

Joe laughed.

The pizza was hot and good enough, Bao was great company on a dull gray day, and it was good to have a partner again, especially one who understood the nuances of cyber warfare. But the clock was running out on the patients at St. Vartan's, and the clock was loud and persistent.

Joe let out a sigh, and Bao looked up as they cruised toward FBI HQ.

"Joe? It's good that we manned the ferry terminal, but it was a long shot. Wooten and Thordarson have the big guns. If or when they call us with a hit—"

"I like 'go' a lot more than 'wait.'"

Bao said, "I know. Get ready. Get set. Stand down." She dropped her eyes to her laptop, where the threat-catcher program displayed attacks in real time.

Joe crossed Market Street, took a left on McAllister Street to Polk to Mission, and was backing into a spot when his phone buzzed.

"It's Steinmetz," he said, pressing the button on his console. "Craig? We're parking a block from the office. You're on speaker."

CHAPTER 53

STEINMETZ'S VOICE FILLED the front compartment.

"Something just came in," the chief said. "There's an abandoned house on Turquoise Way, a teardown. It's been empty since the crypto market crashed. Suddenly, young guys, five or six of them, college age, start coming and going from this shack. Cars are parked all over.

"Our tipster peered into one of the windows just now. Saw these boys passed out on the floor and on furniture, and several expensive industrial-grade computer setups on the dining table. The neighbor's name is Wade McEnroe. He's a former Silicon Valley engineer and what he saw lit up his nervous system. He called Chief Clapper, who called me."

Joe said, "So, a bunch of college-age kids are holed up in an abandoned building. They could be taking control of a hospital network for twenty million—or watching porn in 3D."

Steinmetz said, "You have a better lead?"

"No. Give us the address. We're going to be outnumbered. Send backup."

Steinmetz agreed, read off the address, and clicked off.

Bao said, "It's just weird enough to be possible."

Joe unlocked the trunk, got out of the car, put on his Kevlar vest, and hung his badge on a chain around his neck. He gave a second vest to Bao, then got back behind the wheel and headed toward the house on Turquoise Way under occupation by a handful of squatters who might be holding hundreds of hospital patients for ransom.

CHAPTER 54

THE HOUSE ON Turquoise Way was faded blue, wood frame, one story high, squeezed in between two taller, bigger houses, and set back on its small wooded lot. Joe knew this area well. The small front yard meant that the rear of the house backed up to the top of a hill at the edge of Glen Canyon Park, a steep drop hundreds of feet above the floor of the valley below.

Joe parked across and up the street from the target house. His mood had picked up significantly since Steinmetz had given them this assignment. He took out his phone and got out of the car. He walked up and down, taking photos of the tags on vehicles. Bao tucked her gun into her waist holster, put her suit jacket on over the vest, and when Joe came back to the car, she said, "We need backup before we go into...that."

Joe called Steinmetz. It was midafternoon and the chief was out. His assistant picked up his call.

"Agent Molinari, it's Farah. Chief Steinmetz left you a message that SFPD is on the way. And also you got a call from a Sveinn Thordarson, twenty minutes ago. He said it's not urgent."

Joe thanked Farah and clicked off.

He said to Bao, "Car's on the way. So we still wait?"

"Who's in charge here?" she asked.

"You are. I'm freelance."

"We watch and wait."

Time passed without either speaking, then Bao reached the limit of her patience. "Okay," she said. "Let's move."

The street sloped up from the car toward the house but the driveway was a parking lot to four used American cars. They walked slowly, a nice-looking couple taking in the view, wearing badges, packing. They reached the poured concrete walk leading to the front door of the shabby blue house without seeing another soul on foot.

"We're not too conspicuous," she said, "but I do feel eyes on me."

Joe said, "I'll be opposite you in the doorway with my gun out. You knock."

"Oh, boy," she said.

As the agents started up the walkway in front of the house, a tall, dark-haired man wearing a ball cap, jeans, and a Giants windbreaker came out of the house next door and walked quickly toward them.

"I'm Wade McEnroe," he said. "I'm the one who called the police. You're FBI?" he said, looking at the badges.

Bao said, "SFPD called us in."

"Good," said McEnroe. "There's about a half dozen of them. Maybe they're just rich kids with nothing to do but sleep all day, drink all night, and play video games. But I spent twenty-five years in Silicon Valley and I recognize the tens of thousands' worth of industrial-grade computer hardware they've got there. It's all new, arrayed on the dining table."

Joe thanked McEnroe and gave him a business card, saying, "We're just checking things out. But for your safety, please go home. And thanks for calling the police."

CHAPTER 55

AFTER LEAVING THE Fricke house, I'd flagged down a cruiser, thrown myself against the back seat, and tuned in to my unanswered question. *Who killed the Frickes?*

I pictured their dead bodies on the street. Compared them. Both lying on their bellies, shot from behind. Holly's face was turned to the left. Jamie was cradling his face with his right arm.

Differences without distinction.

I pictured our array of possible subjects: Arthur, Rafe, Patty, and Jamie's other lovers from here to New York. Of course there was also the mystery man in black, who the neighbor had seen shoot Jamie and drive off in his Jaguar. A lot of work had been done, but we were still at square one. Maybe someone would walk into the station with a hot clue or a confession? It happened. But very rarely.

I got out of the cruiser at the Hall of Justice at 850 Bryant, took the main entrance, and, after putting my gun aside, went through the magnetometer. I bypassed the mob at the elevator bank and took the fire stairs to Homicide on four. I stopped at the front desk to check in with our gatekeeper, Bobby Nussbaum.

He said, "While you were out, some goon confessed to killing Jamie Fricke."

"You've got butter on your chin. Also, you are the world's worst liar."

He laughed, swiped at his chin, and told me that three dozen tips had been phoned in. "Here ya go."

He handed me a half inch of messages.

"Thanks. Where's Conklin?"

"He and Alvarez are in Interview One with"—he checked his log—"Patricia Delaney."

I texted Conklin and Alvarez that I would be in the observation room the size of a walk-in closet that shares a two-way mirror with Interview One. The mic and cameras were on. My attention was drawn through the glass to Conklin and Alvarez, who sat in plain gray chairs at a plain gray table. Across from them, facing the mirror, was Patty Delaney. She appeared to be melting over the tabletop. Her face was flushed and her chest heaved as she sobbed over folded arms. This woman of thirty-five was the picture of depression, petulance, and grief.

Team Fricke had gathered a lot of background on Patty from interviews with her and others in the Fricke household after Holly's murder. She'd tested negative for gunshot residue then and no doubt was negative today. When we ran her prints and photo through FBI criminal databases, they'd netted nothing, not even a *beep*. No one we'd questioned about her thought she had motive for or had taken part in executing Holly Bergen Fricke. I felt sure that went double for Jamie.

I pictured Patty in her floral quilt a few hours ago, distraught, angry, and shedding real tears. Jamie was dead. Her entire dream was dead.

My phone buzzed. Alvarez was texting me notes from the interview room, details from her interrogation of Patty to date. The subject was Patty's finances. She was well paid, and most of her paycheck went into her savings account. Her credit cards showed purchases of the Victoria's Secret variety. Cappy had previously checked her bank statements, and her income, expenditures, and savings all added up.

I looked up from my phone. Alvarez had gotten out of her chair. The mood had changed significantly inside the interview room.

CHAPTER 56

ALVAREZ WAS STANDING over Patty. Having dropped the good cop role, she was grilling the subject.

She said, "Are you listening, Patty? Holly and Jamie. Did they have a common enemy?"

Patty lifted her head to say, "You've already asked me that. I don't know. Jamie wouldn't have told *me*."

"Patty, I've asked you this before, too. It's important. Think. Have you heard any gossip since Holly's death? Someone sounding a little too pleased that Holly—"

"Oh for God's sake," Patty spat. "Am I under arrest?"

Conklin said, "No, of course not."

"May I go?"

"Yes, but hang in for another minute or two and I'll get you a ride home."

Alvarez said, "Excuse me," and left the room. She entered the observation room and said, "See anything interesting, Linds? Because, in my humble opinion, if she's behind either murder, she's wasting her life in the kitchen. She can act."

"She could do both, but I don't see her as cold and cunning. In fact the opposite. But that doesn't make you wrong."

I looked again at the wreck of Patty Delaney, who was pulling on her cardigan. Conklin was asking her to sign her statement, wrapping up the interview.

I said to Alvarez, "How do you see Delaney as a killer?"

Alvarez said, "Jealousy as motive? Get Holly out of the way, and then here comes shock and fury when Jamie doesn't make good on his promise."

"How'd she do it?"

"Hired a bad man with a gun."

I said, "Without money?"

"Guile. Promises."

I could almost see it. Patty was fetching. And for some people she'd be a soft place to land. I said, "She is due to inherit a boatload."

Alvarez said, "Huh. From Jamie? How much?"

"Three million."

"Whoa. If she knew, that's enough to pay a boatload of bad guys."

I turned my attention to Conklin: smart, kind, a great cop with women. He was saying, "I feel bad, Patty, about how much pain you're in. We're doing this now to clear you and because you know everyone who lived in or visited the Fricke house for—what is it, ten years you've worked there?"

"Eleven."

"Right. Eleven. So, we need your help."

I watched Patty relax her shoulders, unclench her hands, sit up in the chair.

She said, "What happens to me if I tell you something, and it gets out?"

Conklin said, "Your name will never be mentioned."

A long silence followed. Then Patty said, "I can't prove anything. Not a thing. But if I were you I'd look at photos from Holly's funeral. I wasn't there, but Arthur was, and he took a lot of pictures."

"You're saying the killer was there?"

Patty said, "I would think so. Maybe a woman."

"Tall? Thin? Young? Old?"

She stared at Conklin. Clearly she had finished speaking.

"Okay. Thank you, Patty."

My partner stood up, walked behind the subject, and helped her out of her chair, saying, "I'll get you that ride home."

CHAPTER 57

ALVAREZ AND I moved to the observation room attached to Interview Two and watched the formidable Jackson Brady interrogate Arthur Bevaqua. He tried to pin the Frickes' majordomo with an icy-blue stare from across the table, but the well-dressed house manager couldn't meet Brady's eyes.

Brady said, "Tell me again, Ah-thuh. From the beginning."

Arthur had loosened his tie, and I could see the sweat on his brow from where I stood in the observation room.

"Well, he looks shaken," I said to Alvarez. "Sorry I missed most of this."

"We can watch the tape," she said to me.

Now Bevaqua was saying to Brady, "I've told you the same thing over and over. I only have one story."

"I'm not bored," said Brady. "Run it again."

Arthur sighed. "I was up and dressed at seven, as usual. Mr. Jamie came downstairs at eight. Patty made coffee and brought it into the office for us. While she was making his omelet, Mr. Jamie's phone rang. Same time, Patty leans in through the doorway and says, 'Breakfast is served.' Mr. Jamie turns his back and says into the phone, 'Seriously? Yes. I'll meet you there in five.' And he says to me, 'Have Rafe bring the Jag around.'

"I passed Mr. Jamie's message to Rafe, assuming he'd drive Mr. Jamie where he wanted to go. But then I saw Rafe through the front window walking back to his apartment as the Jag was pulling out of the drive."

Brady said, "Fricke didn't say who was on the phone?"

"No, he did not. He left his breakfast uneaten and a draft of his will on his desk. I gave it to Sergeant Boxer."

"You've told me you liked Mr. Fricke."

"I've been with him for twenty years. He's been very good to me and I'm grateful to him and I miss him…"

Brady leaned across the table, grabbed Arthur by the forearms, and shook him. "Steady, Arthur. Say your life depends on it. Who shot him?"

Arthur tried to break free of Brady's grip and said, "Let go. I'm all right."

Brady released his hold on Arthur, who rubbed his forearms and asked, "Do I need a lawyer?"

"Do you?"

Arthur shook his head. "Don't do that again, Lieutenant. I'm cooperating."

Brady sat back in his seat. Arthur leaned forward and lowered his voice. He said, "One thing I've never mentioned. Jamie had been seeing Mrs. Holly's younger sister, Rae."

"'Seeing' meaning having an affair with her?"

"Yes. When Mrs. Holly was alive, she never said anything about it to me. I never saw any sign of betrayal on her face."

"Tell me about Rae."

"She's wealthy. Has a place in Malibu. She writes screenplays, one of which, according to *Variety,* she sold. Also, I've heard that she parties with big names in Hollywood. That's all I know."

"But Rae came to see Holly, right?" Brady said.

Arthur sighed. "Yes. Sorry. She came a few times a year on holidays. Mrs. Holly always said, 'I love my sister.'"

Brady said, "Arthur, I asked you who shot Jamie. This is your answer? You suspect Rae Bergen? Why?"

Arthur said, "Lieutenant, I don't suspect anyone. I'm desperate to know who killed Mrs. Holly and Mr. Jamie. But the way I do my job is to not see or hear things I shouldn't. What you're getting from me is blindfolded doodling under intense police pressure. Mr. Jamie was seeing Rae Bergen. That's a fact. And Mr. Jamie was seeing her right up till the time he was murdered. He'd call her when I was in the office. On occasion, he had Rafe drive him to the airport to meet Ms. Rae and travel elsewhere. If Mr. Jamie made "forever after" promises to her, I don't know. I was privy to Mr. Jamie's personal life, but I was not his confidant. I answered the phone. I took messages. I opened the mail. I supervised the staff. Et cetera."

"Do you think Rae Bergen had a motive to kill her sister?"

"I did *not* say that. I'm hypothesizing because you're leaning on me. I think it's possible that someone, Ms. Rae or someone else, called Mr. Jamie and said, 'Hey, I've got something for you. Meet me on Steiner Street.' Again, I'm making up scenarios."

"Okay," said Brady. "I think we're finished. Thanks, Arthur. I appreciate your cooperation."

Brady pushed back his chair, showed the Frickes' house manager out of the interview room, and hooked him up with a ride home.

I said to Alvarez, "See what you can find out about Rae Bergen."

Alvarez said, "Are we looking to bring her in?"

"Dig around. Talk to me. If there's a case to be made, we'll talk to Brady."

Crossing her fingers, Alvarez left the observation room.

CHAPTER 58

IT HAD BEEN a long day and I was flagging. I needed coffee, heavy on the sugar. Cappy and Chi were in the break room, conversing over coffee when I walked in and poured myself a mug of dregs. I pulled a chair up to the table.

I was asked for an update and I was eager to share with the team. I briefed Chi and Cappy on what I'd learned that day about Jamie's financial manager, his house manager, his driver, and his cook—all of whom they knew—and that Jamie had been in the process of revising his will.

"How'd you know that?" Cappy asked.

"Bevaqua showed us the new draft Jamie left out in the office."

I told them about Arthur making a reluctant admission to Brady that Rae Bergen had been seeing Jamie Fricke romantically, both while Holly was alive and after she'd been buried.

Chi raised an eyebrow.

"That's new."

Cappy pushed a tin of sugar cookies toward me and I helped myself to one and then another.

After I'd downed some coffee, I said, "Patty Delaney told me to look at the pictures Bevaqua took at Holly's funeral. You guys were there. Did anyone make it into your notebook?"

"There was a lot going on," Chi said. "Retired Olympians breaking down, gut-wrenching eulogies, but when it came time to lower the casket, no one was allowed to stand by the grave except family."

Cappy said, "Rae was there with her twenty-year-old son, Brock Picard. College kid. She's been divorced from her husband for ten years. It's all in the file."

Chi said, "Brock gave a pretty moving eulogy about his aunt Holly. Jamie choked out something heartbreaking about losing his soulmate. He was so sincere. If you didn't know better…"

"And Rae?" I asked.

"Rae was a mess. All she could get out was, 'I'll always love you, Holly.'"

Chi looked pensive, and to me that always meant "big idea coming up." "Paul," I said. "What are you thinking?"

"That a few of us should go to Jamie's funeral."

"Which is when?"

"Friday. Private service at the family chapel in Pacific Heights."

"Volunteers?" I asked.

Chi and Cappy raised their hands.

"Good. You've got it."

"What was in the will?" Cappy asked.

"I'll show you if you give me half your sandwich."

"You like pastrami? I didn't know," he said.

"Deal or no deal?"

Cappy laughed and pushed half a pastrami on rye with mustard across the table.

"Looks, uh, yum," I said. "Can you spare the pickle?"

He gave it to me. When I'd finished my half of Cappy's sandwich and my past-dead coffee, Chi handed me the whole Fricke family file: two thumb drives and a three-hole binder of tabloid clippings. I gave him the draft of Jamie's will and took the files down the hall to begin reading up on Holly Bergen Fricke's family.

CHAPTER 59

I WAS DETERMINED to find a hook, a clue, something that looked wrong that would lead me to a double murderer. But the material in the files was meant for popular consumption. Party photos, award ceremonies, the material all fell under the heading of "Enquiring Minds Want to Know."

Cappy's notes were on one of the thumb drives, Chi's on the other. I'd seen most of this information before, when we'd been working daily on Holly Fricke's murder, but some of Chi's notes were new to me: Holly and Rae's parents, Bill and Susanne "Sassy" Bergen, had both come from old money going back three generations in New York. They served on a number of not-for-profit boards, had a few hospital wings named for them, but also were rumored to party in shades of gray.

Chi's notes included a crisp professional photo of the Bergen sisters at a Hollywood award after-party. It had been taken no more than two years before. Rae wore a thigh-high gauzy white dress and Holly was standing beside her in a sleek gold catsuit with a low neckline. Chi had attached Rae's thin arrest record as a photo file. She had been caught and released with a few ounces of marijuana when she was in high school. She'd later been pulled over for speeding several times and cited once for having an open glass of vodka in her car.

I found other photos of Rae Bergen: party and award show photos where Rae was with A-list movie stars, looking happy and beautiful in every shot. The only exception was one that had been taken at Holly's funeral. Rae's mascara had run below her lashes, her black dress clung to her thighs, and her hair was unruly. She was still beautiful but resembled a rose that had been caught in a late snow.

If there'd been a clue in Holly's "murder book," Chi and Cappy would have found it. Still, the last photo in the book seemed promising: a party photo of a number of well-turned-out guests posed on the Frickes' back lawn. Chi had listed the guests, typed their names on a separate sheet.

I spent some time learning the names of people I hadn't met or who hadn't yet come up in the investigation of Holly's death. For the same reason Patty had said that we should check out the mourners at Holly's funeral, I felt I might see someone in this shot who might take us off square one.

I was still scrutinizing the photo when Alvarez appeared in the doorway. She looked distressed.

I asked, "You spoke to Brady?"

"Lindsay, Rae told Brady she's not coming to San Francisco unless he has a warrant. She has nothing to say about Jamie's death. She just wants to be left alone. The end."

"You have her number?"

"I sure do." Alvarez wrote it down on my notepad.

When Alvarez had left the room, I made some calls. Cindy,

Claire, Yuki. I needed to schedule a Women's Murder Club dinner at Susie's with bottomless pitchers of beer.

But first, I wanted to talk to another of Jamie's recent lovers. I needed to speak with Rae Bergen. She hadn't been interviewed. She was Holly's sister and had had an intimate relationship with Jamie. A nexus. A possible doer. And for sure a real source of information.

I rang her number three times. No answer. Left my number each time. No callback.

CHAPTER 60

IT WAS JUST about quitting time. Claire Washburn was in the autopsy suite with her assistant, Bunny Ellis. Also present was the shot, cut, and stitched-up body of James Fricke III lying on a stainless-steel table, covered in a blue drape. Mostly covered. His right arm lay over the drape, the hand loosely wrapped in gauze.

What about Fricke's knuckles? Was the answer right there? Claire whispered, "Please, God."

A tag lettered with the deceased's name and the number of his drawer hung by a string from his right big toe. Bunny tucked the hem of the drape around the body and wheeled the table through the swinging doors to the storage area.

Claire called out, "After you stow him, Bunny, please stick around until Loomis picks up Mr. Fricke's effects. The carton is under the reception desk."

"The swabs need to be processed immediately," Bunny said.

"Right," Claire said. "Warp speed."

Bunny laughed. "You've only told me six times."

"And now, seven," said Claire. "You understand, right, Bunny? If I have to stop his funeral, I'd like to be correct."

"I totally get it," said Bunny. "I'll make sure Loomis gets it, too."

"They're usually a little early, so stay where you can hear the buzzer. I have a couple of things to do in my office but if I'm needed, come get me."

Inside her office, Claire skimmed the death certificate and the three copies. *Cause of death, five .40-caliber rounds. Manner of death, homicide.* She signed and dated them all.

She turned on the light box behind her desk and put up Fricke's X-rays, which she'd already reviewed at least a half dozen times. Had she overlooked something? Did the five matching shots in the same locations on both Holly and Jamie's bodies mean something to their killer, and if so, what? Was this the mark of a serial killer just getting started in Pacific Heights or was this personal?

She studied the X-rays, animated the murder in her mind. The shooter had taken the first shot to Fricke's back and the bullet had lodged in the fourth rib, grazing his spine. Theorizing now, Claire pictured Fricke spinning around reflexively—a reaction to the shot. She could imagine him seeing the shooter and throwing a punch to his face. Then Jamie Fricke had dropped to his knees. The shooter put a second round in Fricke's heart, then his groin, his liver. And as Fricke rolled onto his side or back, he shot Fricke in the forehead. The coup de grâce. The bullet was still in Fricke's head when she'd gone in after it. The head shot killed him, but Fricke wouldn't have survived the others.

Claire placed one copy of Jamie Fricke's X-rays into a large envelope that she would have hand-delivered to Jackson Brady in the morning. She slipped the second set of files into another large envelope, this one addressed to Dr. Humphrey Germaniuk. Dr. G., the night shift ME for the last fifteen years, specialized in trace evidence. She left the envelope on his desk.

She filed the original of Jamie Fricke's films and paperwork in her open case file drawer, right next to Holly Fricke's. Then Claire stripped off her gown, cap, and gloves, put it all in the trash.

Earlier, Claire and Lindsay had commiserated about the lack of visual evidence in Holly's death. No witnesses. No security camera footage. There was one known witness in Jamie's murder: Dan Fields, the neighbor who'd seen the shooter. His view was partial, seen from three stories overhead with some obstruction from trees and the corner of the building next door. Fields had not seen the shooter's face. He'd said that the killer was wearing black, and he'd seen no identification on the clothing. And he hadn't seen if the victim had punched out at the shooter. Fields had been shocked by the killing and didn't move until after the shooter drove off in Jamie's black Jaguar. It wasn't much, but it was something.

Claire changed from her rubber-soled shoes to street shoes and was ready to go.

She found Bunny straightening up in the autopsy room.

"Bunny. Have you seen Dr. G.?"

"He just texted me. He's parking his car."

"Good."

Claire was eager to compare notes with the good doctor.

CHAPTER 61

DR. HUMPHREY GERMANIUK was not just a highly regarded medical examiner, but he'd taught at UCLA Medical School before joining the medical examiner's office. After retiring from teaching, he came back to the ME, night shift, and he and Claire were friends.

He was just coming through the ambulance bay when Claire said, "Thanks, Bunny. Put in for overtime. Dr. G. will take it from here."

Bunny didn't have to be told twice. She went to the ladies' room and came out shortly in street clothes, hair loose around her shoulders, lip gloss. As she left the ME's office, Claire and Dr. Germaniuk both wished Bunny a good night.

Claire gave Dr. G. a couple of minutes to gown up, then open his office door and ask her what was lying in wait for him. She got right to it. "I left Jamie Fricke's files on your desk. A million dollars for your thoughts."

He said, "You look tired, Claire."

"Is that your professional opinion or a little help from my friend?"

"Both," said Dr. G.

Claire nodded. "I hear you. I'm a brain wreck. Come with me, Dr. G. If you don't mind," she said, going through the swinging doors to the cold storage room. She opened Fricke's drawer and slid his body out.

"What do you think of this here?" Claire asked Dr. G., unwrapping Fricke's hand with great care. Dr. G. cleaned his thick, black-rimmed glasses and, when James Fricke's right hand had been entirely freed from the bandage, peered at the dead man's hand.

Claire told him her theory of the injury and Dr. G. looked closely at Fricke's skinned knuckles.

"Hmm. It sure looks like he got a punch in before the curtain dropped. You swabbed it?"

"I swabbed the hell out of it," said Claire. "I've got the swabs packaged and I called Hallows to make sure he gives it priority treatment. Rapid DNA could be back tonight."

Dr. G. nodded approvingly.

Claire went on. "Contents of the box for the lab: fluids from the tox screen, clothes bagged, fingernail scrapings, slugs, all in the carton under the reception desk with the swabs, five of them in individual tubes. Loomis is careful. I just hope they come early tonight."

"I'm taking over, okay, Claire?"

"Triple okay," she said. "If the lab calls back with the DNA, wake me."

"You're off duty, Claire. I'm in charge and I'm not going to let you down."

CHAPTER 62

BAO WAITED WITH Joe in his car parked on the shoulder of Turquoise Way three hundred yards downhill from the blue house. The road was flanked by homes with small yards overlooking the steep hillside below.

Bao was focused on Thordarson and Wooten's threat-catcher program. She hadn't found a match from Eastern Europe to San Francisco but was not giving up.

Joe was fixated on the east side of the sorry-looking blue house at the top of the road. At nearly five in the afternoon, the sky was overcast, building up to a soaking rain. The target house was dark and silent, shadowed by its taller neighbors, trees, and the darkening sky.

A little while earlier, Joe had peered into the house through a gap in a window shade. He'd counted five, possibly six, fit young men sleeping on the floor and sofa. But there could be others in the adjacent, windowless room. Joe pictured what else he'd seen—the array of computers on the dining table and the box of

.40-caliber ammo on the windowsill. And it was the second item that was keeping him in the car.

He checked his watch again to see how much time had elapsed since Steinmetz's assistant had told him that backup was on the way. It seemed like half a lifetime passed before Bao looked up from her phone and turned to Joe.

"Incoming backup," she said.

Joe got out of the car and stood against the door looking down the road. A white police van turned onto Turquoise Way and came up the hill. Joe held up his badge and the van braked hard next to him.

The passenger door slid opened and a uniform stepped out, introduced himself as Sergeant Brian Whalen and his partner, behind the wheel, as Inspector Ray Lipari. Joe introduced Bao and himself and nodded to the three cops wearing tactical gear seated in the rear of the van.

Whalen said, "Wait a minute. Molinari. You're not a cop. You're an independent whatchacallit. Contractor. Boxer's husband, am I right?"

Whalen had crossed swords with Lindsay in the past. This operation was Joe's responsibility. He was working from a phoned-in tip, and with manpower he didn't know. The outcome for St. Vartan's could be apocalyptic. So, he did what he had to do.

"Whalen, let me be clear. This is an FBI operation. I'm in command. Are you in or out?"

"I was never out. What's the plan?"

Joe pointed out the blue house a few hundred yards uphill. He told Whalen, "I saw five or six sleeping males in that house, mid-twenties, four used cars out front. We have a short time frame in which to unwind a cyberattack on a hospital. There are industrial-grade computers set up in that house's main room and I saw a box of .40-caliber ammo on the windowsill."

"So they're armed."

"Very likely. At the moment they're camping in a property that's not theirs. We can bring them in on trespassing alone."

Whalen said, "We have tac gear and search warrants."

"Good. I've roughed out a plan," said Joe. "It's basic. Form a perimeter around the house. Your men knock and announce, then enter through the back door. If the subjects don't drop to the floor, flush them out the front. Director Wong and I will be waiting for them. If they shoot, we shoot. But we prefer live captives who talk."

Whalen had questions and Joe answered. He described the layout of the house, its location on its lot, and the long drop down a hillside at the rear boundary line.

Joe said, "The van is now our command post. Once the perimeter is in place, Lipari calls you, and you drive up the hill, block off the driveway, trapping their vehicles from leaving the property."

Whalen said, "I've got it, Molinari. Make arrests, transport this gang of whatever to booking, go home."

Joe said, "Right. I think we can wrap this up in under an hour."

Whalen was nodding when everything changed.

The lights in the run-down blue house went on.

The occupants were awake.

CHAPTER 63

JOE'S BRAIN WENT into overdrive, assessing the ways things could go terribly wrong. The young men could see the van and grab their guns, resulting in a Wild West–style shoot-out. Or they could leave the house before the perimeter was set, take off through the canyon, and get lost until night. Or it could go the other way. These kids might be a college study group, armed with nothing more than their cheat sheets. People could get hurt right here in the next few minutes.

Five cops, including Whalen, secured their tactical gear and huddled with Joe near the van as he gave them their orders.

On Joe's go, the team moved out.

It started to rain as Joe and Bao reached the front door of the house. Through a crack in the door, Joe saw that some of the young men were on their feet, pulling on their clothes. Two sat in front of computers. They hadn't seen the cops. Then a bullhorn sounded, and a voice announced, "This is SFPD. We're coming in. Toss your guns. Drop to the floor. Hands behind your heads. Do this now and no one gets hurt."

There was shouting inside the small house. One of the men disappeared from Joe's view. The others fell to their knees. A tall kid with leadership presence shouted to his guys, "Front door. Front door. Let's go."

"Ready, set," said Joe to Bao.

Joe put his shoulder to the front door, which splintered as it broke open. Four half-dressed young men pushed aside strips of wood and ran through the doorway with drawn guns, muscling past Bao and Joe.

Joe fired three shots into the air and shouted orders to halt.

The four dropped to the walkway. The cops seized their guns, wrenched their arms around their backs, and cuffed them. Joe heard, "You have the right to remain silent…" and watched as the captives were marched to the van.

Bao entered the house with Officer Boyd Jamieson to make sure the house was cleared while allowing her to check out the computers.

Joe felt a rush of satisfaction, a feeling he'd missed since he last worked a case in the field. He holstered his gun and was calling Steinmetz's office — when a shot sounded from the canyon to his left.

Joe yelled, "Everyone down!"

The bullet had hit Officer Devon Brown, who was standing just to Joe's left side. Blood spouted from Brown's left thigh as he dropped.

The van pulled up, blocking the cars in the driveway. Whalen got out, wove between the cars, put his arm around Brown's shoulders, and helped him into the van's passenger seat.

Whalen said to Brown, "We'll get you some help, Dev."

"All I need is a Band-Aid," said Brown.

Joe stood behind an open car door, using it as a shield. He was searching the canyon with his eyes, looking for the shooter, when Bao ran out of the house to where he stood.

Joe turned to Bao thinking she didn't look right. Her eyes were red and there were raw spots on the backs of her hands. She smelled of smoke.

"What happened, Bao?"

She said, "I was doing a cursory check of the computers while Jamieson cleared the house. Joe. Those guys were selling drugs. Online. Mail delivery. The house is full of courier envelopes. There were two pill presses in the spare room. Binding chemicals. Plastic bags. The works."

"Anything on Apocalypto?"

"I was moving fast but I saw nothing but lists and addresses and ledgers of receipts. No ransomware. No hospital anything. These are not our guys."

CHAPTER 64

JOE LIFTED BAO'S right hand and then looked at the right side of her neck.

"What happened to you? Are you burned?"

"One of those guys just appeared, Joe, I don't know from where. Next thing I know, he's at the stove and there's a frying pan on the burner. He turned on the gas and dumped the grease onto the burner and the fire got a good start. I'm okay, but it could have been worse. I smothered the flames with wet dish towels. Jamieson got the curtains out of the way and the guy ran out the back door."

Joe asked Bao, "Do you see the guy here?"

As Whalen and Lipari stuffed the modern-day drug dealers into the van, shackled them, checked them, checked again, Jamieson jump-started a rusted Ford sedan in the driveway.

"Dev, hold on to me," he said to the injured cop as he transferred him from the van to the Ford and headed out to the hospital with him. As the used car lot in front of the house thinned, Bao saw a flash of red in the nearby canyon.

She said, "Look," as the red flash disappeared behind a rock.

"That's the guy who set the fire," Bao said. "That's him."

Joe pulled Bao down to the ground just as the guy showed his gun and fired. Joe returned fire and hit the shooter, who howled in pain.

Joe ordered the uniforms into the woods, but they returned to the blue house empty-handed.

Joe said, "Damn. He didn't get away, did he?"

Lipari said, "We identified ourselves loud and clear. But this dude ran behind the house. There's a drop-off back there and the ground was muddy. Look." Lipari showed Joe his mud-caked shoe sole.

"So the jackass slipped. Cafferty and I ran to the edge. Jackass grabbed on to a root about twenty feet down the slope. We couldn't reach him. We got hold of a good branch to lower down to him, and by then it was pouring. Guy calls out to God, slips, hitting rocks and roots and whatever on his way down."

Joe said, "Is he alive?"

"Doesn't look like it. He's motionless. I yelled. Told him to hang on, we'd come get him. He didn't answer. I think he broke his neck. He lost his gun near the top of the slope. We have it and his wallet. His name is Keith Ballantine."

"Can't leave him there," Joe said.

He got back on the phone with Steinmetz, told him he needed a search-and-rescue team. "We need it now."

Joe said to Steinmetz, "We have to retrieve the guy who got away. He attacked Director Wong and then fired on us, hitting Officer Brown, who's on the way to the ER. The shooter slid down a steep canyon beyond reach. Alive or dead, I want to bring him in."

Steinmetz agreed and signed off. Joe saw Bao picking out cops by name, telling them she needed help getting the computers out of the house. Joe called out to her, "Wait for me. I'll be back."

He didn't hear her say, "I'll be right here."

THURSDAY

CHAPTER 65

AT SIX O'CLOCK the next morning, Nick Gaines crossed Bryant from the All Day Parking lot to the Hall. He turned so that he was facing the gray granite face of the Hall of Justice building and called Yuki.

"Yuki, sorry to wake you. The gaggle is stopping traffic on Bryant and starting to pack the sidewalks. Uniforms are outnumbered."

Yuki said, "Aw jeez," thanked Gaines, and slipped out of bed without waking Brady, made coffee, and called Mary Elena.

"Mary Elena, are you awake?"

"Maybe. I'm not sure I was asleep. What's wrong?"

"Nothing. Not yet. Just every journalist in the country is surrounding the Hall. Please get dressed. I'll pick you up in about forty-five minutes."

"Party dress or jeans?"

"Your blue skirt suit, Mary Elena. Or the gray jacket and trousers...I want to get you into the building ahead of the press and they're already stopping traffic."

"I'll be ready," Mary Elena said.

Yuki went to her closet and pulled out the first suit still in a dry cleaner's bag. No one was going to be looking at her. She showered. Soaped her hair. Dried off and dressed. She put on her watch that had once belonged to her mother. Seven o'clock plus a few seconds. She tiptoed back to the bedroom and kissed Brady goodbye. He startled awake.

"What's happening? Are you okay?"

Yuki soothed him back to the pillows and blankets, told him she had to be at court early, kissed him again.

She stepped into her shoes and left the apartment. Yuki's mother's voice warned her, *Drive safe, Yuki-eh*. She said, *Okay, Mother, I'm good*, as she drove her car out of the garage and up the ramp to the street. Checking the time, she was sure she'd be at Mary Elena's place in ten minutes. If the lights were with her.

This was a big day. Mary Elena was going to testify about the assault again, but this time Schneider would cross-examine her. Unordered thoughts flashed through Yuki's mind, but chief among them was this: Would Mary Elena hold up on the stand? Would she stay in her main personality?

Yuki thought over the questions she was going to ask, added one, subtracted another, braking her car as she nearly ran the light on Geary Street. After that close call, she turned on the radio to a light jazz station and kept her eyes on the road.

CHAPTER 66

WHEN COURT OFFICER Louie Mack opened the double doors to Courtroom 8G, journalists and the trial curious stampeded through the wide opening and lunged for seats in the gallery. Cindy fought for the last seat nearest the door, throwing her computer bag onto the chair that she called hers, and nailed it.

Britney Waller, a reporter from the *Sacramento Ledger* who also wanted that seat, stamped on Cindy's instep with her high heel, hard enough to bruise bone. Cindy yelped and cursed at Waller, who was taller, older, and heavier than Cindy. Still, Waller saw something in Cindy that caused her to back off.

Once seated, her computer cord plugged into the socket behind her, Cindy opened her laptop. About then Bailiff Riley Boone entered the courtroom from the side door, filled his lungs with air, and called out, "Alllll riiiise."

The audience stood noisily as the judge came through the narrow doorway from his office and took his seat at the bench. Even from the back of the room, Cindy noted that His Honor Henry William St. John had had a bad night, or maybe hadn't slept at all.

It was clear from the bench that the gallery was packed to the walls, chairs squeezed close together. His Honor was not pleased. He banged his gavel repeatedly, calling out "Quiet," until the volume of voices dropped to a low buzz.

Cindy looked up at the judge as he shouted, "You people in the gallery who've rearranged the chairs. What we have here is a fire hazard. Bailiff, please clear the aisles and everyone standing at the back of the room. That's it. Show the nice people out to the corridor, Officer Mack. No one else comes into the courtroom unless they are part of the proceedings."

While Cindy was drafting her column, a man standing in the rear of the room called out, "Your Honor, Your Honor, I'm Cory Leach from the *Grand Rapids Badger*—"

"Sorry, but no, Mr. Leach. No standing room."

Cindy kept her head down, fingers on the keys, setting the scene, describing her observations, quoting the quotable. She was working fast and well when Bailiff Riley Boone brought in the jurors from their room behind one of the oak-paneled walls of 8G. Once they'd been seated, court was called into session. Judge St. John delivered the rules on court decorum quickly, paused to pass his eyes over the room, then turned to Yuki.

"Ms. Castellano, please call your witness."

Yuki stood, keeping one hand on the back of Mary Elena's chair.

"Your Honor. The People call Ms. Mary Elena Hayes."

CHAPTER 67

MARY ELENA, LOOKING smart and put together in cobalt blue, stepped out from behind the counsel table and set course for the witness stand. She put her left hand on the Bible, raised her right, and swore before God to tell only the truth. And that wouldn't be hard for her. It had been well established that Mary Elena had no memory of being beaten and raped.

As late as last week, after another consultation with Parisi, Yuki and Nick Gaines were convinced that if they didn't call Mary Elena to tell her story in her own words, the defense surely would aggressively present their side; namely, *You asked Mr. Cates for sex, didn't you? The sex was consensual, isn't that right? You hold an important job, don't you, Ms. Hayes? How is it that your psychological disorder hasn't disrupted your job performance in the human resources department at Raymond James over, what is it, four years? Seems a little handy to have a breakdown at Xe Sogni, wouldn't you say?*

It was Schneider's job to bury Mary Elena. When Yuki introduced Mary Elena, she'd present her as credible and the victim of terrible crimes perpetrated by the defendant, Tyler Cates.

When Mary Elena had settled into the witness box, Yuki asked her to state her name, which she did. Then, "You feel comfortable testifying?"

"Perfectly. I could get used to all this attention," Mary Elena said with a smile. She even got a few laughs from the gallery.

"Mary Elena, you remember what His Honor the judge asked me to tell you?"

"Sure. It's about my alters. If they come out, each has to be sworn in individually."

"That's right," Yuki said. "Okay, what do you remember about the afternoon when you entered a restaurant called Xe Sogni to use the ladies' room?"

Mary Elena said, "Well, when I walked in, lunch was being served. I asked the maître d' if I could use the ladies' washroom."

Yuki nodded and asked Mary Elena to go on.

"He pointed me to the stairs and when I got to the second floor, I was inside a locker room, and the ladies' room was to my left. But there was a man near the lockers. I remember that he asked me my name and I didn't like his tone of voice. I told him my name and kept walking toward the door marked 'Ladies.'"

"What happened next?"

"This...this guy said he wanted to have sex with me—demanded it—and I just...freaked out. He had no right to come on to me like that, and he frightened me. One of my alters came forward and tried to protect me. I lost time. I don't know how much time or what was happening to me, but I've been told that when the police came, I was on the floor, mostly naked and quite bruised. And I do remember this: I hurt everywhere."

Yuki stepped aside so that Mary Elena had full view of the courtroom and asked, "Do you see the man who attacked you?"

Mary Elena said, "There. He's right there." And she pointed to the defense table.

"Are you indicating the defendant?"

"Yes. Wearing a blue jacket."

Tyler Cates didn't flinch.

Yuki asked, "He was a stranger to you, isn't that right?"

"Yes. A large, aggressive stranger."

Tyler Cates shot to his feet and shouted out, "*Liar! You're a stone liar!*"

Mary Elena froze. The judge told Cates to sit down and for Schneider to restrain his client or the defendant would be removed from the courtroom and returned to lockup—indefinitely.

Yuki thought Mary Elena's change of tone and expression were extreme as if one of her alters had taken her over. Her eyes were locked on Cates and she looked angry and afraid.

Yuki said gently, "Mary Elena, don't answer him. Answer me."

"Okay. The first. And *only*. Time in my life. I ever saw that man. Was in the restaurant changing room. Six months ago."

Cates jumped to his feet again and yelled, "*Pants on fire, Mary whatever your name is! Try telling the truth. Tell about Brookside Psychiatric!*"

Yuki felt it. The case was falling apart. Mary Elena was no longer Mary Elena. Now, she pulled her knees up to her chest, closed her eyes, and screamed. She took a breath and screamed again. Loudly. Painful to hear. She was Lily.

Yuki called up to the judge. "Your Honor, we need a recess, please."

When Mary Elena's feet touched the floor, Yuki put her arms around her and walked her to the counsel table. Behind them, the judge used his gavel with meaning.

CHAPTER 68

THE EMPTY OFFICE on the thirteenth floor of the FBI's San Francisco branch had been a spare, unadorned space with two metal desks facing each other, a narrow credenza, and a large picture window with a view of the traffic on Mission Street.

Since taking over the office, Joe and Bao had spread out to the four corners. The heavy-duty computers with fifty-inch screens covered the desks, a borrowed table, and most of the credenza. Since they had returned from the blue house on Turquoise Way, the sun had risen over the city skyline.

Joe got up, adjusted the shades.

"Coffee, Bao?"

"Thanks, no. I'm still working on the last one."

Her phone tootled and she picked up, said, "Hey, Sweetie."

Joe left the room to give Bao privacy, and as he headed toward the vending machine alcove, he thought about how rare it was to fit this well with a new partner.

He and Bao had maximized every minute, going from a hospital meeting to a shoot-out, a gas stove fire, a cop down, a dead perp, and four arrests. But while that was all good, they were no closer to putting St. Vartan's back in business than they had been at minute one.

And they were still on it. They'd scrolled through uncountable gigabytes of files as time ambled by. They'd found nothing in all those hours about ransomware, hospitals being held hostage, or Apocalypto. Patients at St. Vartan's were still in danger. The agreed upon forty-eight-hour window was closing despite a well-meaning tip that hadn't paid off.

Joe got coffee from the vending machine along with a bag of M&M's. When he returned to the office, Steinmetz was sitting on a few spare inches of the credenza.

He said, "Fine job you two did yesterday. How about a briefing?"

Joe said, "As it happens, I'm writing up a summary right now. Do you want details or just the bottom line?"

"Cut to the chase. If I need more, I'll ask."

"Okay, then. Starting after our phone call with you from the scene," Joe said, "one of the five squatters took shots at us, hit Officer Devon Brown from Glen Park Station…"

"He's the one in Emergency?"

Joe nodded and said, "It was a through-and-through, inner left thigh. Worse than it sounds. The slug hit a juncture of arteries called the femoral triangle. We tied off the wound at the scene and still Brown nearly bled out. As of now, he's out of surgery, but he's still in critical."

"It's not on you," Steinmetz said.

Joe nodded, but he thought it was. He said, "The shooter is at the morgue."

"He's the one went over the drop-off? Has the body been ID'd?"

"Keith Ballantine, twenty-eight. Technically unemployed. Glen Park Station contacted his parents. Bao, you're up."

Bao swiveled her chair so she was facing Steinmetz.

"These are the six computers that were in the house, and they each have enormous storage capacity. I've strip-searched four of them so far. There is nothing in them referencing Apocalypto or ransomware, nothing about hospitals at all."

"So, what did you find?"

Bao said, "Well. The young entrepreneurs in the house were in the drug manufacturing and distribution game. All of their business records were on their computers."

"Drugs?" Steinmetz asked. "You're sure?"

Bao said, "I have another two computers to go through, Craig. But we found pill presses and the chemicals needed to fabricate the pills and package them in the house. A vast mailing list of bulk buyers and repeat customers. They take orders over the web, ship the product out through any courier service. Incoming funds are auto-deposited in one of six banks. Glen Park has processed the four still standing. No sheets, no outstanding warrants. They're geeks, sir, now with serious goddamn drug and money laundering charges."

Joe looked at his phone, which had pinged with an incoming text.

He said, "Sorry to interrupt, Bao. Chief. Message from CS Inc. They've tracked an incoming signal from Eastern Europe that is seeking a target in San Francisco."

"Brilliant," said Bao. "The IP address of the target should belong to an Apocalypto-operated computer."

CHAPTER 69

BAO WONG CALLED Pete Wooten's direct line and Wooten picked up.

He said, "We have high confidence that this is it. The coordinates are on target—"

Sveinn Thordarson joined in, saying, "There's a Starbucks on Divisadero Street at the corner of Bush Street. Joe, you know it?"

"Very well," Joe said. "Their Wi-Fi is strong."

Wooten said, "I'm guessing their operator is going to look perfectly natural in there. Probably young."

Ten minutes after the call with Cyber Security Incorporated, Joe and Bao drove past the Divisadero Street intersection with Bush and parked across the street from the coffee shop. Bao called Pete Wooten for the second time since leaving the FBI offices.

"Pete, we're across the street from Starbucks now."

Wooten said, "Bao, assuming you're still wearing a suit, Joe should go in, buy something, sit down, and text me. The code from Apocalypto is on the subjects' computer right now."

Joe said, "Copy," and headed across the street to the coffee shop.

Bao slid over to the driver's side in case they had to move fast. And then she watched and waited.

A few customers drifted out of the store with coffee containers in hand, but five minutes passed and Joe was still inside the shop. What was keeping him? This could be their only shot at Apocalypto. Bao patted the gun on her hip, then opened the car door.

CHAPTER 70

BAO WAS WAITING for a break in the traffic so she could dash across Divisadero Street—when she saw Joe moving rapidly toward her. He was carrying something under his arm. Once he reached Bao, he showed her a laptop.

"You've got it? That's the one?"

"Better be," Joe said. "But we still need the operator."

He got back into the driver's seat and buckled up, as did Bao.

She said, "I'm dying, Joe. Talk to me."

"I'll tell you everything. But first, we have to find the owner of this laptop."

Joe flipped on the flashing emergency lights and pulled out onto the road. When the car was in the clear, he turned the wheel hard and headed slowly up Divisadero toward Pine Street. A soft light filtered through the trees that lined the wide two-lane street. Traffic was sparse.

"Joe?"

"So when I walk toward the front door, I see through the window that there's a laptop sitting on a table by itself."

"Noooo."

"I head for the laptop, but someone beats me to it and takes it up to the barista on the other side of the room. Now there's another person between us in the line. So when I get to the front, I pull my badge. I signal for the laptop and ask the barista does she know the guy who left it. Could she describe him? Yes, she could. What was his name?

"She didn't remember what name he gave for his order, but she described him. White male, five ten or so, chunky build, in his early thirties, wearing jeans and a green windbreaker. I realized I saw that guy leaving Starbucks as I was coming in. I saw him, Bao. But since he wasn't wearing an Apocalypto sweatshirt, I didn't think anything of him. Now, we're going to look for him."

A driver behind them honked his horn.

"Bao," said Joe. "Flip that guy the bird, okay?"

She snorted and said, "Joe, slow down, in case we pass a thirty-something in a green jacket."

Joe smiled. "Have faith. After I got the laptop, the barista—her name is Sophie—said, 'There's a note inside.'"

Bao picked the computer up off the floor, opened the lid, and saw a Post-it note with a couple of lines of handwriting stuck to the screen. She read it out loud.

"'I was here. Where were you?'"

CHAPTER 71

YUKI AND GAINES sat at the prosecution table with Mary Elena in the chair between them. She was quiet and as cold as stone.

His Honor Henry William St. John had once again adjourned court for the day, excused the jury, who were returned to the deliberation room. He offered Mary Elena his chambers until "this mess is resolved."

Gaines wrote the word "mistrial" on Yuki's pad and she put a checkmark next to it.

Yuki asked Mary Elena, "Would you prefer to wait in my office?"

She nodded her head vigorously.

"If the judge agrees, I want you to sit in my office until he is through with me, then I'll drive you home."

With permission, Yuki approached the bench and told His Honor her plan. Moments later, Yuki's assistant, Deirdre Palmer, was at the double doors. Deirdre was a kind and resourceful person and Mary Elena had met her before. The transfer was handled quickly, and as soon as the doors closed, Yuki returned to her table. That's when the judge called Tyler Cates, Schneider, and Castellano to the bench.

His Honor stared .50-caliber rounds through the defendant, saying, "Mr. Cates, this is where your presence in the courtroom ends—with one condition. You swear you will make no more comments unless you are on the stand and under oath. Do you understand?"

"I understand, Your Honor. I promise."

Judge St. John wasn't finished.

"If I continue this trial, you will spend the rest of it in a holding cell. No lunch break, no visitors except your attorney. You are dog meat until the jurors have made a decision. Or I will determine that we will have to start all over again. If so, back to jail with you until a new trial is scheduled. So count the months on your fingers. And no discount for time served if you are found guilty. I have a lot of cleaning up to do before I arrive at trial or mistrial."

The judge turned his head a few degrees and said, "Mr. Schneider, you've been a criminal defense attorney for as long as I've been a judge. Today you risked a contempt citation by not shutting down your client and removing him from the court."

"I'm very sorry about this, Your Honor."

"Sorry doesn't cut it. My staff is going to look into this charge your incredibly reckless client has made. We should know by tomorrow if there is such a place as Brookside Psychiatric, and whether or not Ms. Hayes was a patient there—and same for Mr. Cates, and if so at the same time. The results of that research will help me determine how we proceed."

Cates said, "Your Honor, I'm sorry I blurted out what I did. She's making horrible accusations."

Schneider pinched Cates's arm.

The judge turned his back on the sorrys and excuses and disappeared through the door to his chambers. As guards took Cates to holding, Gaines and Yuki gathered their things, left the courtroom, and headed toward the DA's offices.

At the same time, Red Dog was coming toward them in the corridor. In Yuki's current state, Len Parisi looked like a bristling, rust-colored heart attack.

Yuki said to Red Dog, "Len, Gaines will fill you in. I have to make a call. Deirdre is keeping Mary Elena company for a few minutes in my office and then I'm going to drive her home."

Turning away from Parisi, Yuki spoke into her phone. "Dr. Aronson, its ADA Castellano. I need your help."

The frightening scene in the courtroom played over and over again in Yuki's mind as she drove a silent Mary Elena to her apartment. Yuki felt that she had set a bear trap for herself then walked right into it. Could she have known?

Yuki stayed with Mary Elena before, during, and after her telesession with Dr. Aronson. She made tea and then helped Mary Elena into bed.

CHAPTER 72

JOE PARKED HIS car at the intersection of Divisadero and Pine, giving him a 360-degree view of the street and cross streets. If the guy who'd left the computer was on foot, Joe might recognize him. If he was driving, Cyber Security Incorporated was St. Vartan's best or only chance to get the ghosts out of the machine.

Bao said, "I still don't get it. Why did he leave his laptop? 'I was here. Where were you?' What's that?"

"What do you think?"

"He was stood up."

Joe laughed. "Thanks, I needed that."

He really did need a laugh. He was tense, tired, hungry, and exhilarated. If they succeeded, they'd be elated. People would live. If they failed, St. Vartan's was going to have to find millions and Apocalypto would still be in business.

Bao leaned toward him. "Joe. See that?"

"What? Where?"

"That dark SUV parked across the street. The driver just flashed his lights. Joe. Flash ours."

Joe turned on the lights and flashed them.

Bao said, "He's waving. To us. I think he could be wearing a green windbreaker."

"Great freaking catch, Bao. I recognize him."

Bao had called CS Inc. and spoken to Pete Wooten, who'd pinged the laptop she'd put in the footwell. He'd confirmed that it was the one Apocalypto was seeking. Joe reached Craig Steinmetz and brought him up to date. "I'll call you if we nab him."

Bao held the laptop. She would coax, untangle, trick, and in every way deploy her technological chops on that box. CS Inc. could extract the key to the malware implanted in St. Vartan's network. But they still needed the Apocalypto operator to give up what he knew.

"Joe. I think we should go talk to green windbreaker before he drives away. What about you?"

"Okay. Bao, you go around to the passenger side of his car. I'll go to the driver's side. Keep your gun down at your side."

Joe got out of the car. Keeping his eyes on the SUV but totally aware of where Bao was coming up on the passenger side, he stepped up to the driver.

"I'm Joe Molinari, FBI. We need to talk. Raise your hands. I'm opening your door now. Don't make any sudden moves."

Joe opened the driver's-side door with his left hand and showed the driver his Glock.

The driver asked, "You have my laptop?"

"Maybe," said Joe. "What's your name?"

"Robert. Nicholson. Bob."

"Bob. My partner to your right is Director Wong of the FBI. I need you to keep your hands up and get out of the car."

"Okay, I'd like to talk to you, too."

Joe's inner voice asked, *Why?* Was this the Apocalypto connection? Or had he just taken some kid's homework?

Bob said, "I'm not armed. I'm going to roll my legs out and try to stand."

Joe watched Bob awkwardly angle his way around the door frame. He tightened his core muscles and eased his legs out until he was standing.

Bao joined Joe as he threw Bob across the hood and frisked him. The guy had no weapons. His wallet held his driver's license and another picture ID. Bao first pulled Bob's right arm behind his back, then the left, and Joe cuffed him.

"Hey, take it easy," Bob complained. "And by the way, where's your warrant?"

"You had no expectancy of privacy, Bob. You left the laptop on a table in a public place. Look it up."

Now Bob Nicholson was laughing.

"Wait until I tell my friends I got arrested by the FBI for leaving my laptop at Starbucks. Oh. Am I under arrest?"

Bao said, "We're bringing you in as a person of interest in an ongoing case."

Bob said, "Starbucks is open. Why don't we—"

Bao said, "Let's talk here, Bob. What are we going to find on your laptop?"

"That's why I want to talk to you. Depending on what you can do for me, you're going to be able to liberate St. Vartan's hospital. And I can expose Apocalypto—all you want to know. Locations. Active operations. Weak links. Okay? But, right now, I'd say the deal is that I stay a free man, and the FBI makes sure that I don't get murdered."

CHAPTER 73

BAO WONG, Joe Molinari, and Bob Nicholson, the self-described negotiator for a global ransomware enterprise, sat in a semicircle of office chairs facing Craig Steinmetz's desk. The section chief was dressed in sweatpants and a gray cardigan with a cowl neck and leather buttons, loafers, no socks. Joe knew that Craig, who'd been in bed when he'd called him, had thrown on after-work clothes and made it to his office PDQ.

All of the lights were on. Papers were stacked in neat piles on Steinmetz's desk, which was bracketed by two standing flags; one the Stars and Stripes, and the other a plain blue banner with the insignia of the FBI at the center. Beyond the plate glass window, the evening sky was broken by streaks of headlights thirteen floors below. No beverages were served nor offered. Nicholson struggled out of his jacket and, with Joe's help, hung it on the back of his chair. Did he know Apocalypto's secrets or was Bob just full of crap? Craig would know.

After forty years with the Bureau, Steinmetz couldn't have been more ready for this critical interrogation. He straightened a line of pens in front of him and spoke.

"Mr. Nicholson, you're employed by a firm called Apocalypto?"

"Not exactly, sir. I work for a toy company in Amsterdam that markets toys internationally. But that's their cover. On one floor of their building, about a hundred software geniuses run the real profit center. That's Apocalypto."

"Got it," said Steinmetz. "And how did you come to work for this toy company in Amsterdam when you're a US citizen?"

"They scoped me out. Found out my grades at Caltech. My skills in advanced software technology. My job history with HP and Intel. Then I was recruited by remote interviews with flattery and mounds of shiny objects and I fell for the pitch. This was about four years ago, sir. My US citizenship doesn't come into it because I live, work, and pay my taxes here. Also, Chief, the job wasn't fully explained to me. I thought it was experimental. I typed code into my laptop—like always. Then, it got real. Am I talking too much?"

"No," Steinmetz said. "Please go on."

Bob nodded and continued the story of his life as a criminal.

"Over a few years, I was given increased incentives to negotiate with targeted firms. Most of them were industrial, but not pivotal to anything. Lawn mower manufacturer. Aluminum cans. This was all a tryout but I didn't know. The job seemed great. Creative. Challenging. I got rich. For me. But this year with the hospitals… Well. I'm disgusted with myself, sir."

"Convince me."

"Okay. I want to clarify, Chief. I don't select the targets. I don't create or deliver the malware. I'm just what they call the closer. I negotiate the ransom with the target, and after the payment is secured, it goes to the first of many banks who wire it to other banks. I am not part of that, sir, but eventually it gets back to a bank in the Netherlands. For a while I rationalized that once we were out of the victims' hair, we left them more secure than when we broke in."

Bao said, "Big of you, Bob. Did you assign a value to the people who died because of the malware?"

"No. No. I tinkered with the program, I talked to executives by internet, but when I asked about a human toll, I was iced. 'Not your job. Hospitals are insured'…"

Steinmetz said, "All right. I get it, Bob. You're a go-between, you're saying, an upstanding citizen with computer skills who got duped by terrorists."

Joe was watching Bob carefully. It seemed to him that Bob had never imagined a moment like this. He was scared. Leaving his laptop at Starbucks hadn't prepared him to confess to the Federal Bureau of Investigation's top man in San Francisco. He wiped his eyes with his sleeve.

Steinmetz rooted in his center drawer, found a packet of tissues, and slid it across the desk.

Bob was stammering now. "Sir…I was willfully blind and I don't forgive myself…But for context, this was very heady stuff for a fat kid from a factory town who got scholarships and grades and a way out of Nowheresville…I want to earn a clean reboot…"

Steinmetz said, "So you're going to quit your job, whether or not you get protection from the FBI?"

"Yes, sir. But without protection, I'll be killed. And Apocalypto will live."

CHAPTER 74

CLAIRE AND I drove separately to Susie's and parked about a half a block away. Just the sight of those windows blazing with light was enough to buck me up. I linked arms with Claire as we walked toward the entrance. I did all the talking, as Claire was unusually quiet.

"Something eating you, Butterfly? Talk to me."

Claire's sigh was long and deep.

"Claire?"

"Sorry. I was thinking about some results I'm waiting on. I was collecting scrapings from under Jamie Fricke's fingernails yesterday and noticed that his right hand was a little swollen and the knuckles were slightly abraded. Like he'd punched someone. Probably just before he dropped dead."

"Claire, this is huge. You're thinking he slugged his killer?"

"Or he scraped the sidewalk. All I know right now is that he skinned his knuckles. Anyway, I swabbed each knuckle, segregated the swabs, covered his hand with gauze, and asked the lab to rush it through rapid DNA. Maybe it'll match to his killer."

I asked the air, "How did we miss this?"

"Linds. When I got to the scene, there were ten people inside the perimeter—say, a hundred square feet. And twice as many true crime addicts were outside the tape, taking pictures, shouting questions. Fricke was lying face down in pooling blood. We got him into the van quick—"

I said, "No, it's okay. I'm feeling some hope..."

"Me, too," said Claire. "Some. But I'd advise you to keep it in check."

And then we were at Susie's front door.

I pulled it open and the aroma of spice billowed out to the sidewalk along with light, laughter, and the jazzy beat of steel drums. I held the door for Claire and she smiled as the Yellow Bird Band launched into an original tune. The room itself calls up the image of a yellow bird. The walls are the color of ripe mangoes and hung with hand-painted market scenes in the Jamaican style.

Susie was setting up the main floor for the limbo competition and the long bar to our right was packed with regulars who were tossing 'em back without falling off their stools. The barkeep was half-past thirty, played trombone, had a mop of yellow hair, and was wearing a flowered shirt with a name tag reading "Fireman."

He waved and called out to us as Claire and I pushed through the main room, then took the corridor that skirts the kitchen's pass-through window and opens into a smaller, quieter dining area.

Susie's back-room waitress, our friend Lorraine O'Dea, whistled to get our attention and pointed to "our" booth. Yuki was already seated there, scrunched back in the corner wearing a designer suit and a smile that fell short of happy. Claire slid into the booth next to her. I took the bench seat across from them.

Claire said, "Let's get something to drink. I'm ready."

Lorraine read our faces. She brought over menus and a pitcher of draft plus three frosty beer mugs, and asked Yuki if beer was okay.

Yuki's "go wild" drink is a fruity margarita—she downs tequila like soda water. Then she giggles and sings. I was glad when she said "Sure" to the brew.

I said, "Lorraine, chips and dip until Cindy gets here?"

"You bet."

Claire waited for Yuki to put down half her beer, then placed her hand on Yuki's arm and asked, "You got something to share, sweetie?"

Yuki said, "Oh, boy. I hate to have to say this."

I said, "This is about Mary Elena?"

Yuki nodded. "Wasn't her fault. It was all going well. She was fine in court and on the stand. Then Tyler Cates, that SOB, jumps up and says that he *knew* her. *That they were in a mental institution together.* Brookside Psychiatric. And he hadn't been sworn in. He was at the counsel table when he got to his feet and bellowed this crap out to the jury."

CHAPTER 75

MY JAW ACTUALLY dropped as I pictured Tyler Cates blowing up Yuki's case with his news that he and Mary Elena had both been patients at Brookside Psychiatric.

Then I sputtered, "That's bull, right?"

"We don't yet know," Yuki groaned. "It's near impossible to get hold of medical information. But I googled it. There's a Brookside Psychiatric in Bangor, Maine; in Louisville, Kentucky; and in Pensacola, Florida. Also a Brookside Wellness—a chain of clinics—and a couple of Brookside Mental Health Spas. Those are all in different states, with different laws, and given HIPAA rules, the patient has to sign on the dotted line or you can't find out beans."

I heard myself say "Oh, man" just thinking of the legal hurdles that would have to be cleared to get protected information.

Claire said, "Hold up a second. Just so I understand. If Cates really did know Mary Elena—just sayin'—how does that affect the charges of an obvious violent rape and beating?"

Yuki said, "Mary Elena's credibility is at stake. There were no witnesses to the crime, so it's 'he said, she said.' Yes, she was brutalized, but she also said she didn't know Cates. She said under oath that a stranger demanded sex. He said she's the one who asked for it. So. If she demanded sex from someone she used to know, some people would say it wasn't rape. Aggravated assault? Very possible. Still. One vote could hang the jury, and Cates could get a hall pass."

I asked, "Can Cates document his time at Brookside?"

"No idea," Yuki said.

"And what about Mary Elena?"

"She says it never happened. No way." Yuki went on. "Red Dog would have to move mountains to get this information if Brookside was in San Francisco. Even then, he'd have to pull a million strings. He's barely speaking to me because he said this case sucked from the beginning."

Yuki, Claire, and I had all been at the scene of the crime. This was a case that had to be tried and won, and I said so.

Yuki continued, "Our best chances are with Judge St. John. He's fierce and he's furious. He also doesn't want to lose this jury and have to start over. We're hoping he instructs the jurors to ignore all references to Brookside, as there's no actual evidence or sworn testimony."

"Or?"

"Or he can call a mistrial. Even Red Dog would rather get a mistrial and forget it. We'll find out in the morning. I wish Cindy was here to give you the eyewitness journalist's version. Where is she, anyway?"

In an exception to the "no phones" rule, I turned on my phone, as did Claire. There was a text for me from Joe.

I'll be home late, Blondie. I called Mrs. Rose and she's got the kiddo and the doggo.

That's when Claire called out over the restaurant racket, "Here she comes."

I turned to see Cindy dressed in a pretty floral dress coming down the corridor and into the room.

She wasn't alone.

CHAPTER 76

CINDY HAD BROUGHT her mother.

Darcy Thomas was right behind her daughter as they entered the Women's Murder Club special dining room. We'd all met Darcy before at a party for Cindy's first book, *Fish's Girl*. We'd had dinner together with paper plates in hand at Book Passage in Corte Madera, and had unanimously liked her. The family resemblance was there. Darcy had the same bone structure and curly hair, and she also had an easy laugh over stubborn determination.

Lorraine moved a chair to the end of the table so we could all fit at the booth. Darcy slid in next to me and reached out for a hug, which I was glad to give and receive. She reached across the table and bumped fists with Yuki and Claire.

"So good to see you all. Am I interrupting a serious Murder Club meeting?"

Claire spoke up, saying, "Not at all, Darcy. We were summing up. We know the menu and can make recommendations."

"No time to eat," she said. "Time for a drink, maybe."

Lorraine had her pad in hand and took our dinner orders,

Darcy's order for a glass of Chardonnay, and Cindy's request for a mug of beer, then disappeared as if in a puff of smoke.

Darcy said to the table, "This was a one-day turnaround trip. I'll have dinner on the plane, but I do have a problem for the club's consideration, and I hope you all can help out."

Cindy groaned, "Oh, God."

Lorraine brought wine for Darcy, a mug for Cindy, and I used the moment to call Joe. He picked up.

"Can't talk now, Linds. Sorry."

"Later?" I said. "I'll be home in an hour. Or so."

"Don't wait up," he said. "I've got no idea when…I gotta go."

He clicked off and I hung up on dead air.

Lorraine came back quickly with our food, and as Darcy was dipping chips, I said, "Darcy, you wanted to brainstorm with us?"

When Cindy's mug was topped up, Darcy said, "Let me say first, no guns are involved. No one gets injured. No ambulances are needed."

CHAPTER 77

DARCY WAS A natural comic, and the three of us laughed, of course, until Cindy said, "Mom, spit it out, will you? You're being overly dramatic."

"Cindy, you tell it, okay? I'm exhausted," said Darcy.

"We went shopping!" Cindy said. "For wedding gowns."

"Ohhhhhh," two or three of us said in unison.

Darcy jumped back in. "There are three semifinalists down from thirty. Cindy is not even committed to a type of dress. You need to write a column about this, Cynthia. Find out how other women deal with the life-and-death decision of buying a wedding gown."

Yuki started to laugh, her bell-like chortle so full of glee, it was impossible to hear without joining in. Even Darcy, who was clearly all worn out, blew wine out of her nose, and Claire slapped the table repeatedly as she guffawed.

When we were all breathing normally again, Claire asked the table, "Where's the rub? Cindy looks good in anything. And for the something borrowed, wear my pearls."

Yuki said, "Please put me on the gown jury. Do you have pictures of the contenders?"

"Why, yes we do," Darcy said.

While we dug into our dinners, Darcy passed around her phone with its picture gallery open to the three top choices. Cindy peered at the time on her phone, then asked her mother if she should call her an Uber.

"That would be great, honey," Darcy said.

Cindy requested the ride and got a confirmation. She wasn't in the mood for fiery food or more interference in her gown selection, but she bore up, and made comments about the last three standing: "That one," she said, "makes me look pregnant and I am definitely not. Number two," she said, "looks like it was made on the cheap in a sweatshop."

Darcy said, "Designer gown, by the way."

Cindy ignored her mother. She said, "This, the third loser, looks good on Mother, but it's a closeout and it's two sizes too big for me."

Darcy scoffed.

Just then, Cindy's phone pinged.

Cindy said, "Your ride is here, Mom."

"I should go, too," I said.

I gave Claire some folding money to cover my share, said good night to her and Yuki, then Cindy and I walked Darcy Thomas out to her ride. I gave Darcy a good hug, told her I'd see her at the wedding.

"Cindy will be wearing white," I said. "I guarantee it."

"Cross your heart?"

"Uh, no."

Cindy gave me a soft punch in the arm.

I was laughing again as I opened the car door for Darcy and waved goodbye. I hugged Cindy, too, saying, "Let's talk tomorrow."

We kissed cheeks, then I jogged down the block to my blue Explorer, the third nearly identical model I've had in the last several years due to on-the-job gunfire. Yes, this is truly what I do for a living.

Skipping past that, I focused on how in twenty minutes I'd be bringing Julie and Martha home from day care with their nanny, our neighbor Mrs. Gloria Rose, and that I'd be home for Joe when he came through the door. Whatever time that was.

CHAPTER 78

JOE WATCHED BOB SWEAT.

Bob Nicholson was speaking from his heart, but he hadn't seen around this corner and the consequences had just gotten real. He asked for a glass of water and Steinmetz shook his head no.

"Keep talking, Bob."

"I see it like this," Bob said. "I can show St. Vartan's protection team how to put the hospital behind a virtual wall. I can destroy the Apocalypto program from the root, and I can tell you how to shut down the decision-makers. All tonight."

Steinmetz sat forward in his chair, said, "Did you negotiate with Oakland Pediatrics?"

"Yes, sir. Sorry to say. I saw the headlines. And the photos. Before you ask me 'Then, why St. Vartan's?' there was no way to turn down the assignment. One guy I know did that, and I heard that he'd gotten a bullet and a wood-chipper funeral."

Steinmetz grunted his ambivalence, but Joe knew that he had decided.

Steinmetz said, "And what you want from us is a new identity and location in exchange for putting the hospital's computer network back together, protecting it, and destroying Apocalypto."

"Yes, sir."

Steinmetz said, "Okay, Bob. I've had you checked out. Quantico. Interpol. Seems you are who you say you are."

He turned his chair a few degrees and said, "Bao, call Wooten and Thordarson and have them get LaBreche down to the hospital."

Joe said, "And the IT guy, Walters."

Steinmetz said, "Fine. Joe, US marshals are waiting downstairs to take you three to St. Vartan's. Call me when you're on-site. Marshals will be responsible for Bob. You and Bao stick with him until CS Inc. confirms that the hospital is in the clear. I'll be here and available. Joe, I need a few minutes with you alone when the job is done. Bob, if you fail, you'll be detained and charged. Understand?"

"Yes, sir."

Steinmetz took a sheet of paper from a folder on his desk and offered it to Bob, saying "This agreement protects both parties. You do your part to our satisfaction and you get a new ID and relocation to a small town in Bulgaria."

Bob laughed. "Let me see."

Steinmetz handed him the agreement. Joe saw by Bob's nods and uh-huhs that he accepted the terms that he would be relocated to a city in the USA with a new identity. Bob picked up a pen from the line of them on the chief's desk. He signed the document, Steinmetz signed, and Joe witnessed the signatures. Steinmetz put the document back in his drawer.

Steinmetz said, "Take care of this tonight, Bob. Save some lives. Redeem yourself."

FRIDAY

CHAPTER 79

AT 2:00 A.M., five hours after the meeting with Steinmetz, Joe was back in the chief's office with vending machine coffee and cinnamon rolls in front of him.

Steinmetz said, "Bao called. She says it all went like quicksilver. St. Vartan's network has been repaired, tested, and approved. You agree?"

Joe said, "Craig, I watched. I looked the part and asked questions, but really, my technical knowledge has its limits. Bao and CS Inc. were satisfied. I'd say more than satisfied."

"Tech speech is irritating, isn't it?"

"Yep, language from outer space. The marshals have Bob in lockup while we work out his part of the deal."

"Very good. And I've got something for you," Steinmetz said.

He opened his drawer and took out a folder and handed it across the desk to Joe. There was a number two envelope inside the folder, Joe's name typed on the front.

Joe wondered if it was another job offer. Steinmetz had tried to lure him back full-time, but so far Joe had resisted.

Steinmetz said, "I fast-tracked this."

He sat back in his chair and had a bit of a grin on his face. Joe put his thumb under the flap, pulled it across the back of the envelope, then fished out the enclosed sheet of paper. There was one double-spaced paragraph.

"Craig, thank you. I want to discuss this with Lindsay."

"Fine. I need an answer by this time next week. Okay?"

"Thanks again, Craig. I'll let you know."

The two men stood up, shook hands, and took the elevator down to the street together.

CHAPTER 80

I WAS STARTLED awake at some time before dawn. My bedside clock tells the day and the weather as well as the time. Six forty. Friday. Overcast, no chance of rain. My clock never lies.

I closed my eyes, hoping I'd fall back asleep, but no. I was thinking about Jamie and Holly Fricke, their bodies spread out on the street, killed only six months apart.

I had a nine o'clock meeting with Rae Bergen. Holly's younger sister had resisted cooperating with the investigation but had finally agreed to meet with me and Rich at the Frickes' house before the funeral service at ten. Not much time for us to question Rae, who'd known Holly her entire life and was also one of Jamie's longtime lovers.

I was determined, though, to get what I could from her in the time allowed, with Conklin's help. We had under an hour to put a dent in the case, but Rich was an ace at interviewing women.

I rolled over and reached for Joe.

"You awake?" I whispered.

"No," he said. "What day is it?"

"Friday. How'd it go?"

"Hmmmmm?"

"Laptop guy?"

"He saved the day, hon. He wants to make good."

"For St. Vartan's?"

"Sure. He was Apocalypto's. Man with Oakland. Pediatrics. Too."

"Seriously? And you caught him?"

"He grew a connn…"

"Conscience?"

"Mmmmm."

"Joe?"

He had slipped right back to sleep. I kissed my fingers and touched his cheek and whispered, "I've got to hustle. Got a funeral to go to."

Joe smiled and held up crossed fingers without opening his eyes, then, "Gloria's coming at eight."

"Excellent."

I gave him a full body hug and got out of bed.

Getting a too-short explanation of how or if Joe had closed the Apocalypto business down was like having the power go out while watching a thriller. Joe had said that the ransomware guy had saved the day. Good to know, but I could have used a few more details. Where did things stand now?

I was still thinking about the possibilities, trying to solve the crime with nothing to go on, as I got ready for the day. I spent five minutes in the rain box, then blow-dried my hair. I stepped into pointy shoes for the first time in so long, my feet protested. I slid my smart black dress over my head and hung a gold cross on a chain around my neck. I was brushing my hair when the doorbell rang. I greeted Gloria Rose, our saving grace. She was early.

We had one of our shorthand conversations where I ticked off the few items on the Molinari to-do list. I wrote a note to Joe, and when Julie stumbled out of her room with Martha I was grinning. Julie's curls, black like Joe's, fell over her blue eyes. She put her arms around my waist. I kissed the top of her head, ruffled Martha's ears, and last, asked Mrs. Rose how I looked.

"Like you're going to a funeral."

We laughed, and sandwiching Julie between us, I hugged Mrs. Rose. I kissed Julie again and told her how much I love, love, love my little girl.

"When Daddy wakes up I'm going to teach him a new game," Julie said.

"Make sure he's had his breakfast first, Bugs, okay?"

"Put on some lipstick," said Mrs. Rose.

Copy that.

CHAPTER 81

ONCE I WAS buckled up in my Explorer and headed to Pacific Heights, I replayed my waking thoughts around and around on a closed loop. The Fricke conundrum. The Holly and Jamie executions. The clueless house staff. Claire's sharp observation of Jamie's skinned knuckles. She'd pulled a rabbit out of her scrubs pocket.

And I thought about Rae Bergen, divorced mother of one, seen in Los Angeles's hottest playgrounds, known as a party girl with writing talent that might eventually pay off.

I was dying to meet this woman who'd been having a long-term affair with her sister's husband. It wasn't unheard of but it was uncommon. Is that why Rae had put me off until now?

I reached the Frickes' house about fifteen minutes after leaving home. A moment later, Richie's old Bronco rolled up the house's curving driveway and braked behind me. He got out of the car, handed me a container of coffee, and I smiled. The kindness of this man.

I said, "You didn't sleep, either?"

"It wasn't the case," he said. "It was Cindy."

"What about her?"

"She was flipping. Flopping. Getting out of bed. Coming back. Kicking the mattress. Talking in her sleep."

"It's not about you, Richie. It's about marriage in general. She never imagined it for herself. You know this."

"You didn't sleep, either," he said to me.

"Joe had a big assignment from Steinmetz. He didn't get home until about three."

"Apocalypto?"

"Bingo," I said. "All good. St. Vartan's is back in business."

"Thank God."

Richie crossed himself, sighed. "Details?"

"I wish. Joe fell asleep while talking."

We both laughed.

"I'm going to sleep all day tomorrow if I have to go to a hotel," he said.

I said, "Great idea. Meanwhile…"

"Yeah. Will Rae talk to us? Or will she not? Do you get why she wouldn't talk?"

"I think so. My guess is, she loved Holly and Jamie, both at the same time. Or, the obvious: something she doesn't want to tell us. We'll find out, but it would be easier if she didn't live in Malibu."

I took a deep breath, then said to Richie, "After the funeral she's going home."

Rich put an arm around my shoulders and gave me a little squeeze. "She'll talk to us," he said.

Most of the time, Rich was right. He had sharp instincts and could tease out the truth from a sphinx. But no one scored 100 percent on breaking down a suspect without having leverage and in a short time. Not even my partner.

We walked up the pathway to the front door, then I reached out and rang the doorbell.

CHAPTER 82

ARTHUR BEVAQUA OPENED the front door.

"Sergeant, good to see you."

"Same here, Arthur. You remember my partner."

"Of course. Inspector Conklin. Come in."

I asked Arthur, "How are you doing?"

"I feel lost. Do I have a job?"

"This is a big one, Arthur. See what Rae has in mind. And I suggest don't make any sudden moves."

He showed me that his hands were empty, prompting us to grin. We three walked together down the long carpeted hallway lined with old masters that today held no magic for me. I knew the way from the hallway to the domed glass room with its exotic plant life and wide view of the Pacific.

There were a dozen small round tables in the solarium, one of which was set for three. A dark-haired woman in black was sitting at one of them with her back to the entrance. We followed Arthur to the table. He said, "Ms. Rae, this is Sergeant Boxer and Inspector Conklin from the SFPD."

I thanked him, and Rich and I took our seats. I heard Arthur calling Rafe on the phone, asking him to move the cars. I told Rae that we were sorry for her tragic loss, after which Arthur took our order and disappeared.

I said, "Ms. Bergen."

"Call me Rae."

"Rae. I'm the lead investigator on James Fricke's murder. I know we have very little time today, so with your help, we'd like to get some basic information, and any ideas you may have on whoever killed James and Holly."

"I want to help, Sergeant. You don't have to persuade me."

"Good."

I took out my phone and showed her what I had for her address in Malibu, her phone numbers and email addresses, and she confirmed them.

"I'm going to record this interview, Rae. It will save a lot of time. You can ask me as many questions as we have time for. And we can follow up on the phone, or here, or in Malibu."

"Fine with me. May I have your card?"

I passed a card to Rae, and Conklin asked, "I'd like to hear this from you. What was your relationship with James Fricke?"

"I loved him. He loved me. Yes, he was married to my sister, a complicated story. But my sister knew about his free-ranging social life. And that went both ways. Holly had lovers, too. She didn't love Jamie anymore. Or even like him. Or so she told me."

I asked, "How often did you and Jamie see each other?"

"When we could. I live some six hours away by car. I don't like to fly. So, I only saw Jamie about once a month."

Rae told us what she knew about Jamie's schedule since Holly died, that his sons from his first marriage were living in Switzerland as was his first wife, Talia, and that Arthur would have the soccer schedule.

Conklin asked Rae if she knew of anyone who'd threatened Holly or Jamie, if either of them had made big changes in their lives, if Jamie had gambling debts, if Holly could have been the target of a rejected lover.

Rae answered the questions credibly and without hesitation. Four nos one after another. And when she looked at her watch, I knew that our breakfasts of tea and freshly baked rolls would go untouched. That in five minutes or less, our interview with Rae would be over, we would be inside the Frickes' private chapel, and we might not have a chance to speak with Rae in person again.

I put my hand on her forearm and asked, "Rae. Where were you on this past Tuesday morning?"

"When Jamie was murdered? I was at home," she said. "My ex-husband, Christophe Picard, had stayed overnight."

I said, "I've read about Christophe. He has a restaurant here in Presidio Heights."

"Yes," Rae said. "He lives here in San Francisco. On Monday, the day before Jamie was shot, Christophe drove down to LA. We spent the day at Venice Beach with our son, Brock, and then Christophe stayed over with me, which was fine with Jamie. There were no issues there. I can introduce you to Christophe at the funeral."

We thanked Rae for her time, and on my way out the door, I stopped to have a few words with Arthur. He liked Rae. But although he'd known her for twenty years, he didn't know her well.

"Arthur, yes or no? Would you trust her?"

"I couldn't say," said Arthur.

That meant no.

CHAPTER 83

YUKI BUTTONED THE jacket on her red "closing statement" suit. The case against Tyler Cates had been going as well as Yuki had hoped; she'd been steady, believable, hadn't dropped a single stitch—until Cates had set off an H-bomb saying that he had known Mary Elena when they'd both been patients at a mental institution called Brookside Psychiatric. That was his explanation for why she'd asked him for sex in the changing room at Xe Sogni. He said that they were old friends, both of them crazy.

An advanced computer search showed no fewer than thirty mental institutions with "Brookside" in its name, and as she'd lamented to Lindsay and Claire, they crisscrossed the United States from Bangor to Pensacola, from Baton Rouge to Seattle. Mary Elena had no living relatives who could support or deny Cates's whopper, and if either the DA or the defense found a Brookside Mental anything, the institution would be highly unlikely to turn over records to any lawyer without a subpoena. And there were too many reasons to count why no subpoena would be forthcoming in her lifetime.

Red Dog had been against Yuki taking this case, but he was sympathetic to her current dilemma.

"You did your best. No. Yuki, you did great. And after you give your closing, it's out of our hands."

At 9:00 a.m. Yuki and Nick Gaines took their seats at their counsel table in 8G. Normally, Gaines was as put together as an actor playing Young Dad in a cereal commercial. Today, he looked as though he'd slept in his car. Too much lack of sleep.

Returning Yuki's appraising look, Gaines said of her suit, "Red for the win?"

"I also have my toes crossed and a four-leaf clover in my pocket. I don't think Mary Elena will feel better by lunch recess."

"Is she actually sick?"

"She was re-traumatized, Nicky. There was the original trauma by her grandfather, the attack in Xe Sogni, and now Cates shouting his stinking trash and calling her a liar. Do you think she was actually in a mental institution with Cates?"

"I didn't say that," Gaines said.

But Yuki knew he'd thought it. If Brookside was a real place, and Mary Elena Hayes and Tyler Cates had both been patients there, Mary Elena's multiple personalities would protect her from the shock if Tyler Cates was found not guilty. But her attorneys would have no protection against the crushing disappointment. The loss. Six months gone. Trust in their client gone.

This wouldn't be the first or last time they'd be whacked by a case that had gone upside down without warning. The feeling was certainty that you'd screwed up, despite the facts and the hard work, and it never got easier. Hell.

But Yuki believed in that woman. She'd put her money on Mary Elena over that shit Cates any day.

CHAPTER 84

THE COURTROOM WAS packed, just shy of standing room only. Officer Louie Mack signaled a guard to close the double doors, then he escorted the jurors into their box and swore them in. When they were seated, the door cracked open between the courtroom and the judge's chambers, and the Honorable Henry William St. John entered and took the bench.

Yuki turned her head a few degrees to the left, surprised to see that defense counsel Ed Schneider wasn't yet seated when every other day he'd been early. She said so to Gaines.

He said, "Maybe he's talking sense to Cates."

"Hmph," said Yuki. "So, what's he saying?"

"'Retract this Brookside garbage or you're going to have a lifetime in a cell to regret it.'"

Yuki said, "Maybe. Cates is vile, but to this day, I don't think he gets it."

Gaines said, "Makes him a psychopath, doesn't it?"

Just then, their conversation was derailed by a rising buzz in the gallery. Judge St. John slammed his gavel down, demanding quiet, which he got. Everything about him, from his precise haircut and trimmed mustache to his controlled scowl and the neat pleat of his robes, said that this judge meant what he said. Quiet.

When the room was silent, the judge cleared his throat and the bailiff called the court to order.

Yuki and Gaines turned their heads at the sound of the double doors opening. Louie Mack opened them wide and Ed Schneider stumped through, unapologetic as he took his seat at the defense counsel table.

The judge acknowledged him with a nod, then called on Yuki. "Are the People ready with their closing argument?"

"We are, Your Honor."

Yuki got to her feet and stepped out into the well to face the jury. At the same time, the counsel for the defense stood and asked if he might address the judge at the bench.

"Mr. Schneider, Ms. Castellano, please approach."

Two minutes later, the judge ordered the courtroom cleared.

CHAPTER 85

DURING THE RECESS, Cindy grabbed two cans of sparkling water plus a sandwich and a fruit salad from the snack cart outside the Hall and brought them up to Yuki's office.

"Chicken and bacon with mayo okay?" she asked. "If not I'll trade you for my fruit salad."

"Either way," said Yuki. "I don't think I can taste anything."

Yuki seemed to have no appetite but looked glad to have Cindy as company. Cindy was thinking of the *Chronicle*'s six o'clock deadline and had hopes she could update the Hayes v. Cates story in time. It was rare for Yuki to give her exclusive news on the record, but today might be one of those days.

Cindy passed a can of sparkling water to Yuki, pulled the tab on hers. She slid the sandwich to Yuki's side of the desk and unsealed the container of fruit salad, took a bite of melon, and dialed down whatever feverish expression might be giving her real hunger away. Yuki took a bite of her sandwich, apparently determined not to let Cindy bully her for any front-page tidbits.

Cindy, sitting across the desk from Yuki, was finding it hard not to interrogate her friend. What did Yuki know? And would she tell her? She watched Yuki take her sandwich apart, push a strip of bacon around with her fork, pick it up with her fingers and chew on it for a while. Cindy drank her seltzer and waited. And then, she had to ask.

"Yuki, what caused St. John to call a recess? Schneider asked to talk to the judge, then the judge asked for the prosecution, too. You all spoke for exactly two point seven seconds. You and Schneider went back to your tables and St. John said, 'Court is adjourned until further notice.' I was there, Yuki. I can write that."

"Sure, Cin. Not a problem."

"So, Yuki. Judge says, 'Court is adjourned.' But you and Schneider don't leave when the room is emptied, so I think there's some story here."

Yuki said, "Cin, I would give you a *kidney*, but this is…"

Cindy said, "Let me guess. Off-limits. But. What if I give you one of *my* organs? How about my liver?"

Yuki laughed, and Cindy was laughing too when Len Parisi's shadow crossed the doorway.

Yuki looked up. "You need me, Len?"

"Judge wants to meet in chambers. Now."

CHAPTER 86

THE FRICKE FAMILY chapel, circa 1853, had been built on a treed quarter-acre lot behind the Frickes' house. The white, wood-frame structure was hidden from the road below by the house and a large copse of trees. There were stained glass windows on the long sides, a red painted front door, and a simple cross at the top of the steeple.

By a quarter to ten, Fricke friends and family had gathered on the freshly mown chapel lawn while Conklin and I stood at the edge of the tree line. I had brought Cappy's annotated photo from Holly's funeral and we were attaching names to faces and getting a feeling for the gathering. Some of the mourners were dabbing at their tears or crying out loud. Some were enjoying themselves. Looked like they were at a class reunion or party of old friends.

After scanning the crowd, I put the photo away in my bag and we waded in. Conklin went over to Patty Delaney and cut her from the herd. I couldn't hear their conversation, but she wasn't hysterical the way she'd been a few days ago. I found Judy Borinstein, looking smart in a navy-blue suit and gold accessories. She was speaking to a tearful woman I recognized as Marilyn Stein, a.k.a. Marly, Holly's assistant and another of Jamie's lovers, now living in New York City. Borinstein was in business mode as was I, and I broke into their conversation. Marilyn stiffened her face to me and started to move away.

Borinstein caught her by the arm and said, "Marly, we're lucky to have Sergeant Boxer leading this investigation. Spend a few minutes with her, why don't you?"

Then Judy was called away.

Marly asked me, "Have you gotten anywhere in Holly's death?"

"Not yet. It's possible that this investigation into Jamie's death will turn up a clue in Holly's."

Marly shrugged and looked past me, her expression meant to convey, *Whatevah. I couldn't care less.*

I said, "Ms. Stein, I know that Mr. Fricke cared about you very much. We need your help."

"I can't tell you anything. I left the Frickes' employ after Holly was murdered. It's been six months."

The lawn had emptied and this might be the last time I'd spend time with this woman.

"Marly, very simply, who wanted Holly dead?"

"Holly would say that I did."

Conklin came over in time to hear this exchange. He said to Marly, "Why do you say that?"

"I knew too much about her," Marly said. "I signed a six-page NDA but that didn't stand up to how much Jamie loved me. I was a servant by day and a madly in love idiot a few nights a month when he and I were together. Holly knew all of that. It's a humiliation that will cost me thirty years in therapy and I doubt I will ever trust a man again. But I didn't kill Holly or Jamie. I have a job and a roommate and a doorman in New York, all of whom can testify to where I was when Jamie was killed."

I asked for names and numbers and Marly gave them to me. I had other questions. Had there had been any hate mail or threatening phone calls to Holly, any aggression from Jamie toward Holly, anything that at that time, or in retrospect, made her suspect that Holly or Jamie might be in serious danger?

Marly said no to everything, her face frozen to stop her emotions from breaching the banks of a lake of bitterness. She emphatically claimed that she was and had been an ingenue when Holly hired her, unprepared to handle the complex emotions of both of the Frickes.

"Arthur can back up everything I've said," she spat. "There are no secrets from Arthur Bevaqua. He knows everything. Good luck, Sergeant. I'm a dead end."

CHAPTER 87

I WATCHED MARILYN STEIN walk away; stiff, angry, and not afraid to show it. I wondered if she was the one who'd made the phone call to Jamie on his last morning, if she had summoned him to his death. Had she hired someone to put him down? Had she done it herself? It would take a few phone calls to airlines to see if Marilyn Stein had flown from New York to San Francisco earlier this week.

I looked around for Richie, saw he was still working the crowd. I also saw brooding women, men drinking alone under shade trees who looked away as I caught their eyes. There was a touch on the back of my arm. I turned around. Rae Bergen was there with a tall, good-looking man of about forty.

She introduced me and Conklin to Christophe Picard, her ex-husband and companion of two decades. Christophe, a chef, said, "By the way, I have a bistro on Sacramento Street—Chez Bonhomie. You are both welcome to drop by and speak with me anytime. I doubt I know anything useful, but I'll definitely serve you a meal you won't forget."

Rae said, "See that gloomy young man over there by the drinks? Gray jacket? That's our son, Brock."

I looked and saw a college-age boy standing beside the bar area. Brock was taller than Rae, had an athletic build, and had a look on his face I couldn't read.

I mentioned wanting to speak with Brock, get his impressions of his uncle.

Rae said, "Good luck. Brock barely even talks to us. I had to plead with him to come to the funeral for my sake. Don't be offended if he just walks away from you."

Christophe said, "Sergeant, Brock's generation would rather text than talk, and he's in his own world at school—four hours from here."

The door to the chapel opened, and the guests filed inside. I took Richie's arm and followed the mourners into the chapel, where we took two seats on the aisle at the rear.

The service was ecumenical. The officiant was Judge Susan Anderson. She had not known James Fricke III, but she spoke as a woman who understood the loss felt by those saying last goodbyes to the dead. Anderson exhorted them—us—to think of the good life Jamie Fricke had lived.

She asked who would like to speak, and hands went up. Arthur Bevaqua stood, took the podium, and spoke of Mr. Jamie as a man who'd shaped his life and taught him to strive for excellence in all things. Arthur said that he loved Mr. Jamie and Mrs. Holly and always would.

Most of the eulogies were given by people I didn't know well. I noted that neither Jamie's first wife nor his sons had flown in to attend his funeral. Not even by Zoom. Rae took the podium to say that she'd known Jamie since before she'd been maid of honor at his and Holly's wedding.

"Although I don't believe in an afterlife, if there is one, Jamie will be having a party for Holly, for their friends who have passed. God bless Jamie and Holly. God bless us all."

I took note of these rehearsed speeches, especially those from Jamie's former lovers, and excepting Patty Delaney, no one fell apart or crossed a line. A prayer was offered by Judy Borinstein, and Sage Dugan, a member of the staff, sang a hymn in French, "J'irai la voir un jour." At one point her voice had cracked, but she'd taken a breath, then picked up where she'd left off.

Conklin and I paid our respects to Jamie in his casket at the front of the chapel; a man no longer powerful, narcissistic, charming, unfaithful. We signed a visitor's book, and I left my phone number and email address in the space provided.

We left the chapel before the hearse and the limos took the long drive out to Cypress Lawn in Colma. Rafe Talbot brought our cars around to the front of the house.

"Good luck, Sergeant," Rafe said to me. "You still have Greta's number? My girlfriend? Please call me there if I can help in any way."

I wondered again about Rafe, this pleasant middle-aged man who'd done time for car theft at nineteen. He lived on the Fricke property and was closely tied to Jamie's movements. We would need to talk to Rafe Talbot again.

As Conklin and I walked down the path to our cars, I composed a short email on my phone to Team Fricke, copied Brady, and pressed Send.

CHAPTER 88

THE JUDGE'S CHAMBERS were lined with bookshelves, carpeted in Oriental rugs, and appointed with midcentury modern furnishings. Judge St. John himself looked as though he'd stepped off the cover of a plump 1955 *Life* magazine featuring the California Department of Justice.

He sat behind his desk facing the door, with the window behind him looking out on Bryant Street. Red Dog sat to the judge's right. Yuki Castellano and her deputy sat at right angles to Parisi. Schneider sat across the room from the prosecution, with an empty seat beside him for Cates.

Also to the judge's right was a thirty-two-inch TV on a stand, Tyler Cates's image on the screen. Cates was sitting on a metal slab bed, with a blanket, no mattress. His head was in his hands and his body language told all. The young man was depressed or worse. On the screen, court officer Robert Wells, who was well-known around the Hall, approached the holding cell.

Cates asked, "What's up?"

Wells said, "You, your attorney, and the prosecution are meeting with the judge now. If I were you, I'd behave."

"Who asked you?"

"Do as you wish," said Wells and unlocked the gate. He cuffed Cates and walked him out of the holding cell.

His Honor turned off the CCTV and phoned his assistant.

"Susan. When Wells arrives with Cates, ask them to wait outside with you for a few minutes. I may ask you to take them to conference room A."

CHAPTER 89

THE JUDGE TURNED back to the attorneys in his chambers.

He said to the defense counsel, "Ed, because of Mr. Cates's eruption in court, I had to check it out. I put every free hand in the justice department on duty yesterday, last night, and early this morning. They made calls to every mental institution with 'Brookside' in its name. There are thirty in the country. And we hopped over the Canadian border while we were at it. None of the institutions had ever had a Tyler Cates or Mary Elena Hayes as patients, ever. One or two of them had closed, but we chased down heads of these defunct places who were working at other mental institutions. As Mr. Cates produced no documentation of his time spent in a mental institution, we not only went as far as we could go. We went farther.

"In my heavily researched opinion, Tyler Cates lied to confuse the jury, to get them on his side. I can't let it stand. I could call a mistrial but it would only serve to encourage your client to repeat this performance in a new trial.

"Ed, when Cates gets here, I suggest you talk to him in the conference room. Tell him this is a come to Jesus moment and if he doesn't tell the actual truth, I'm going to put him in jail and throw away the key for all of eternity.

"Len. If Cates confesses, will you consider giving him a break?"

"Meaning?"

There was a knock on the door. Court officer Susan O'Connor opened it about ten inches, looked back toward the judge, and said, "They're here."

Judge St. John said, "Give us another couple of minutes."

Susan went outside the room. The judge answered the DA.

"Len, I'm suggesting that the rape and aggravated assault sentences run concurrently so we can lop a few years off if he satisfies you with his full-throated 'I did it, and accusing Ms. Hayes of knowing me was a vicious thing to do to her on top of the other vicious things I did to her.'

"Mr. Cates should apologize to her and ask her forgiveness. Something approximating all of this. And, let's say, he'll be eligible for parole in thirty years. Sound all right?"

Red Dog said, "I'm open to it."

CHAPTER 90

DEFENSE COUNSEL ED Schneider left the judge's chambers and followed Susan O'Connor to the conference room to have his stern talk with Cates, repeating what the judge had offered almost verbatim.

Tyler Cates, having had a brief taste of life in a cell, wasn't convinced that his lawyer was fairly representing his interests. And he said so.

Schneider said, "Tyler, this is the point of no return. Confess. Apologize and you'll be eligible for parole sometime in the very distant future. Otherwise, life in prison is your future with a life sentence for rape and the additional sentence for aggravated assault. If you don't confess, you will never be free again. I'm going back to the judge's chambers, where I will try to keep that deal in place. Ms. O'Connor will bring you back to chambers in two or three minutes, so think fast."

Schneider returned to the meeting, took his seat, and a few minutes later, Susan brought Officer Wells and Cates into the judge's chambers. Cates looked defiant. Even the last few hours in a cell hadn't softened him. Still cuffed, he took the chair beside his stern and florid attorney. Wells sat on a window ledge behind Cates so that he could reach him instantly if needed.

Yuki and Gaines sat opposite Cates and Schneider. Red Dog Parisi sat in the side chair beside the judge's desk. The table was set.

Tyler Cates was on the menu.

Judge St. John said, "Mr. Cates. You've had time to reflect on your actions. Do you have anything to tell the court?"

"Like what?"

"Like, do you take responsibility for your actions against Ms. Hayes?"

"I have nothing to say that I didn't already tell everyone in court and probably on national news. Were you listening?"

"Yes I was, Mr. Cates. Mr. Wells, will you please take Mr. Cates back to his cell."

The attorneys remained in place and when the door was closed, His Honor addressed the room.

"Court will resume Monday at nine."

CHAPTER 91

I'D HOPED THAT by going to Jamie's funeral, his killer or a lead to that person would reveal himself, but the opposite had happened. I'd cleared no one, while adding additional potential suspects: Marly, Rae, and Christophe, to name three, and possibly Rafe, to add another.

I thought about Arthur: his attachment to Jamie, his twenty years of loyal service, his access to all things Jamie, and not least, his inheritance of more money from Jamie Fricke's estate than he would earn in three lifetimes as house manager.

I was so absorbed in reviewing the funeral attendees that the fifteen-minute drive home felt like it had only taken a minute. Lake Street was just ahead. I parked around the corner on Eleventh and entered our building, hoping that Joe was awake, his feet on the ground, watching *World News Today*.

Inside our place, I locked my piece in the gun case in the foyer and by then Martha had found me and greeted me with wagging and slobbering and shoving me backward by planting her front feet on my waist. I told her she was a good girl and called out to Joe.

"Help!"

Julie shouted back. "Mom! I'm giving Dad combat training. We need to concentrate."

Meaning, *Don't interrupt us, okay?*

Okay.

CHAPTER 92

INSIDE OUR BEDROOM, I stepped out of my black silky everything and changed into jeans and an SFPD T-shirt. Back in the living room, I dropped into my Mom chair. I wanted to talk to Joe and knew he wanted to talk to me. But this was Dad and Julie time, and Julie wasn't giving that up without a fight.

"Daddyyyyy. This is important. No talking."

I saw what was happening and stifled a laugh. Julie is one of the funniest people I know, but she takes herself very seriously. When it came to combat training, Julie Ann Molinari, clothed in lavender unicorn pj's, was in charge.

She called out her moves.

"Daddy. This is called 'kicking and punching.'"

Joe covered his eyes and our little combat trainer kicked him in the shin with one bare little foot, then socked him in the biceps with the opposite fist.

"Ooo. Oww, Julie," Joe called out in mock pain.

"Now," she said, "this is what I call 'dodging.'"

She leapt from side to side making, I guess, war cries. "Yah. Pow.

Powee. Yahoo." Joe played his part as victim until a laugh escaped him.

"Don't laugh, Daddy. These moves could save your life! Now, this one is 'karate chopping.'"

"No, no more, Julie," Joe said, falling over sideways. "You've killed me."

"Okay. Last one today," Julie announced. "This is advanced training. It's 'using weapons.'"

Julie picked up her plush stuffed cow she'd named Mrs. Mooey Milkington and swung it around her head singing out, "Whoop, whoop, whoop," then slapping those few ounces of fluff and foam rubber against Joe's forearm.

"Julie, I can't take any more. Pleeease stop."

"We're done," Julie crowed. "I promote myself to combat trainer level two," she said, and jumped into his arms. Joe hugged her until she squeaked, "Dadddddyyyyy, you winnnn."

"Thank you, Julie. I can take on anyone now: kung fu fighters, even Superman," said the actual G-man in the family.

I said, "Julie—"

"Mom! You want combat training?"

"Not now, sweetie. I need to talk to Dad. It's confidential police business. How about we set you up with a movie in your room so Dad and I can catch up?"

"Okay. This time. What movie, Mom?"

She ran across the floor, climbed into my lap, and threw her arms around my neck.

I said, "You tell me."

"*House of Cats*," she told me.

Done.

CHAPTER 93

I SET JULIE up in her bed with Martha, a glass of milk, and the extended two-hour version of a cartoon musical filling her TV screen. When she was calling out advice to multicolored dancing cats, Joe and I went to our bedroom and got into bed.

We hugged and rolled around, and I got up to check that the door was locked. Then I got back to bed. Joe was quiet for a full minute. I thought he may have gone to sleep. I shook his arm and he said, "Steinmetz offered me a job."

"Again?"

"This time in writing. And it's a great offer."

"Oh, my God. What did you say?"

"That I wanted to talk to you."

"And here I am. Listening…"

"Well. There'd be a very decent raise, other perks. It's a full-time job. Which doesn't mean nine-to-five. You remember."

"Vividly."

I remembered, too, gunfights, touch-and-go nights in the ER, the "Chinese wall" between us, meaning talking about our cases was forbidden, Joe's absence for days at a time, and the worst, still animated in my mind—the evening when a museum made of glass and steel had exploded with Joe inside.

He said, "I could turn down the job again, and keep doing what I've been doing for a few more years. There's a lot to be said for that."

"Like what?"

"I'm the boss. No-brainer work. Afternoon naps. Long walks with Martha. High-fat, salty snacks in the kitchen. Drop off and pick up our little girl at the school bus. But that's not all. Did I mention afternoon naps?"

His delivery was priceless and I laughed out loud.

"No screaming," he said, then tipped my face to his and kissed me long and hard. I kissed him back and then his hands were under my clothes and I was tugging at his.

"Hey. I love you," he said.

"I love you, too."

We made sweet love, panting but not screaming, aware of the little girl in the next room watching a movie that would soon be over.

We dressed reluctantly but stayed in bed and made a circumstances-permitting date for tomorrow night: dinner out, home again, same place, and with some screaming allowed.

I rolled onto my back. It would be good for Joe to go back to work, but we both knew that everything would change.

Joe spoke. "Steinmetz wants a decision next week."

"That stinks. How about we talk again about this a few more times? I have to get used to the idea of it, but the decision is yours."

"Ours."

I squeezed his hand. I rubbed his head and traced the scar from the Sci-Tron explosion that had parted his hair.

It was a rare pleasure to be in sync like this. In the same circadian rhythm with my husband. Even tired, our minds racing from the other's touch, from anticipation, from knowing, loving, trusting each other. Joe and I just had a great, memorable night together.

The best in a long time.

SATURDAY

CHAPTER 94

JOE HELD THE front door for me and I felt transported back to a more elegant time, at least as it was portrayed in black-and-white movies.

The jazz was hot, the patrons looked cool, and Joe and I held hands as we took the grand staircase to the mezzanine floor. To my eye, Joe looked a little bit like Clark Gable without the mustache, and I'd swept up my hair, worn my red, scoop-necked cocktail dress, giving me a glam Ginger Rogers look.

Bix had been named for Jazz Age musician Bix Beiderbecke, and the restaurant in a brick building in an alley off Gold Street felt like a 1930s supper club or speakeasy. The waiters wore white jackets, and ours, a young man named Randall, said, "Welcome back to Bix." He showed us to a table with a view of the ground floor dining room and handed us the menus. In fact, we ordered from memory and Joe and I were alone again.

Over a light white wine, I updated my combat-trained husband on the recent high points of the Fricke case.

I said, "We got an unbelievable break, Joe. Maybe."

"Let me have it. I'm braced."

I told him about Claire's eagle eye, that the first shot at Jamie Fricke was a .40 fired at close range to his left shoulder. That Claire suspected he'd been adrenaline-charged enough to turn around and punch the shooter in the face.

"That's plausible..." Joe mused.

"The next four rounds killed him but the DNA on Jamie's knuckles told the tale on the shooter. He's male and get this, Joe. He shares DNA with James Fricke."

"Nice catch on Claire's part," said Joe. "I guess the lab was unable to ID anyone from the DNA comparisons?"

"Not yet."

"Hunh. So if a suspect has no Fricke DNA, he's out of the running. On the other hand, Jamie Fricke was such a hound with women..."

"I was thinking the same," I said. "Who knows how many offspring he's produced in the last thirty years..."

We paused as the waiter brought our entrées.

When he had left the table, I prompted Joe to tell all about his stress-packed save-the-hospital week. He told me about his partner, Bao Wong, whom he liked and admired.

"How much?"

"Hmmm?"

"How much do you like and admire her?"

Joe pinched my knee. "You goofball. She's a high-tech agent, cyberterrorism director, actually. Lives in DC, but if I take the job, she may move here with her family to work with me and Craig. We make a good team."

CHAPTER 95

OVER DUNGENESS CRAB and sautéed asparagus, Joe described the shoot-out at the blue house. And then described the thirtysomething coder with the green windbreaker who'd left his computer for the Feds, then helped save St. Vartan's Hospital.

Joe said, "I really like that guy. I hope I'm right about him." And then said nothing for a full minute. I shook his arm and then he gave me his straight-on, blue-eyed gaze and said, "So, I'm thinking I should take the job. Here are the whys and why nots…"

"Joe, it'll be good for you."

"Not so good for you, though."

"Here's how I see it. If it makes your life more interesting, challenging, and you don't get killed, I'll be happy enough. We'll offer Mrs. Rose a full-time job."

"Well. I'll be getting a good raise, more than enough to cover Gloria's salary and fun for the kiddo. As for the job, it's full-time. Which doesn't mean nine-to-five. You remember."

"I sure do," I said. "It was like living inside a sci-fi thriller and getting out of the theater is not guaranteed. That said, I think it's now or never."

Joe showed me his palms, first one, then the other. "On the one hand, assuming Gloria says yes, it could be the perfect life. On the other, early retirement, and I'm already bored with myself."

"Go for it, Joe. With my full support. Tell him yes."

We held hands under the table, kissed, spooned up criminally delicious chocolate mousse with our coffee, and kissed again. We made it home before Julie was in the sack. Mrs. Rose wanted to hang out for Julie's review of *Super Mario Bros*.

"Four rotten tomatoes," Julie said. "No. Four and a half!"

We thanked our good friend Mrs. Rose, tucked our little girl into her big girl's bed with my old friend Martha. Then Joe and I went to the room next door. We dressed in pajamas and crawled under the covers in the dark and snuggled in for a long night's love. It was Joe who screamed into the pillow. As for me, I held him tight and I prayed to God that we had made the right decision. That all of us would be safe.

I fell asleep remembering nights when Joe hadn't come home. But we were together now. Amen.

MONDAY

CHAPTER 96

I SAT AT the head of the scarred oak conference table, Jackson Brady to my left, Claire Washburn to my right, eight Homicide inspectors filling the remaining chairs. The Frickes' autopsy photos were taped to the far wall. There was also a list of suspects tacked to the adjacent corkboard.

Although our persons of interest list had dropped in number, the energy in our shabby war room was high. By process of elimination, we might be getting closer to Jamie's killer. And maybe Holly's.

Brady said, "Claire, why don't you start us off."

Dr. Washburn was ready. She opened the folder in front of her, then told the group about the Fricke DNA/knuckle connection.

"So far, it's just a good idea," she said. "Which it will be if we have a viable suspect with Fricke DNA. The samples I took from Jamie's hand are now at Quantico. The FBI's database might spit out a name."

It looked to me like Claire's explanation hit Sergeant Paul Chi like a shot of adrenaline, straight to his brain.

"I want to be in on this, Doctor," he said. "Let me know how I can help."

Then Cappy, wearing his undercover leather jacket, denim cap, and jeans, reported that Holly's Bentley had been discovered, sold to a dealer in Acapulco; Jamie's Jag had also been found, demolished. He took off his cap, placed it over his heart, and said: "Every window was broken, the upholstery slashed with a carpet knife. The electronics were gutted, the VIN numbers had been burned off, but one was legible enough to identify it as Jamie Fricke's vehicle. The hundred-thousand-dollar sports car was deliberately run into a brick wall and totaled. Looked personal to me. I'd call it a hit. By proxy. Or to make sure it was really dead."

Chi added, "The perp was wearing gloves. There were no, none, zero prints in the remains of the car."

Conklin then spoke for a couple of colorful minutes about Fricke's funeral, and when he paused for a sip of coffee, I stood, apologized, and said that I had to dash off for what might become an important interview.

I said, "I'm having lunch with Christophe Picard. Like Arthur Bevaqua, he's been entwined with the Fricke family for over twenty years — through his former marriage to Rae Bergen, their son, and his friendship with the Fricke clan. Plus. He wants to talk."

"Free food, Sarge?"

That was Cappy, being a wise guy.

I said, "I hope. I skipped breakfast this morning. I get the sense that Christophe likes to talk. So, he's either going to give me a lot of bull or steak frites."

Folks laughed, wished me luck, and soon I was in my car headed northwest on Seventh Street toward Christophe Picard's trendy, four-star-rated Chez Bonhomie.

At a stoplight, I opened a text from Claire: "FYI. Three new homicides came in this week. Unrelated to Fricke, but still murders."

Feeling time slipping away, I burned some rubber when the light turned green. Inevitably new homicides would drag us away from Jamie Fricke just as had happened with Holly. New cases had come in with an urgency that had turned Holly's case cold. A week in, Jamie's case was still fresh. But every day that passed would lower the odds of finding his killer.

That much was clear.

CHAPTER 97

CINDY WAS IN her protected seat inside the doorway of Courtroom 8G. The placement of furniture and people, the time court was due to go into session was all normal, but at the same time it didn't seem normal at all.

The room was packed and the tension in the air gave Cindy goose bumps. Something was about to happen.

Yuki was at the prosecution table just beyond the bar with Gaines and Mary Elena Hayes in the seat between them. Red Dog entered the room, and a split second later, Bailiff Riley Boone called court to order.

The door behind the bench opened and Judge St. John entered his court as Boone called out, "All rise." The hundred-plus people in the gallery and the lawyers came noisily to their feet. The judge took his place at the bench, looked across the oak-paneled room, and asked the gallery to be seated. The bailiff ushered in the jury, all twelve of whom looked somewhat dazed, as if they'd been sleeping in a closet or under their beds.

Cindy focused her eyes on Mary Elena Hayes, but her face was turned toward the front of the room. Cindy typed a silent note on her tablet that the victim in this case seemed at ease. Mary Elena had information about what was to come while court was in session that Cindy could only guess at, so she typed a line of question marks across the midline of her electronic page.

Judge St. John asked for quiet. It took several long moments and a bang of the gavel to get it. The jury had already been sworn in. The assemblage now sat quietly. No one coughed or dropped a handbag or a phone charger.

When he was ready, the judge addressed the jury, saying, "The court wishes to thank the jury for their time and diligence in hearing the case regarding the defendant, Mr. Tyler Cates. The time you've spent on this has not gone to waste. There will be further proceedings forthwith and the jurors are invited to leave or to remain in their jury seats and observe these proceedings. The press will be admitted. If you are neither a juror nor the press, regrettably, I must ask you to exit the courtroom."

Cindy unclenched her jaw and checked to see that her battery charger was still snugly in the wall socket as the guards moved the grumbling audience through the double doors.

When the doors were closed again, the judge said, "The defendant, Mr. Cates, has confessed to both the crimes of rape and aggravated assault. Mr. Cates and Mr. Schneider, please stand."

"Mr. Cates, to the charge of rape, how to you plead?"

"Guilty, Your Honor."

The judge asked the defense counsel to verify his client's plea, which he did.

Judge St. John addressed the defendant again.

"Mr. Cates. In the charge of aggravated assault, how do you plead?"

Cindy saw the defendant shift his weight from one foot to the other. The judge opened his mouth to speak and Cates preempted him speedily.

"I plead guilty to that charge, also."

"Mr. Schneider?"

"Yes, Your Honor. My client accepts the responsibility and the penalty for his actions, and he would like to say a few words to Ms. Hayes from their respective seats."

Judge St. John asked if that was all right with Ms. Castellano. Yuki bent her head toward Mary Elena, and they exchanged two or three words. Then Ms. Hayes stood and faced her rapist and abuser. She was rigid. Not as at ease as Cindy had thought.

The judge said, "Go ahead, Mr. Cates."

Cindy typed as Tyler Cates turned and faced Mary Elena and whichever of her personalities, maybe her own, had stiffened her spine.

"I'm very sorry," said Cates. "You didn't do anything to bring down my anger and violation on yourself. I hope someday you can find a way to forgive me although I will never forgive myself."

The judge asked all to sit while he pronounced the sentence.

"Mr. Cates, for the charge of rape, you are sentenced to thirty-five years in prison with the possibility of parole. For the charge of aggravated assault, you shall receive an additional fifteen years in prison, also with the possibility of parole."

Ed Schneider asked the judge to waive time, which Cindy understood and noted. It meant that imposition of the sentence would begin immediately.

Looking at St. John, Cindy saw that his expression had been fixed for the length of the trial. In this, the afterword, he finally cracked a small smile. He thanked the jury again and after they had filed out of the jury box and had been returned to their room, Judge Henry William St. John left the bench. Guards escorted Tyler Cates out of the courtroom by the side door, and Cindy stood in the aisle until she could throw her arms around her dear friend Yuki.

"Great job, Yuki. Great job and on the record."

CHAPTER 98

LATER THAT MORNING, Sonia Alvarez got a call from Rob Bailey, a former Las Vegas cop she knew and trusted. Bailey had connections with official CIs and unofficial snitches and now had what he called "a smoking hot tip" for her: A known but unindicted killer-for-hire named Samuel Rochas, who went by the unlikely street name of "Padre," was being held in South Lake Tahoe, Nevada, today before extradition tonight to Mexico City, where he was wanted for killing a high-ranking politico.

Padre was known to have associations with James Fricke via gambling and had been dropping hints to gang members and petty thieves that he may have been involved in the Fricke murders.

Rochas's blabbing to local criminals, insinuating that he had killed the Frickes, seemed suicidal — or maybe his way of evading Mexico's court order. Returning to Mexico was dangerous for Padre. Convicted or not, someone would get to him and put him down.

On the other hand, Bailey had sent an attachment — a mug shot of Padre. Alvarez had a very strong and somewhat supportable hunch that Padre had been at Holly Fricke's funeral, something for which she might have evidence.

Alvarez had the mug shot side by side on her phone with Cappy's color photo of mourners at Holly Fricke's funeral gathered outside the chapel and a black-and-white copy of that same photo with Cappy's handwritten names of the individuals in the shot.

Not all the individuals had been identified. Even with Arthur Bevaqua's help, there were a dozen individuals without names. And Alvarez was particularly interested in the one who might be Padre.

Her eyes had settled on an unidentified Mr. X. He looked to be fortysomething, white, average height and weight, with medium-length dark hair. His sunglasses obscured a quarter of his face and his clothing was unremarkable: a dark sports jacket and trousers. He was standing alone, looking out at the bay, his face in profile to the camera. No matter how much Alvarez enlarged the photo, she couldn't say with a real degree of confidence whether or not this person was the man in the mug shot she had on her phone.

But Bailey had said, "Alvarez, Padre's a psycho. If you want him for killing Jamie Fricke you need to get to Tahoe today and stake your claim before he's transported back to Mexico City."

There was a flight to Tahoe leaving in an hour and a half, but Alvarez needed authorization to make the trip, stay in a motel, buy breakfast.

She'd left a message for Brady, who was in a conference and hadn't called her back. Even Brenda couldn't reach him.

Likewise, she'd left messages for Conklin, who was at the crime lab in Hunters Point, and Lindsay, who might have turned off her phone during her meeting with Christophe Picard, Rae Bergen's ex-husband. At any rate, none of the three had called her back and she couldn't make the plane wait for her.

Alvarez was still at her desktop, her eyes fixed on the screen while obsessively checking the time on the blinking clock app. If she didn't get a call back, Padre Rochas would be in Mexico City tonight and she wouldn't be able to question him.

As point person for the SFPD, it looked as though Alvarez was going to have to bring Rochas in on her own.

CHAPTER 99

THERE WAS MOVEMENT at the halfway point in the bullpen. Alvarez looked up to see Cappy arriving at his desk, dropping his weight into his chair.

She called out, "Cappy. Can you please take a look at this?"

He called back, "Sure, okay. Ten minutes. I have some stuff I have to do."

"Cappy, this will be fast. Two minutes. I swear."

Cappy muttered, "Whose definition of two minutes?" He hoisted himself out of his chair, went to Alvarez's desk in the pod she shared with Conklin and Boxer. He took Boxer's seat, rolled the chair closer to Alvarez's computer.

She said, "I got a reliable lead on a hired gun, gambling pal of James Fricke. Given name, Samuel Rochas. Goes by Padre. Apparently, he says 'Rest in peace' when he pulls the trigger."

"I don't know the guy," Cappy said.

Alvarez said, "Look here, Cappy. That photo you took at Holly's funeral service, the one on the chapel lawn."

"Ya-hunh. That's mine."

Alvarez pointed to a man in the photo who might be Sam "Padre" Rochas, standing alone, staring into the distance in profile. She zoomed in on his face.

Cappy peered at the color image. "I don't recognize him. I don't even remember seeing him. There were swarms of people moving around. Circling swarms."

"I have a mug shot," said Alvarez. "Check this out."

She opened her phone, scrolled through her photo gallery, and opened the mug shot of Sam Rochas. Was he the no-name guy who'd been at Holly's funeral? She had to know.

Alvarez filled Cappy in on Rochas's background. Bailey had told her that Padre was from Chicago, had a sealed juvie record, including gang activity, misdemeanors. Later, he'd been accused of shooting a liquor store owner, raiding the cash register, and getting away. Next stop, Nevada. More shootings, and although no one had made a successful case on him, the Mexican police wanted him for killing a popular politician.

Extradition papers had been submitted and signed up the line, and this shooter, with a reputation as a first-class silent killer for hire...

Cappy said loudly, "Alvarez, you saying this guy shot the Frickes?"

"Cappy, I'm going by this. A close source of mine from Vegas PD, now in Tahoe, told me that Padre hung with Jamie when they did a tour of the hotels and casinos. That Padre was a big fan of the Bleus and bet on Jamie's team to win. He went all in. And lost. Big-time. And Padre held a grudge."

Cappy said, "I want to look at some of the other shots I took of the funeral party. Find a different angle on this guy's face."

"Can you do it now?" Alvarez asked. "There's a flight leaving any minute. I've gotta meet with some cops I know about whether Padre was the last person Jamie Fricke saw before he died."

Cappy said to Alvarez, "How would anyone know that?"

"I guess he said so."

"Fine. Let's see that mug shot again."

Alvarez scrolled down in her photo gallery and passed the phone to Cappy, who began memorizing the man's features.

He took out his phone and looked at the four shots he'd taken of the crowd outside the chapel at Holly's funeral.

He said, "My last shot catches this guy's head from the back. No help. But I'll say this, Alvarez, he's not seen talking to anyone here. Not even Jamie, who was the bereaved. If this dude was checking out the family, Holly's funeral was a scouting operation. In my opinion, Padre's worth a look-see and a chat with the arresting officer and the CO."

"Okay. I'm going. I need you to say, 'Go for it, Alvarez,' and sign off on moderate expenses, okay?"

"Go for it. I'll sign a requisition and email it to Brady. Just call home. And if you think he's the doer, call Clapper and demand to be put through."

"Thank you, Cappy."

"Sonia, be careful. Call me every couple of hours and let me know where you are."

"Will do."

CHAPTER 100

I'D KNOWN OF Christophe Picard's jewel of a bistro in Presidio Heights for years. I'd never been inside but had driven past its outdoor café and thought that someday I'd come here with the girls for dinner. Yet now, I was sitting at a small square table by the fireplace without the girls, dressed in my usual work clothes, badge hanging from a chain around my neck, holstered gun at my waist. I was appropriately dressed. I was working.

While waiting for Christophe to leave the kitchen and join me, I listened to French folk music and thought about Rae Bergen's ex-husband. I was hoping that I was going to learn something from Christophe that would lead to an arrest. He'd invited me to drop by and talk with him. Maybe he wanted to gauge what I knew about the killer. Either way, he'd opened a door and I'd walked through.

While waiting, I mentally reviewed Paul Chi's earlier interview notes with the restaurateur, which ended with "Christophe Picard; alibi checked out, not suspected." I was tapping my feet, twiddling my wedding ring, when Christophe slipped into the chair opposite mine wearing chef's whites and a red scarf knotted around his neck. We shook hands.

Christophe asked if I trusted him to order for me.

"Wouldn't have it any other way."

"Excellent."

Minutes later, a waiter delivered the first course.

Oranges? I looked up at my host.

"Blood oranges," he said. "With caraway seeds and a Champagne vinaigrette. Have a taste, Sergeant. I think you're going to like it."

He was right, and I told him so.

"Just getting started," he said.

"Me, too. I think you invited me to lunch so you could tell me something."

"Did I?"

"Yes. Talk to me, Christophe. Do you know or have any idea who hated Holly and Jamie enough to have killed them?"

"You get right to the point, don't you?"

"Yes. I hope you do, too."

"Shoot," he said. "I mean..."

"I get it," I said to the good-looking guy in blazing white sitting across from me. "I've spoken with Rae, but briefly, and she was guarded. I just want to understand her, and you, better."

"Ask me anything."

"Here we go. Where were you on Tuesday morning last week, between eight and eight thirty?"

"That's when Jamie was murdered? That's easy," he said. "I was in LA, and a lot of people can vouch for that. Also, I paid tolls with my card."

I had my phone in hand and typed notes as he spoke. He went on.

"I drove down to LA on Monday night and stayed with Rae in Malibu. On Tuesday we picked up Brock on campus at Pepperdine University and went to Venice Beach for the day. Look." He removed his watch so I could see a tan line.

I didn't look impressed.

"And then?"

"Then we all went out to dinner, Chinese restaurant en route. I'll have the name on my credit card receipt if you want it. Then we drove the kid back to school. We didn't know about Jamie's death until we got back to Rae's place. I had another overnight with my ex-wife and we talked about Jamie's death all night. I was in the kitchen here by eleven fifteen. I can account for my time and Rae's."

I asked him to go through his wallet now and give me the toll and restaurant card receipts and he did it.

"I'd like these back, okay?"

"I'll get them back to you this afternoon. Now, I'd like to know more about Rae and James Fricke."

"That's a very long and old story. Let me put some more food in front of us, before I start talking."

He called the waiter over, spoke a dozen words in fluent French, and turned back to me.

Christophe said, "Sergeant, most of what I know about Jamie comes from Rae. We were brothers-in-law, of course, but I didn't socialize with him, especially after the divorce. It's whatchacallit, hearsay, Sarge. Personal stuff through Rae, or what I read in the media. Theory seems to be that the same person killed both Holly and Jamie? Is that true?"

"It's still a theory. We have no proof."

A waiter removed our dishes, then put down more surprise food from Christophe. It was a baked ravioli dish. "What is it?"

"Go ahead, Sarge. Taste it," he said. "Then, you tell me."

I took a taste and guessed. "Ravioli stuffed with some kind of squash."

"Very good. Butternut squash."

"Delicious. So, Christophe…"

"Chris is fine."

"So, Chris. What do you know about the relationship between Jamie and Rae?"

CHAPTER 101

CHRISTOPHE SAID TO me, "Too late for that long old story now. See that pretty woman who just came in?"

"Short print dress. Long wavy hair?"

"That's the one. Moira Benet."

She was coming toward us, right up to the table, when Chris stood up, gave her a good hug, and introduced us.

"Moira Benet," said Chris, "meet Sergeant Lindsay Boxer. Sergeant, Moira is the heart of gossip central, right, Mo? And Sergeant Boxer is the top cop on the Fricke murder cases."

"Lindsay Boxer," Moira said. "Nice to finally meet you."

"Moira is an old friend of Rae's," said Chris. "You two should talk. I have a nice table opening up on the patio. Lunch is on the house."

We moved to seats at a teakwood table under a striped umbrella outside. Chris moved Moira's handbag out of the aisle and said, "You need anything, just ask."

"He's such a dear," Moira said of Chris.

Turned out Moira wasn't one for banter. She took the reins and talked through the first course. Her key point was that she and Rae were tight.

"We share many friends, have attended many red-carpet events together, countless parties and after-parties."

Moira told me that she wrote a column for the *Tribune* and also had a podcast that was offered by invitation only and not available at any app stores.

There was no way to say it modestly, so Moira smiled broadly as she told me that she had the inside track with the rich and famous. I hoped that was true. I didn't know enough about Rae Bergen to keep her name on the persons-of-interest list or cross her off. And doing that was my number one goal.

Moira had no questions about me and our investigation, and I was relieved. I wanted information from her, but I wouldn't be able to tell her anything.

When the main course came to our table, Moira left a space between words. I grabbed it.

"Moira, what can you tell me about Rae and Jamie Fricke?"

"I thought Rae told you. She utterly loved Jamie and he loved her, too. Since the day they met. It was complicated, of course. Rae got together with Jamie whenever it was possible. He sent her to the moon and drove her back to the airport. She is devastated that some mofo blew him away."

I said, "Yes, I know. But did Rae's love affair with Jamie cause trouble in her relationship with Holly?"

"Oh," said Moira. "I get it. You're asking, was Rae so jealous of Holly that she killed her? No, no, no way. Not ever in this world." She pushed her chair back a few inches from the table.

"Moira, don't judge the question. I'm a cop trying to solve a very bloody puzzle and the longer it takes, the less chance we have of finding out who killed Holly and Jamie Fricke."

"Yeah, yeah, yeah, I get that. But you don't know Rae. She and Holly were so close, they were like twins."

"Please go on," I said and meant it.

Moira said, "Well, do you know about Christophe and Holly?"

"I don't know about that. Please fill me in," I said as I typed "Chris + Holly" on my phone notepad.

Moira put down her fork and leaned in toward me.

"It's not a secret," she said. "Not anymore. May I call you Lindsay?"

"Sure."

"Well, Lindsay. Once, a couple of years ago, Christophe and Holly ran off together for a week to an absolutely amazing hotel in the South of France. Cannes, I think. Rae showed me the pictures. Frisky ones. I had to look at those images over and over because Rae and Holly look so much alike. But it was Holly, confirmed by Rae."

That was a bombshell — and news to me.

I said, "Did Jamie know?"

"Sure, he did."

"That must've ticked him off."

"He wasn't that way. Neither was Holly and neither is Rae. I, too, thought there would be ramifications. I'd forgotten how the Bergens, the Frickes, and their social peers played around and how they were raised. It was all allowed."

I could imagine rampant promiscuity, maybe. But had I learned anything germane to cold-blooded murder?

"How long did the Holly and Chris, Rae and Jamie crossover last?" I asked, even using my hands to do a crisscross pattern.

Moira said, "In Rae's case, she was with Jamie off and on for twenty years. Before Holly and Jamie were married, and during, and after she and Chris were divorced. But those two, Chris and Rae, are still the best of friends and Brock loves them both."

I followed Moira's comments onto a track of my own and when I tuned back in, she was saying, "Brock's a complicated kid. Smart and clueless at the same time. He was smoking, drinking, failing classes. Rae got him into rehab, and then back into school."

"That's why Rae lives in Malibu."

"Exactly. And Chris is very devoted to his son. What a wonderful man he is."

CHAPTER 102

ON MY WAY back to the Hall, I had a dark thought about a missed opportunity. One that threw shade on Moira. It had taken me too long to figure out how to pose this question and still keep her at the table.

Her phone had rung. She'd answered and had gotten into a lengthy conversation with her producer about people I didn't know, movie people, events and designer names that hadn't even grazed my consciousness.

Meanwhile, I was wondering how well Jamie and Moira knew each other. Sexually? And if so, what would that mean? I tried to imagine Moira as a double murderer. I couldn't picture it.

Moira had said over her phone, "Thanks, Peggy. I'll call you after I do the podcast."

Then, she clicked off, saying, "Lindsay, I have to go. Here's my card. Send me your contact info."

She gathered her bag, phone, sunglasses. She blew me a kiss and waved down the driver of her smart-looking car. She opened the back door and with a flip of her skirt, a kick of her heels, disappeared into the back seat. The door closed.

And Moira was gone, leaving me with a headache and a lot to think about.

CHAPTER 103

I HAD JUST parked my car in the All Day lot off Bryant across from the Hall when my hip pocket chirped out my ringtone. I looked at the screen. Arthur Bevaqua calling.

"Arthur?"

"Sergeant, I'm walking on Bay Street. Heavy traffic."

"Same here," I said, locking my car, picturing the former Fricke house manager I'd talked with so many times in the last year.

"You okay, Arthur?"

"Pretty much, Sergeant. Feeling sad about, well. You know. Listen, I got a call from Ms. Borinstein this morning."

"Something wrong?"

"Mr. Jamie's will, the draft I gave you when we were in his office."

"Uh-huh. What about it?"

"Well, Ms. Borinstein and Mr. Jamie both signed the original and she's a notary. So it's stamped. It's good."

"Arthur, may I call you back? I'm going into the Hall—"

"Mr. Jamie left the house to Ms. Rae."

I paused a few beats to take in this news, and it surprised me. That Jamie had loved Rae had been established. *But how did that affect Arthur?*

I asked, "Arthur. How does that affect you? Did you think Jamie would leave the house to you?"

"Hold on, Sergeant. Garbage truck. Okay. I'm here. I was just surprised, you know? That he didn't want it sold. Money for his sons. Or turn it into a school or a soccer camp."

"Is Rae at the house now?"

"No. She's back in Malibu. She'll be coming next week to look around. I'm just letting you know in case this changes anything."

"I wonder if Christophe knows. He didn't tell me."

"And I haven't spoken with Ms. Rae. It's all so sudden. Call if you want to talk about this," he said.

"Arthur, you sound worried. Why?"

"Ahh. So many questions. No answers."

"Welcome to my world, Arthur."

"I don't think I would have guessed Ms. Rae was his principal heir. Well, Mr. Jamie always did follow his heart."

I climbed the steps, pulled open a decorative steel and glass door, and walked toward the security station.

I was still on the phone with Arthur.

"Please keep your ears open and your phone charged. Call me anytime day or night. Yes, night's okay."

Then we signed off. I had known Arthur for six months and, strangely, I both cared for and mistrusted him. He was distressed.

I didn't know why. And he hadn't really told me.

CHAPTER 104

DETECTIVE SONIA ALVAREZ sat across from her former colleague, Sergeant Robert Bailey, at a plain metal desk on the second-floor squad room of the Tahoe police station. Bailey was forty, shaggy-blond-haired, steel-blue-eyed, a former middleweight boxer, high school math teacher, undercover cop with the Las Vegas PD and now at the police station in Tahoe. He had called her this morning with a lead that went straight to the front of the line.

According to Bailey, Samuel "Padre" Rochas was a known contract killer who'd been dropping hints just short of taking credit for the Frickes' murders. Why? Was he the doer? Did he want to get caught to forestall his imminent extradition? Or was he stupidly attaching himself to the crimes in order to muddy the opaque waters of these sensational murders and boost his street cred?

Either way, Alvarez was charged up by this unexpected development. She had questions when Bailey picked her up at the Tahoe airport about how much Padre had told his street buds.

"Just crumbs," Bailey said. "Based on facts."

He filled in Alvarez on the details of Padre's claims.

"Witnesses of the seedy kind tell us that Padre definitely knew Jamie Fricke well. He dropped names, knows a lot about soccer… But mostly he described Holly Fricke as an addict and a whore and Jamie Fricke as a spiteful bastard, which Fricke certainly could be. Have you seen any of the clips of him chewing out various team players? Fricke was a brute. He fired one of the assistant coaches right off the field a couple of years ago. Got into fistfights in locker rooms and hotels—he really thought he was some kind of god."

Alvarez said, "I never thought about Jamie Fricke at all until his wife was killed, and soccer was definitely never on my mind. I'll study up."

Bailey grinned at her. Good-natured teasing went both ways in their partnership and Alvarez had almost forgotten the fun they had injected into their dangerous undercover work.

"No," Alvarez insisted. "I will. Study up."

"Okay. I'm convinced." As they pulled into the station, Bailey said, "So we have Rochas in the cage on the third floor getting his shit together for his flight tonight."

"I need to talk to him if there's a chance he's our shooter."

"No problem, Sonia. If you need coffee, the machine is down the hall, turn left. It's right there. But you'll want to talk to Rochas first and fast."

"Lead the way, Bailey. And stay close. If I get into trouble, I'll give you our help sign."

Bailey put his thumb on his forehead, fingers splayed out like a fan, and he wiggled them.

He and Alvarez both laughed at their old gag. Then Bailey said, "That's it. I think we're good to go."

Alvarez was expectant as she followed Bailey up the stairs to the jail. Padre, serial killer for hire. And she was going to interview him within a hand's length of the bars.

When they reached the landing, Alvarez caught up with Bailey and grabbed the crook of his arm.

"You okay?" he asked.

"Good to go," she said, smiling into Bailey's face. "I really am."

CHAPTER 105

THE INTERVIEW ROOM was a ten-by-ten screened cage at the far end of the cell row. It wasn't private, like the interview rooms Alvarez had become accustomed to, and the acoustics on the tier were crystal clear. She walked alongside Bailey and as they approached the cage Alvarez glimpsed the prisoner.

Bailey said to Alvarez, "I'm armed. And he's not. He's shackled and we're not. He's ruthless but you'd never know it. His charm is charming, but—well, you'll figure him out, Alvarez."

Rochas was sitting at a table inside the cage. His ankles were shackled, his hands were cuffed in front of him, and a chain ran through the cuffs, then a metal loop in the tabletop, and fed down to connect with his shackles.

Bailey led Alvarez to the door to the cage, opened it to let her inside. He said, "Padre, this is Inspector Alvarez from the San Francisco PD."

Padre turned to look up at her. He gave her a second look and whistled through his teeth.

Alvarez ignored the whistle and took the seat facing the

prisoner, with a clear view of Bailey, who was standing to her right outside the cage.

"Mr. Rochas—"

"You can call me Padre."

"And you may call me Inspector Alvarez," she said.

"*Como esta?*" he said with a smile.

"Pretty good, Padre, and you?"

"I guess we'll both know after we talk. If I board a plane to Mexico City tonight, I'll be hanging by my neck in my cell in a week. What do you want me to say?"

Alvarez said, "I'm going to tape our conversation, Padre. Save us a lot of time."

Alvarez set up her phone on the table and pressed the button to record.

"Let's start over again, Mr. Rochas. I'm Inspector Alvarez, SFPD Homicide. Sergeant Bailey has reported comments from confidential informants—"

"Snitches."

"—that you had a relationship with Jamie Fricke. Did you go to his wife Holly's funeral service in Pacific Heights about six months ago?"

"Says who?"

Alvarez picked up her phone, went to the photo gallery app, and opened Cappy's photo of someone who may have been Rochas. She held it up to his eye level, out of reach of his cuffed hands. "Is this you?"

Rochas laughed. "I was there."

"But you didn't know the deceased."

"I went out of respect for her husband."

"Did you have anything to do with Holly Fricke's death? Did you know about a plan for her death or take some role in a plan? Did you pull the trigger?"

Rochas grinned. For a second, gold teeth flashed under the fluorescent lights.

"Inspector, you think if I had anything to do with that whore's death I should tell you?"

"Up to you, Padre. If you took part in her murder, you might not be going back to Mexico and life in prison. Life might be as long as a few days."

Rochas laughed. "What you might call an interesting proposition. I have a better one. Take me back to the City by the Bay for questioning. See what I say."

Alvarez said, "Answer the question, Padre, or I'm saying, '*Vaya con Dios.*'"

"Okay, okay, I had nothing to do with Holly Slut's death. Nothing. Not word. Not deed."

"Thank you," Alvarez said. "Same questions about Jamie. The street is talking, saying you feel James suckered you into a sports bet on the Bleus while you were cruising around Vegas. That you held a grudge against him because he wouldn't make you whole."

"What does 'make whole' mean?"

"It means to reimburse you, pay you back for your loss."

"Right. I lost a quarter of a million dollars. He wouldn't pay me back. He was a snake and everyone knew it. You want me to confess to killing him, so we go back to Frisco? I await trial. And maybe go free? Maybe take you to a good restaurant to celebrate."

"Did you have anything to do with Jamie Fricke's murder, Padre? Yes or no. If yes, tell me your role."

"I wish. I wish I had seen his face when he knew he was about to die. I wish I could have caused him mortal pain. I heard about it on the block."

"On which block?"

"This one. Cell block. I was here when he was gunned down, babe. I mean, Inspector. I was in a cell when Jamie Fricke was killed, and I had no foreknowledge or nothing. Snitches were playing a game with Detective Bailey. I think so."

Alvarez looked up at Bailey, who came over to the cage and said, "Padre. You shitting me?"

"You weren't here," Padre said. "But I was. Corcoran picked me up the night before. *Estupido.*"

Bailey opened the cage door and said, "Come on outta there, Alvarez."

To Rochas he said, "Be right back."

Alvarez followed Bailey down to booking on the first floor.

The desk sergeant opened a computer file, said, "He's right, Rob. Checked in on Sunday, never checked out."

"I love to look stupid in front of a dirtbag. Sorry about this, Sonia."

Alvarez laughed. She said, "Tell Padre I said it was good meeting him. And he has a perfect alibi for Jamie's murder."

"What about you? What are you going to do?"

"Ask you to run me out to the airport." She reached up, tousled his hair, and said, "Good seeing you, Bailey. Going home without a suspect, a confession, any kind of evidence, or even lunch, but it's been great."

"We'll have to do this again," he said.

Just before Alvarez boarded her plane, he kissed her goodbye. She stowed her carry-on bag in the overhead rack. She thought about Padre. There was nothing, not even circumstantial evidence, suggesting that he'd killed Holly. He hadn't killed Jamie, either, having the perfect alibi. He was in jail at the time. Now he was going to jail in Mexico…where he would surely get jailhouse justice.

TUESDAY

CHAPTER 106

CHRISTOPHE TEXTED ME the following morning, inviting me to lunch again, saying he needed to talk to me. The word "need" hooked me. I was 95 percent sure that the restaurateur had fobbed me off on Moira the day before so that he could avoid telling me something I had to know. I hoped we would have time alone without distraction and bull. If Christophe had inside knowledge of the Fricke murders, I was determined to learn something that would advance the investigation. Or God willing, close these open cases.

I agreed to be at Bonhomie at one. I spent the morning meeting with the team, a somber group of detectives who had nothing to bring to the war room but hope. Even Brady was pinning hope on me getting the name of a killer from Christophe Picard.

I arrived at a crowded Bonhomie on time and Chris greeted me at the door. He looked different than he had a day ago. The ebullience was gone. His face was drawn and he had dark smudges under his eyes.

He led me to an inside table, in a nook between the kitchen and the dining room. The table was up against the wall and the light was low. Chris opened a bottle of wine. I refused the drink but encouraged him to go ahead. Not a problem.

Once Chris had downed his glass and poured another, I crossed my arms on the table, leaned in, and said, "Chris. I need you to tell me the truth. What do you know or surmise about Holly's and Jamie's killers? No ping-pong—"

"Ping-pong?"

"No games. No diversions. I need information. Understand?"

He nodded miserably. Filled my glass with something I'm sure was rare and wonderful, but I pushed the glass aside and waited.

"If I knew," he said, "I would tell you."

I placed the flats of my palms on the table, pushed off, and got to my feet. "That's too bad, Chris. If something comes to you, call or write."

I edged out of the privacy booth and was heading to the exit when he said, "Wait. Please."

I turned and looked into his sorry hound-dog face and walked back to the booth.

When we were both seated, Chris said, "I don't know who killed them, Sergeant, but this I know. I loved Holly. I've loved her for decades. What happened to Holly destroyed me. Thinking how she was gunned down! That she had time to realize she was going to die. I wake up every morning wanting to kill myself."

His voice broke and tears came. He covered his eyes with his hands and cried. I didn't speak. I. Just. Waited. Him. Out. After he mopped his face with a cloth napkin, he said "Sorry" three times.

"It would be a relief to join her in death, but I can't," Chris said. "People depend on me."

A waiter put a charcuterie board of cheese and sausage in front of us. Aromas from the kitchen filled our small space. I quashed my hunger pangs and did a gut check.

I believed Chris had told me the truth about his feelings for Holly and his grief at her loss. But I felt just as strongly that he was leaving out the answer to who killed her and Jamie.

I tried him on as the killer.

If Chris had killed Holly for rejecting him, if he'd killed Jamie for winning the prize so long ago, it was hardly even a theory. I had nothing to support it.

That really ticked me off.

CHAPTER 107

I STOPPED OFF at MacBain's for a take-out BLT and cursed myself for declining a meal at Bonhomie. I had a small brown bag with the sandwich in hand when I breezed through the gate to the squad room. I said "Hey" to Bobby Nussbaum, our gatekeeper, as I passed his desk on my way to our pod just beyond him, but he stopped me.

"Sarge, I've got a message for you." I turned and he told me, "Anonymous tip."

I groaned, "Great."

He said, "I think this one's good."

"Hit me," I said.

"It was a woman. Her voice was muffled, like she was whispering or blocking the receiver with her hand. She asked for you, then gave me a message but not her name. Says she saw you at Bonhomie and won't ID herself."

"I'll take any old scraps, Bobby."

He said, "I know, I know, Lindsay, so I took it down verbatim. I didn't hear every word, but…"

He handed me a sheet torn from a message pad.

The handwritten note read, "Chris is shielding his son who's threatened people at school. You should check him out."

Bobby asked me, "Does this help?"

"Maybe. Is Brady in?"

"He'll be back in five."

I thanked Bobby and set course for the pod, where Alvarez and Conklin were having sandwiches together. I squeezed in behind Alvarez and claimed my spot between them.

"Is Christophe the man?" Alvarez asked me.

I leaned back in my chair and rocked a little. "I can't nail him and I can't clear him," I said. "But a tip came in for me while I was out."

I handed it to Alvarez and she passed it across the desks to Conklin.

"Check out Brock," he said. "Uh. As our killer? Why? Christophe gave him an alibi for Jamie's shooting, didn't he?"

"Right," said Alvarez. "Christophe told you that he and Rae and Brock were together. Venice Beach."

I said, "Yep. So says Chris."

"I'm sure Brock was at Holly's funeral," she said. "He gave a eulogy."

Conklin said, "He was also at Jamie's funeral, for sure. Rae pointed him out."

I agreed, saying for Alvarez's benefit, "Rae said he attended only because she asked him to be there."

Conklin said, "I'll run his name. Brock Picard?"

"This is like my Padre lead," said Alvarez. "It almost fits but doesn't fit at all."

She passed me her favorite snack, the family-sized bag of truffle oil potato chips. I snatched it before she changed her mind—and that's when a scuffle started at the front desk. Bobby was tackling someone who'd tried to charge past the desk. Bob had been a court officer before coming to the Homicide desk and he still knew how to jujitsu a man.

Through the shouting and thudding of bodies hitting the floor, I heard my name being shouted from under Bobby's thick body twenty feet away.

"Sergeant!"

I launched myself toward the sounds of men fighting and saw that it was Christophe, red-faced and struggling to get out from under Bobby's weight.

I was joined by Conklin and then Brady appeared, coming through the bullpen entrance. He told Bob to step aside.

Brady is instinctively battle-ready. He grabbed a frenzied Christophe Picard with both hands, jerked him to his feet, threw him against the wall, and pinned him there. Then Brady stared around furiously until his ice-blue eyes found me.

"Who is this man, Boxer?"

"Christophe—"

I didn't finish the introduction. Chris interrupted me, pleaded to talk only to me, and in a fashion he did. His voice was a hoarse, paralyzing scream.

"Rae is dead! She was murdered!"

CHAPTER 108

CHRISTOPHE'S SCREAMS NEARLY stopped my heart. I'd seen him less than an hour before, and he'd told me how much he loved Holly. And now he was here, reporting Rae's murder.

Was it true? Or had he mentally skidded off the rails into a ravine? No one moved. His next directive broke the spell.

"*I sent you the video!*" Chris shouted at me. "*Open it!*"

I shifted my eyes first to Conklin, then Alvarez, then Brady. Christophe was keening.

Brady said to me, "Go ahead. I'll keep him here."

A torrent of dread washed over me. I went to the pod, took my chair, and opened my inbox. I stared at the long stack of email on my screen but I made no move to open any of them. Alvarez got up and walked behind me. She reached over my shoulder and found incoming mail from CP@Bonhomie. She clicked on it with a forefinger.

Alvarez is fearless.

The email was blank with a video attachment. Alvarez stood

beside me as I opened it. I was looking directly at Rae Bergen's face, full screen and animated. She was alive, in what looked like a home office, speaking to Christophe, visible in a small window in the corner of the screen.

Chris was saying, "You can't baby him anymore, Rae—"

There was movement behind Rae's image. It was the camera's-eye view of a male torso, from waist to right shoulder, coming into the frame. The figure pointed a .40-caliber at the back of her head and fired.

Rae's eyelids flashed wide-open for a split second as the bullet sped from the back of her head through her forehead, blowing out a hole the size of a golf ball.

Instinctively, my eyes slammed shut and when I opened them a second later, Rae's head and upper torso had fallen forward across her laptop. I heard Chris's voice coming over Rae's computer. He screamed "Rae!" and the picture went black.

The image of Rae's last breath had burned into my brain, and I couldn't blink it away. I heard Alvarez repeating my name. Christophe bellowed from the wall beside the front desk.

"He killed her, Sergeant. Rae is dead."

"Who? Who did it?"

That was Conklin crossing in front of Bobby, calling to Christophe.

Christophe's answer was an anguished, wordless cry. I sat with my elbows on my desk, palms over my eyes, knowing that I would never forget what I'd just seen. It was as if I'd been sitting across the table from Rae Bergen myself, watching as a bullet tunneled through her head.

CHAPTER 109

BRADY SAID, "BOXER, I'm calling the LA Sheriff's Department. Get ready to move out." I snapped out of it, as Bobby called for medical assistance and Brady dialed the LASD and asked for the sheriff. He waited as the desk sergeant hunted him down and then explained what he wanted to do. Ten minutes after placing the call, Brady hung up the phone.

He came to our pod and summarized ground zero for me and Conklin. He'd reported the murder to the LA sheriff, who knew Clapper and was happy to cooperate with us. LA's CSU would leave the scene intact until we arrived, then they would process it, give us the results. Uniformed officers were being dispatched to Rae Bergen's apartment now.

I told Brady I wanted to see Christophe while we waited for transportation to the airport. I took the elevator up to the seventh-floor jail, where I asked desk sergeant and old friend Bubbleen Waters where I could find Christophe Picard.

"I'll let you see him, Lindsay, but EMTs just gave him a tranq to knock him out. He was hysterical, banging his head against the bars."

"He's unconscious?"

"Yup. I know you're going to ask for how long, and I asked and was told that time out differs from person to person."

I said, "When he wakes up, call Brady."

"Copy that, Sarge," she said, saluting me.

It was the first time I'd smiled that day.

I peeked in on Christophe, who was lying on his back on a slab inside a cell. He was out cold. I tried to rouse him by calling his name, but he was way under.

Because Rae Bergen's murder was attached to the Fricke murders, and all three had happened in California, the case was ours. Rae Bergen went on the board back in our squad room.

A few minutes later, Conklin and I were in a patrol car speeding toward SFO, and from there we shuttled to LAX, where a pair of uniforms were waiting for us when we landed. They also had the keys to a loaner squad car and handed them to me.

Once we were on Pacific Coast Highway, heading to Malibu, I dialed up the radio, introduced myself to dispatch, and got a dedicated channel. Conklin typed Rae's address into the GPS while I had a conference call with Brady and a sheriff's deputy.

Two teams were assigned to us as backup and once the administrative formalities were buttoned up, an APB was put out so that every officer in LA was on alert to a murder with no actual suspect. Our squad moved out and, with all lights on, sirens blaring, we headed to the murder scene: an apartment building in Malibu.

CHAPTER 110

FOUR PATROL CARS were already parked outside a three-sided grouping of town houses on a bluff in Malibu. They were all white with red tiled roofs and decks with a view of the ocean. The building where Rae had lived was the first condo in the A block, the one closest to the street.

Conklin double-parked and our backup teams got out of their cars and cordoned off the street. We badged the uniforms at the entrance to the compound. The ranking officer was Chief William Taverno. I introduced Conklin and myself and asked him if he'd seen the crime scene.

"I was there. Left my lunch in the toilet." I nodded as he added, "We're waiting for the ME."

A CSU mobile was parked at the curb unpacking their gear. I wanted to get into Rae's apartment right now and get out, leaving everything as I found it. I hoped that before I left Rae's place, I would uncover a clue to the identity and whereabouts of Rae's killer.

Taverno said, "Don't worry, Sergeant Boxer. Nothing but nothing moves until after you've seen it."

As if Taverno had conjured it up, the ME's van rolled up the street and double-parked.

Taverno said, "That's Dr. Camille Gray, the ME."

The ME exited from the rear of the van with her bag and camera. She looked to be in her early forties and lithe, moving with speed and purpose. I intercepted her as she reached the sidewalk.

"I'm Sergeant Lindsay Boxer. My partner, Inspector Conklin," I said. "I'm the primary officer—"

"The sheriff called me," said Gray. "Good to meet you, despite the circumstances. I hear that the cause of death is apparent. Let's see the scene. After we've got pictures, I'll take the victim to my offices and send you a full report after the autopsy."

Dr. Gray, Taverno, and two uniforms headed into the A building. Conklin and I followed them to 1A, Rae's apartment. Rae's office was too small to accommodate all of us at once. The others stayed back as Conklin, Dr. Gray, and I approached the nightmare that had been Rae Bergen.

The manner of death was as shocking now as when I had seen the shooting in action earlier, because now there was no screen separating us. A massive amount of blood had poured over the laptop keyboard and desk, dripping onto the floor and forming a pool the size of a kitchen sink. I stepped around the puddle to the opposite side of the desk and saw brain matter and fragments of bone, the shattered remains of Rae Bergen's skull.

I turned away and tapped Brady's direct line into my phone.

"We're in Rae's house," I said. "Did Christophe give up who killed her?"

"He wouldn't talk to me. So I sent in Paul Chi."

Brady is heavily muscled and rarely smiles. From a perp's point of view, Brady looks like he could mash human flesh into pulp. Chi, on the other hand, is about five six and cagey. So regardless of whether or not Christophe could read people, Chi could likely outfox him.

And he did.

CHAPTER 111

CONKLIN TURNED THE car off Pacific Coast Highway south to John Tyler Drive, the entrance to Pepperdine's Malibu campus. There was a parking area at the junction where the road split and continued along the perimeter of the campus while the other road forked into one of the parking lots.

We were looking for a late-model silver Porsche convertible registered to Brock Picard. We had to track him down.

First, locating his car would tell us if he was on campus. There was no place we could park where we could see all the cars in the main lot. So, we drove between the rows, weaving a path, passing many expensive cars, some of them silver, all with parking stickers on the windshields, many with Greek affiliation bumper stickers on the back.

I saw the car at the end of the row we were plowing.

"Slow, Richie. I think that's it."

My partner braked behind the Porsche, blocking it in. There were vehicles on both sides of the car and, since it was the last row in the lot, a curb behind it with landscaping in an enclosed bed.

The Porsche was a convertible, and the top was down. A young man wearing a brown jacket was lying in the front seat, his knees bent, his feet on the passenger-side upholstery, his head on the driver's-side armrest. His eyes were closed.

It was Brock Picard, Rae and Christophe's son. I recognized him from Jamie's funeral.

Using hand gestures and one-word sentences, Conklin and I unlocked and opened our doors. Brock was a light sleeper or maybe not sleeping at all. He bolted upright, saw Conklin, and vaulted out of his car. He ran alongside the Porsche, through the curb-contained plantings, and ducked under the branches of a sapling. And he kept going.

My partner and I yelled at Brock to stop running, that we were police, but a bullet whizzed past my ear as he headed uphill toward a block of buildings. We chased him up the twisting walkway from the parking lot, where he ran across the street and into a large building marked ADMINISTRATION. Conklin and I were of the same mind. We split up, Conklin following Brock into the admin building while I circled around the right side of it in the hope of cutting him off, should Brock attempt to escape through the back entrance.

It was a large building and circling around it was no joke, but I forced myself to move as quickly as I could without stumbling and falling to the ground. As I finished circling the building, I saw up ahead to my right a semi-cylindrical building that looked like a large tube lying on its side.

I spotted Brock running down the steps of what appeared to be a small amphitheater with Conklin several lengths behind him. Brock was making for the semi-cylindrical building and was able to reach it before I could cut him off or Conklin could overtake him from behind.

Brock opened the heavy double doors in the tubular structure and entered just as Conklin and I converged a few steps from the doors and a few seconds late. Out of nowhere, two campus cops appeared.

I flashed my badge and shouted, "We're detectives from San Francisco! The guy in the brown jacket. He's wanted for murder. Please clear students from the area."

One of the campus cops dropped away. The other stayed with us as backup. I peeled off my jacket as I ran and left it on the grass nearby. The Kevlar vest I wore under my coat was stenciled SFPD front and back, ID in case of gunfire.

As I turned to the campus cop and asked him what building this was, I was struck by the wall facing the amphitheater. It consisted entirely of stained glass.

The policeman said, "That's Stauffer Chapel."

Conklin asked him about ways inside.

"There is a pair of double doors, heavy ones, inside the grillwork protecting the glass. But there are also a couple of service doors down toward the other end that open near the altar."

"Please lead the way," I said. Conklin was quick off the mark. I was still breathing hard and I had somehow turned my ankle. The pain was catching up with me. Even so, I ran toward the chapel with the campus cop and kept my partner in sight.

CHAPTER 112

CONKLIN FOLLOWED THE path Brock had taken toward the glass wall of the chapel. I had fallen behind Conklin, and the campus cop—twenty years my senior—was jogging behind me.

"Hey, hey, slow down," he called out.

"Catch up!" I shouted back.

"I'm Jerry," the campus cop shouted to me. "Stay with me."

"I'm with you," I panted.

Jerry caught up then took the lead. We ran along the length of the chapel. He reached the side door, opened it, and went in and I followed him inside. We were standing on the dais at the far end of the chapel facing the enormous wall of stained glass. There were four people in the pews facing us, praying, meditating. I told them to please leave quickly by the side door to my left and that there was no time to answer questions.

The students jumped up from their seats, whispering and clutching at one another, and quickly filed out the side door. I saw Conklin at the far end of the chapel from me, but I didn't see Brock.

And then I did.

One of the side doors was kicked in and Brock entered pushing and dragging a female student, a brunette with two braids, wearing a cardigan over a long blue skirt. She was one of the girls who'd been praying moments ago, and when she made her exit, Brock had scooped her up. His left arm had a vice grip around her neck. A gun was in his right hand. The girl struggled and cried out and begged him to let her go.

Conklin, having hidden behind a pew, now came up behind Brock, his gun drawn, yelling, "Release her, Picard! Let her go. Drop your weapon and no one will get hurt."

Jerry and I had both pulled our guns and moved toward Brock and his hostage at the front of the chapel. Including Conklin, the three of us triangulated Brock Picard. He didn't look frightened. Rather, he had a twenty-year-old boy's bravado.

"Move back," Brock said. "Move back and drop your guns or I will put a bullet in this girl and we won't need to talk."

At that moment and in these circumstances, there was only one thing to do.

We backed off. No guns were dropped.

CHAPTER 113

WE WERE IN a standoff with a killer who had blown his mother's brains out. Now he had a hostage in a choke hold. If we didn't pull a miracle out of our hats, more people were going to die.

I called out to Brock down the length of the chapel.

"Brock. I'm Sergeant Lindsay Boxer, SFPD."

"Yeah. I know. What do you want?"

"I want you to release that young lady and let her walk out of here. She has nothing to do with any of this."

Brock, haloed by stained glass, loosened his grip on his hostage, who was red-faced and gasping for air.

"Get out of here, okay?" he said to the girl. "Sorry I had to do that to you, Becky."

Becky stumbled for the door closest to her and pushed it open without looking back. The door slammed behind her, and for a full ten seconds, no one moved or spoke.

Then, I said to Brock, "Thanks. Now, what do you want?"

"I want to know why you're after me."

I said, "Okay. Christophe recorded his video conversation with your mother this morning. You know what I mean? Bloody horrific in-real-life images of what you did to your mother."

"Aw, Jeez. That's not good. I guess that's what you call direct evidence."

I shot a glance toward Conklin. Had Brock really not known that we'd seen him fire a cannonball through Rae Bergen's head?

Brock asked me, "Now what?"

"There's no reason to keep Jerry here."

Brock nodded, then said, "Go, Jerry. Hurry."

"Are you sure?" the campus cop asked me.

"Go ahead. We're good. Don't let anybody in here. Okay?"

"Okay," he said. He holstered his gun. "Brock. You know me. Take my advice. Don't fire that gun."

"Okay, Boomer."

Jerry shook his head and left the chapel.

I said, "Brock, this is my partner, Inspector Conklin. Let's all of us put our guns down and talk, all right? You okay with that, Rich?"

Conklin nodded. What could he say? Disarming a volatile, violent killer could be done, but it was a calculated risk. I was showing Brock that he was safe. That killing us wouldn't get him anywhere. Would he surrender? Or kill us because right now he had nothing left to lose?

I thought the odds were even. We hadn't hurt him. Maybe he would give up once his gun was out of the picture.

I walked past the altar to the edge of the dais and sat down with my legs hanging over it. I put my gun down, and pushed it away, out of my reach. What would Brock do?

Conklin said, "Now you, Picard."

"Put yours down first," said Brock.

If this maneuver didn't work, my last thoughts would be about what I was leaving behind: my husband, our daughter, my partner, and how Brady wouldn't have done this in a thousand years. Conklin walked to the first row on the aisle, ten feet away from where I sat on the dais floor.

He sat in a pew with his gun still in his hand.

Haloed again in a rainbow of many-colored glass, Brock Picard walked the aisle to the front of the chapel. He took a seat in the first row across from Rich Conklin. From my position on the dais, backed by the altar, I had a twenty-twenty view of both my partner and a young man who, in the next few moments, could end both our lives.

Brock said to Conklin, "Put your gun on the floor, then kick it over to me."

Conklin's expression was clear. He didn't want to drop his weapon, but at the same time, Brock could shoot him dead where he sat, now or anytime. He was trusting my judgment and I had no idea if I was right. But "Keep the guy with the gun calm" was one of the first rules when the gunman was ready to die.

Conklin put his gun on the floor, raised his right foot, and kicked his gun across the aisle to the twenty-year-old killer.

CHAPTER 114

BROCK SAID TO Conklin and me, "Well, you got me on shooting Moms. But you might like to know, Chris isn't my father."

"How do you know?" I asked him.

"Because my father is Jamie Fricke. I thought Chris told you."

"No," I said.

I thought about Moira Benet, Christophe's friend, the gossip queen. She'd told me that Rae had had an ongoing multi-decade affair with Jamie before, during, and after she married Christophe.

Brock said, "It's fucked up, right? You grow up thinking that this sweetheart foodie dude is your father. You call him Dad, hang out at his cool restaurants. I thought maybe one day I'd work for him. Maybe one day I'd take over the business.

"You know who told me the truth?" Brock asked.

I shook my head no.

He was passing his gun from right hand to left. I thought about reaching for my piece, just out of reach, firing on Brock. I was a good marksman. But unless Brock's gun was empty, he didn't have to reach. He could shoot me where I sat. My ride-or-die partner—he, too, would die.

I tuned back in to Brock Picard, who was talking easily to us.

"It was Holly. Yeah. That Holly. I loved her to death. She was my beloved aunt Holly, former Olympic champ. We played tennis together from when I was five. Then when I was sixteen, she took me to bed. I didn't protest. I was the luckiest guy in the world and Holly was my dream come true.

"One morning about a year ago, we were in bed at the Ritz hotel. Holly says to me, 'You know you should ask your father to take you to Switzerland. See if soccer appeals to you.'

"She was half asleep. I figured she misspoke. I joked around. Like, 'I don't think my dad knows much about soccer,' something like that, but funnier. Holly didn't laugh. She realized what she'd said and got dressed. She kissed me goodbye and just like that, she dropped me. I called her, texted her, asked her to talk to me. She says, 'I'm sorry. I don't love you anymore.'"

I think I said, "Oh, no." Brock didn't hear me.

He said, "No more lovely Holly in my arms. No more funny food daddy. You getting this? Jamie Fricke was my father."

He was angry now, saying, "All those years. All those lies, and I didn't know it."

I heard him, but I was working out the DNA puzzle. Jamie had punched Brock. It was Brock's DNA on Jamie's knuckles. Brock had Fricke genes. Brock had killed his father.

"I killed Holly first," Brock said. "I called her to tell her that I had something of hers and wanted to give it back. She came out to meet me. When she got out of her car, I shot her. Took some things off her to make it look like a robbery. Diamond jewelry. Her car.

"I was still furious at everyone, still couldn't get over it or make it stop. Months later, I called Jamie. Told him I was in town and Mom had a book for him, asked me to give it to him. He met me on the street and I gunned him down. Are you getting all this, Detectives? These people played huge roles in my life but never gave a shit about me."

Conklin said, "And your mother?"

"What can I say? She was loose and selfish. She kept Chris hanging all those years and he's screwing Holly. I love Chris, though. Still, he was a dummy in a lot of ways. My mom told him Jamie was my biological father, but never told me. There's your capital murder offense and punishment.

"Heard enough?" he said. "Any more questions? Because I'm not sticking around to answer."

"Brock, we appreciate you telling—"

He said, "You're welcome."

He put his gun on the flat of his right hand and stretched out his arm to Conklin.

"I won't be needing this anymore," he said. "Oh, wait. I forgot something."

He got a grip on his gun, pointed it at his temple, and as Conklin and I shouted "*No!*" in unison, he fired a round into his head and fell off the pew and onto the floor.

I checked. No pulse. No breath. No heartbeat.

Brock was dead.

EPILOGUE

CHAPTER 115

CINDY HAD A question for me.

"Will you be my maid of honor?" She looked shy, hesitant, as if she was afraid I would say no.

"Aww, Cindy. You know I will."

But when I looked her square in the eyes, she squirmed and looked down. I had to ask, "Are you sure you're ready?"

"Lindsay, I am. Of course I am. I think I am. I'm sure, right? How can you know more than that?"

As my expression changed from hope and happiness to doubt and consternation, she cracked up and said, "You should see yourself. Don't you know me by now? Don't you know how much I love him?"

Yes, I did. But. Richie was an honest and kind man who loved Cindy entirely, and I really wouldn't forgive her if she hurt him now in front of God and everyone. At the same time, my stubborn friend Cindy had been building her writing career and doing it very well. She'd said from the beginning that she had to devote herself to her work. And Richie had been supportive even though it had hurt him, and he was pretty sure that Cindy might never move off that position.

"So, Linds," she said. "Is that a promise?"

I said, yes, yes, yes, and after she hugged me she asked Claire and Yuki to be bridesmaids, and now here we all were, flanking Cindy in the Chapel of Our Lady at the Presidio.

Cindy was wearing a white gown even her mother loved, with buttons and bows and satin to her toes. I was standing to Cindy's left, Yuki beside me, Claire beside her. Richie was standing to Cindy's right and four of his brothers were lined up beside him.

The officiant was a young reverend named Michael Romano, and he smiled as he asked if Rich and Cindy had prepared vows. Richie said they had and Cindy, clutching a small white square of paper, said, "Right. Here goes."

"I, Cindy Thomas, take you, Richard John Conklin, to be my partner in marriage and in life. To love you, to give thanks for you, and to honor you, with my wit and my strength—"

Cindy stopped speaking, shook her head, and, veering off script, crumpled the note card. She looked at Reverend Romano and said to him, "That was my first draft. May I start over?"

"Of course," said the reverend. "Go right ahead."

"Thank you." Cindy cleared her throat. She looked up at her groom and said, "Richie, I've loved you since our first date at Ruby Tuesday, no lie. I want to tell you…I'm sorry I've been so difficult—" Her voice broke. She took some breaths and swallowed, then said, "—but I can be stubborn, you know."

I laughed first but not last. All the people on the left side of the aisle, Cindy's family and college friends and coworkers at the

Chronicle, joined in. Cindy turned her head to the audience as the groom's side also fell apart—and she laughed along with them.

Cindy had always been a good sport, and watching her crack up at the altar filled me with more love for her than I'd ever felt before. I knew she was all in.

"Richie," she said, "I want to thank you for picking up after me, putting up with me, going out to my car in the rain to get my radio, sitting up front for my little readings in tiny book clubs, rolling with my shenanigans, letting me cry in your armpit, giving me funny nicknames, and for saving my life. There are a million other things I'll tell you later. But right now, I want to say, I love you so much. You can count on me to support you every day and in every way. I believe in you deeply and will always do so, even when you doubt yourself. I promise never to take you for granted but to let you know that you're a giant and my hero. I promise that I'm yours, Rich. All the way, in all ways, and for all time. I swear to you and to God."

Richie laughed, hugging this precious woman who was just tall enough to come up to his shoulder.

"You're one of a kind, Cindy," Rich said. "And I love that about you. I love you for more reasons and in more ways than I can say, and I trust you with my heart and my life. I promise you, Cindy, it doesn't matter how many rainy nights I go out to the car or run the dry cycle in the washing machine or call you Bunny Toes, I am grateful that today you are making me so very happy. And I will be by your side, always."

Applause broke out in the chapel. Darcy Thomas got to her feet and clapped hard, and so did Cindy's dad. Henry Tyler, Cindy's boss at the *Chronicle*, gave her two thumbs up while Richie's brothers roughed him up, messed up his hair, and called him their own pet names as the laughter rolled from front to back before returning again to the altar, where Rich and Cindy grinned while looking deeply into each other's eyes.

Standing between Lindsay and Claire, Yuki was also grinning along with the bride and groom. She then turned toward the congregation, and as if he were sitting under a spotlight, Yuki's eyes fell on her own fair-haired, good-doing husband, Jackson Brady, Homicide lieutenant, who winked at her as he clapped for Rich and Cindy.

Yuki had never asked Cindy if she'd had sleepless nights when Richie hadn't answered his phone, when he hadn't come home, or had come home in the morning so tired he couldn't sleep or tell her what was wrong. And then having to rip herself away from him and go to work.

Yuki smiled at the sounds of approval from the congregation. She fingered the angel skin coral necklace that Brady had given her as a wedding gift, and she thought about their honeymoon—on a cruise ship that had been boarded by pirates, all armed and dangerous. Every person on the Finnstar could have died but for Brady's sharp thinking and courage. Richie, too, had those qualities.

Claire, standing beside Yuki, reached out and took her hand, nodding once as if she could read her thoughts. Or maybe she just saw the worry on Yuki's face. Yuki tried but couldn't wish the worry away.

She recalled the day she married Brady. Yuki had had little experience with men, and for the most part, had kept to herself. On her wedding day, she'd had a vision of her mother, Keiko, saying to her, *He is love of your life, Yuki-eh. This life and next one. Tell him that.*

Yuki had said those words to Brady, who'd hugged and kissed her, lifting her off her feet and telling her in his soft southern-tinged voice, "Sweetheart. Ah'll be right here with you."

Now Yuki beamed those words and feelings at Rich and Cindy.

Claire took in full sight of the handsome couple, her friends who were about to make official a marriage that had already put down deep roots during their years together. She thought that Cindy and Rich were more alike than they knew; courageous, committed to their careers, loyal to their friends.

Cindy had never shied from anything. Claire remembered well when Cindy had fatally shot a killer who'd had Lindsay in her gunsights. Claire had done the autopsy. No charges had been pressed against Girl Reporter, who'd never looked back.

Claire also remembered a time when Rich had taken a .38-caliber round through his right shoulder at close range. It had been a painful injury that could have cost him the use of his arm or even killed him. But Rich had been stoic.

Claire had conferred with his doctors and had spent seven hours with Cindy in the hospital waiting room while Rich underwent surgery and was still under anesthesia.

When the surgeon had come out and asked for Mrs. Conklin, Cindy hadn't corrected him, but she'd been visibly shaken and had sobbed when she'd lost her fight to stay with Rich at Metro Hospital overnight.

Now, Claire watched Rich and Cindy stand together as the minister asked Eddie Conklin, best man and Richie's oldest brother, for the rings. She dropped Yuki's hand, covered her mouth as if to stop herself from shouting, "Whoo-hooooo!"

CHAPTER 116

REVEREND ROMANO NOW posed the two show-stopping questions.

"Do you, Richard, take Cynthia to be your lawful, wedded wife, for richer or poorer, through sickness and in health, as long as you both shall live?"

Rich said, "I do," and before the minister had fully repeated the question to Cindy, she replied, to the delight of the audience, "I do, *too*."

The rings were exchanged, and Reverend Romano said, "I now pronounce you husband and wife. Richard, you may kiss the bride."

The bride didn't wait for the maid of honor, her dearest friend, to lift her veil. She pushed it back herself. Richie kissed Cindy and buried his face in her curls, while nearly hugging the breath from her. Then he kissed her again to more applause.

As the organ started up, Claire felt as elated as she had on the day she'd married her own best friend. And after all these years, and four blessed children, she thought that they should celebrate their good fortune by renewing their vows. She wanted to get married again and would propose it to Edmund tonight.

Without knowing exactly why, Claire felt warm tears on her cheeks.

As the recessional music continued and the pews emptied from the rear first, Cindy felt the entirety of the wedding flooding through her and with it, a deeper awareness of herself. She was no longer afraid.

The long years of turning away from marriage to Richie and his longing for children were all about fear. Hers. She'd had a fear of failing, fear of giving up her independence, fear of not living up to Richie's belief and faith and love for her.

She also felt a sadness for all the years that she'd denied and delayed. She looked up at her new husband, who looked concerned as he gazed down at her.

"You okay, Cindy?"

"Yes, of course. It's just that I'm sorry for being such a jerk for so long, Richie. But I'm a hundred times better now.

"Thank you for waiting for me to wise up. I think I needed each of those years to learn to believe in myself as a wife. Your wife. To accept that we could be a team and that I could make you happy."

"Cin, we used those years to benefit our future."

Cindy nodded and reached up on tiptoes to kiss her husband as their guests surrounded them, enclosed them in a tight knot moving toward the door. Her parents worked their arms around them, and so did their friends and siblings as they left the small chapel through the narrow doorway and gathered on the front steps.

The photographer was waiting and quickly lined up her shots of the brand-new married couple and the wedding party. Cindy gripped Richie's hand. He squeezed and released hers so he could wrap his arm around her waist.

The photographer said, "Cindy, Rich, look at me."

Enveloped by love, a beaming Cindy posed for many pictures, all the while keeping her one precious secret. She would wait until tonight when she and Rich were in bed. That's when she would tell her best friend, her dear, sweet husband, what only she knew.

Tonight would be the beginning of her married life with the only man she'd ever loved.

ACKNOWLEDGMENTS

Our thanks to these experts who shared their experience with us in the writing of this book. Philip Birney, retired judge, and chief trial attorney for his San Diego law firm, WFGH&B, has practiced law for more than fifty years. Laurie Catherine Birney, licensed clinical psychologist and Phil's daughter, advised us on the mental disorders depicted in this book. As always, we are grateful to the real-life Richard J. Conklin, assistant chief of police, in charge of investigations at the Stamford, Connecticut, PD.

We also want to thank Professor Pierson Clair, instructor of cybersecurity and digital forensics at the University of Southern California, and Oli Thordarson, business executive, ransomware restoration expert, family man, and race car enthusiast. And we thank seven-year-old Lucy Murray for her lessons in combat training.

Ingrid Taylar, wildlife photographer and rescuer, our researcher for a dozen years, has once again virtually guided us around San Francisco and environs. And thanks, too, to Mary Jordan, traffic controller of innumerable parts and pieces, for whom we are always grateful.

Dedicated to our readers, the unofficial members of the Women's Murder Club, with our thanks.

ABOUT THE AUTHORS

James Patterson is the most popular storyteller of our time. He is the creator of unforgettable characters and series, including Alex Cross, the Women's Murder Club, Jane Effing Smith, and Maximum Ride, and of breathtaking true stories about the Kennedys, John Lennon, and Princess Diana, as well as our military heroes, police officers, and ER nurses. He has coauthored #1 bestselling novels with Bill Clinton and Dolly Parton, told the story of his own life in *James Patterson by James Patterson*, and received an Edgar Award, nine Emmy Awards, the Literarian Award from the National Book Foundation, and the National Humanities Medal.

Maxine Paetro is a novelist who has collaborated with James Patterson on the bestselling Women's Murder Club, Private, and Confessions series; *Woman of God*; and other stand-alone novels. She lives with her husband, John, in New York.

DON'T MISS THE 25TH ANNIVERSARY OF THE WOMEN'S MURDER CLUB

JAMES PATTERSON

25 Alive

& MAXINE PAETRO

WOMEN'S MURDER CLUB

I PHONED MY boss, Jackson Brady, from the car to let him know that Claire had called me to a murder scene at Golden Gate Park. "She wants me to see the body in situ in the park, ASAP."

Brady said, "Check in with me when you get there. I don't know squat about this homicide."

I copied that and strapped in. I took a quick detour on my way to the park, stopping at the car pool in front of the Hall of Justice just long enough to exchange my blue Explorer for a squad car. I translated Claire's urgency as Code 3, meaning all lights, sirens, and maximum speed.

The street that accessed the park's Lily Pond was blocked by three squad cars, and both the Forensics unit and the coroner's van. I pulled up to the curb, disembarked, and followed a spur of pavement to a parking area that was cordoned off with yellow barrier tape—a warning to joggers and curiosity seekers to stay the hell out.

I badged a uniform named Maggie Cannon. She held up the tape and gave me a warning look, like I was headed toward a five-car pileup. I didn't question her, just ducked under the tape and kept going. I found Claire standing with four uniformed officers inside a smaller taped-off perimeter within the larger one. Even from a dozen paces, I could see that the victim was lying face down in a pool of blood.

"Who's in charge?" I asked.

"I just spoke to Brady," said Claire. "You're it."

I knew two of the uniforms protecting the scene: sergeants Nardone and Einhorn. I texted Brady to give him an update and gloved up.

Einhorn handed me a pair of booties, and Nardone said, "Lean on me," which I did as I slipped the booties over my shoes.

I entered the smaller perimeter and looked at Claire. She shook her head and said of the victim, "I just can't believe this. It's…it's so *bad*…" Her voice cracked.

I didn't understand what she'd said. "Are you okay, Claire?"

She didn't answer me, just looked down at the dead man, whose face was turned away from me. I could see that he had bled profusely from wounds in his lower back, and from a ragged tear halfway around his neck and face. The only other things I could really determine from where I stood was that he was a gray-haired white man dressed in camouflage pants, a matching sweater, a tactical vest, and rubber-soled shoes. A CSI flag was next to a pair of binoculars lying just outside the tape, half hidden in the shrubbery.

Was this guy a bird-watcher?

Claire's primary investigator, Sage Dugan, had stooped beside the body and was taking photos. Since Claire seemed unresponsive, I asked Dugan, "Did he have a camera?"

"If he had one, it's gone," she said. "Just a cell phone. And the binoculars are not the photographic kind."

"Any sign of the murder weapon?"

The CSI held out a plastic evidence bag with a knife inside. It was a KA-BAR and it was made for killing. The blade was sturdy, good for jabbing and slashing. The handle was equal in length to the blade, rounded for a firm grip and designed for bludgeoning.

I remembered that there'd been some holdups in this neighborhood. A masked robber, or a pair of them, had stolen expensive camera gear—thousand-dollar cameras with German lenses—but nothing more violent had been reported than shouts of "Don't make me hurt you! Hand over the camera!"

"We've got his wallet?" I asked.

Claire spoke up. "No wallet. Had some loose cash and credit cards, and an ID in his vest pocket. He's carrying, too, but the gun is still in his waistband." She paused, then said, "Linds. This is going to hurt."

I don't know the victim—do I? Something was trying to break through the smoke screen obscuring much of my working memory.

Claire called my name, and I turned to her.

"What is it, Claire? Who is the victim?"

She sputtered, then said, "It's Warren Jacobi. He was...killed."

I STARED AT the dead man, but I didn't believe what Claire had said. I said, "This can't be Jacobi. He…He…He's retired."

"I'm so, so sorry, Linds," said Claire.

She put her arms around me. Her sobs released mine, and Claire and I both cried into the other's shoulder until, somehow, I finally accepted the unimaginable.

When we let go, Claire asked, "Can you handle this?"

"No. But I have to."

Another tidal wave of disbelief and grief washed over me. I loved Jacobi. He'd been my first partner in the Homicide squad. Everything I hadn't learned in the Academy, he'd taught me by example at crime scenes or explained to me inside a patrol car. We'd bonded early, and our deep friendship had continued before and after he cut loose from his job, his career, his reason for being.

And now Warren Jacobi was dead, lying curled up at my feet. I leaned down and put my hand on his shoulder.

"I'm so sorry this happened to you, my dear friend," I said, looking into my former partner's face. "You have good friends working to find out who did this to you. And that person who did this will damn well pay. I hope that you know I'm here."

I smoothed his hair and kept my hand on his forehead. I couldn't be sure if it was true or my imagination, but I thought he still felt warm. Everyone around me was quiet. I took another moment to pray, and when I said, "Amen," the little group echoed that solemn word.

Then I inspected Jacobi's injuries, snapping photos with my phone. My vision was blurred by tears, but from what I could see of the degree and angles of his wounds, Jacobi hadn't seen the attack coming. He hadn't even pulled his piece. From what Claire had told me so far, this assault didn't sound like a robbery.

But then why? What had been the killer's motive? Had it been a personal beef? Someone who'd hated Jacobi? Or was my old friend a victim of circumstance?

I turned and asked Claire, "What do we know?"

CLAIRE CLEARED HER throat, then ran the facts.

"Time of death, approximately two, two and a half hours ago, so, say 6 something a.m. The killer surprised him from behind and knew how to use a blade."

Einhorn said, "Plus a matchbook we found in the ferns over there."

"Let me see."

CSI Dugan opened her kit and held up a small, clear plastic evidence bag containing a matchbook with JULIO's printed on the cover. I recognized the design. It matched the look of the sign belonging to a dark hole of a bar on Valencia Street at the edge of the Mission District. I'd driven past it but never been inside.

"Don't know if it belonged to the victim or it's been there for days. But either way, it's interesting," Dugan said. "Look at the writing inside."

I managed to open the matchbook without removing it from the evidence bag and saw that someone had used a ballpoint pen to inscribe a message in block lettering on the inside cover. I could just make out the words: I SAID. YOU DEAD.

What? What the hell does that mean?

I handed the bagged matchbook back to Dugan and addressed the people around me. "'I said. You dead.' We're assuming this was left here by the killer. Is the killer bragging? Fulfilling a prophecy? Has anyone heard this statement before?"

There were no ideas at that moment, but we were just getting started.

I edged out of the scene to let the CSIs and the Forensics unit do their work as ME's team raised the tape, hefted Jacobi's body onto a gurney, and rolled it toward the van.

I walked like a zombie to my squad car. I turned it on, released the brake, backed up, then headed east on Nancy Pelosi Drive and toward the Hall of Justice.

At a stoplight, my mind was flooded with fresh images of Jacobi's lifeless, bloodied body, the horrible sight of his head half sawn off by a strong hand with a killing knife. Tears spilled and I didn't try to stop them. Warren Jacobi had been a great cop as well as my mentor, partner, and friend to the end.

That made his murder personal.

CINDY THOMAS WAS at her desk at 8 a.m.

The petite, curly-haired blonde wearing a rhinestone-studded hair band and loose-fitting clothes looked nothing like what she was—a tenacious investigative reporter, twice-published best-selling true-crime author, and leading writer on the *San Francisco Chronicle*'s crime beat.

Cindy's coffee mug was beside her right hand, her police scanner crackled on the windowsill, and her laptop was open. She was completely absorbed in her reading: the editorial page of a New York tabloid called the *City News Flash*. The top letter to the editor took up most of the screen—and it was making her sick.

The headline above the letter read, NEWS FLASH. "I SAID. YOU DEAD."

The text read, "NOT a joke. I just stumbled upon the blood-soaked body of corrupt former San Francisco Homicide cop Warren Jacobi inside Golden Gate Park."

That sentence raised the hairs on the back of Cindy's neck. *What kind of crap is this? Warren Jacobi was* not *corrupt and he was* not *dead.*

She reread the letter, which claimed to be a first-person account of a passerby who had just come across Jacobi's dead body, wrote it up, and sent it to the *Flash*. The second graf described the clothing Jacobi had been wearing as "a bird-watching outfit" and said that he'd been "knifed to death." It went on to say that a matchbook with the message "I said. You dead" had been left nearby.

The author was "Anonymous," and nowhere did the writer say that the crime or the victim's name had been verified by law enforcement. But the last time Cindy spoke to Jacobi, he *had* told her that he was photographing birds, recording their signature songs. Bird-watching was his new hobby.

Oh, my God. Cindy clapped her hands over her eyes. This could not be true. No newspaper, not even a rag like the *Flash*, would print anything about a murder without a statement from the police. But there was no such confirmation. Nothing from Chief Clapper or Lieutenant Brady. She'd tried reaching her cop husband, but her call had gone straight to Richie's voicemail. Had she missed a mention of it on the scanner? No. This crime hadn't happened. No freaking way.

Cindy dropped her hands from her eyes and printed out the nightmare from the *City News Flash* letters to the editor.

Beyond her desk was a large window in her wall that looked out onto the newsroom. Her coworkers were all on deadline, working hard and fast on their columns and assignments. There were shouts across the floor to "Look at this," the voices penetrating the glass.

She took the printout from the printer tray and read it again. The bombshell was time-stamped 9:15 a.m., East Coast time, today, so 6:15 a.m. local. A little less than two hours ago. If true, the writer had emailed his or her findings to that infamous New

York City tabloid in the time it took a second hand to sweep around a clock's dial.

Why had Anonymous sent this letter to the *Flash*? To take credit? To win a bet? To get revenge? To get published? One thing was sure: Whoever wrote and sent that smut to the *Flash* knew something that she did not.

CINDY'S PHONE BUZZED with an incoming call. She grabbed it, hoping it was Richie calling her back. But no. It was a reporter from the *Examiner* who had also read the letter in the *Flash* and was asking her for a comment.

"I have nothing, Sarah. Just what you have."

"How about a quote about how you miss him or something?"

"Take care, Sarah. I've gotta go."

There was a tap on Cindy's wall. She saw Phil Balshi standing outside her office. He signaled that he wanted to come in, and didn't wait for an okay.

Once inside, he said, "Something big just broke. Warren Jacobi was found dead this morning."

"It's a rumor," Cindy said.

"Oh. I see. No corroboration from SFPD?"

"Right, Phil, it's *gossip* until or if Clapper verifies this. Sit on it, okay?"

As Balshi returned to his desk, Cindy sent a text to Jacobi. She hoped he'd answer, then after they laughed, they'd track down the bastard who'd made up this garbage. When Jacobi didn't reply immediately, Cindy stared out the window into the city room for ten minutes, then texted him again. There was still no reply, so she tried her good friend Lindsay, Richie's SFPD partner. No answer from her, either. She tried her husband again, typing *URGENT* in all caps. And when she *still* got no reply, she phoned Frank Barto at the SFPD.

Barto's job was to keep the police blotter, an ongoing, constantly updated record of all incidents phoned in by police officers, citizens filing complaints, and witnesses reporting crimes.

He picked up on the second ring and said, "Make this quick, Cindy. I'm taking incoming."

Cindy said, "Frank, d'you have a murder in Golden Gate Park?"

Barto told Cindy, "Uhhh. Can't say. A call came into dispatch a few hours ago about a potential victim in the park," he said. "I notified Sergeant Nardone. This is between us, Cindy. Do not quote me."

Cindy pressed Barto for more details, but he dug in his heels and claimed not to have the victim's name. "And even if I did, I wouldn't share it with you."

"Frank. Just tell me this. Was he or she with the SFPD?"

"I don't know. Maybe." Cindy's stomach dropped as Barto continued. "Remember, Cindy. Leave me out of this. I like my job."

"Thanks, Frank. Don't worry. You've told me nothing."

"Use your wiles," Barto said. "I'm hanging up."

Barto had given her an unquotable hint, but it was verification enough for her. Jacobi was dead.

Cindy spun her chair around so that she was no longer facing her window onto the newsroom. Then she bent over and cried into her hands.

For a complete list of books by
JAMES PATTERSON

VISIT
JamesPatterson.com

Follow James Patterson on Facebook
JamesPatterson

Follow James Patterson on X
@JP_Books

Follow James Patterson on Instagram
@jamespattersonbooks

Scan here to visit JamesPatterson.com and learn about giveaways, sneak peeks, new releases, and more.